'I ... scene, ... think of no other way to ob... to dance with me!'

At her unexpected words, Wyvern's heart hammered almost to a stop, causing him to miss his step and necessitating the nearest couple to swing hurriedly out of harm's way.

Stifling his exasperation, the Earl corrected his error and guided Jessica to a less populated area of the floor, whilst racking his brains to conjure up some non-committal remark.

'I had not noticed that you were suffering from a dearth of dancing partners, Miss Beresford,' he managed eventually.

'I cannot imagine how you would know that!' she flung back at him. 'You only turn up when it suits you to do so!'

When he did not immediately respond, Jessica's indignation increased. 'Do you dislike me so much that you cannot even bring yourself to converse with me, sir?' she challenged him.

'I do not dislike you, Miss Beresford,' he replied heavily as, doing his utmost to ignore the tantalising feel of her soft, warm body beneath his fingers, he strove desperately to focus his attention on the manoeuvres of the dance.

Dear Reader

As you are probably aware, 2008 is the year in which Mills & Boon celebrates its 100th Anniversary, which gives me the opportunity to thank the company for the pleasure that its publications have given me over the years.

Having always been an avid reader of romantic fiction myself, I was delighted when, in 2003, Mills & Boon accepted and subsequently published my first novel, A HASTY BETROTHAL, including me in its world-wide team of authors.

Since then I have derived immense satisfaction from my association with this renowned company, and wish to offer my congratulations as it celebrates this truly historical event.

If you have previously read THE OFFICER AND THE LADY, you will be able to renew your acquaintance with several of the characters in my latest offering, AN UNCONVENTIONAL MISS. I hope you will enjoy Jessica and Ben's story as much as I have enjoyed writing it.

Dorothy

AN UNCONVENTIONAL MISS

Dorothy Elbury

MILLS & BOON®
Pure reading pleasure

First published in Great Britain 2008
Harlequin Mills & Boon Limited,
Eton House, 18-24 Paradise Road, Richmond, Surrey TW9 1SR

© Dorothy Elbury 2008

ISBN: 978 0 263 86258 4

Set in Times Roman 10½ on 12½ pt.
04-0508-79326

Printed and bound in Spain
by Litografia Rosés S.A., Barcelona

Dorothy Elbury lives in a quiet Lincolnshire village, an ideal atmosphere for writing her historical novels. She has been married to her husband (it was love at first sight, of course!) for forty-five years, and they have three children and four grandchildren. Her hobbies include visiting museums and historic houses, and handicrafts of various kinds.

Recent novels by the same author:

A HASTY BETROTHAL
THE VISCOUNT'S SECRET
THE OFFICER AND THE LADY

For John, in gratitude for his wholehearted support and continuing encouragement.

Chapter One

'No luck, I'm afraid, Jess!'

His face a picture of utter dejection, Nicholas Beresford hurried into the tiny parlour of the wayside inn where, for the past half-hour, his sister had been anxiously awaiting his return.

'The pole is totally shattered,' he went on, flinging his slight form into the seat beside her. 'And it seems that they can't get a replacement until tomorrow. Added to which, it would appear that there's not a single decent carriage for hire in the whole blessed place!'

Casting yet another uneasy glance at the clock on the mantelshelf, Jessica's wide green eyes clouded in despair. 'But what on earth are we to do, Nicky?' she queried. 'It is almost five o'clock and Harry promised Imo that we would be back well before six. Matt will just about crucify me if she starts to worry.'

Leaping to his feet, her young brother began to pace the floor. 'Not you, Jess,' he groaned. 'It was my fault that we left Hampton Court so late—if only I hadn't wasted all that time in the maze…!'

'If only you had listened to Harry's instructions, you mean,' began Jessica crossly, but then, seeing her brother's disconsolate expression, she sighed and, for the umpteenth time that afternoon, reminded him that it was hardly his fault that the carriage pole had snapped. In any event, surely they should just be thankful that none of them had been more seriously injured.

'The doctor told Harry that a good night's sleep will soon put Olivia back to rights,' she then informed him. 'And, thank heavens, Cartwright's wrists are not broken after all—merely badly strained.'

'Well, that's something, I suppose,' replied her brother, nervously polishing his spectacles. 'I imagine Harry is still with his sister? Has he managed to sort out rooms for us all, do you know?'

'I told him not to book for us,' said Jessica, getting to her feet. 'We simply have to find a way to get home, Nicky. Are you sure that you asked everyone? There has to be some sort of conveyance somewhere in the village, surely?'

Nicholas shook his head. 'Only one small, rather disreputable-looking gig out in the yard here,' he replied. 'Barely big enough for the two of us, let alone Cartwright. Besides which, how on earth do you expect him to drive with his wrists strapped up?'

But Jessica was already making for the door. 'Good grief, Nicky! Surely it is not beyond your capabilities to handle the thing!' she flung at the dismayed young man and, ignoring his protests, quickly exited the room, adding, 'Go and tell them to harness one of our leaders to it, right away! I'm off to find Harry—we will need to sort out some arrangements for Cartwright—Matt will probably want to send someone to fetch him home.'

Lieutenant Harry Stevenage was not at all happy when Jessica informed him of her intention to return to Dover Street with only her seventeen-year-old brother as escort. What had started out as a jolly day's outing to Richmond Park and thence to Hampton Court had, as far as he was concerned, turned into something of a nightmare.

Due to his refusal to take advantage of Stevenage's whispered instructions, Nicholas had set off into the Court's maze of hornbeam hedges on his own and had then proceeded to lose himself completely! Since both young ladies had elected to accompany Stevenage—who had mastered the puzzle some years earlier—the three of them had made their way to the centre and back out again in little over half an hour. After a further half an hour had passed without any sight of Nicholas, Stevenage had deemed it necessary to ask the guide to mount his platform and direct the crestfallen Nicholas back to the exit.

Thus, having promised to have the Beresford carriage, along with Jessica and her brother, back at their Dover Street residence no later than six o'clock, this unlooked-for delay had then obliged Stevenage to instruct Cartwright, the Beresfords' coachman, to whip up the horses. Which command had been followed by constant urges to the distracted driver to make even greater haste.

Not, perhaps, the smartest decision he had ever made, Stevenage now admitted to himself. Taking that corner at such a speed was almost bound to have had disastrous consequences. Hence their present predicament. The pole had fractured, the driver had been wrenched from his box and Olivia, Stevenage's young sister, had been catapulted across to the opposite side of the carriage, hitting her head on the door frame. He could only thank his lucky stars that none of Matt Beresford's matched bays had suffered any damage!

'I do wish you would reconsider, Jess!' he pleaded. 'A fine fellow your brother will think me for allowing the pair of you to go off on your own like this!'

'You do talk absolute nonsense, Harry!' she replied, laughing at his injured expression. 'Nicky and I are perfectly capable of seeing ourselves home—it is barely six miles from here and we could practically walk it! Besides which, you must know that Matt would expect you to stay with your sister. Now help me up, there's a dear boy—and do tell Nicky to make haste!'

Lieutenant Harry Stevenage's acquaintanceship with Jessica, though relatively short, had been of sufficient duration for him to have learned that any attempt to dissuade her from a course upon which she had set her heart was likely to be met with dogged resistance. Ever since he had first laid eyes upon her at his godfather's Lincolnshire seat, some seven months previously, he had counted himself amongst her most devoted admirers, regardless of the fact that Sir Frederick had earnestly cautioned his godson not to allow himself to become too attached to the capricious Miss Beresford. He had taken pains to warn the lieutenant that Jessica's father, the late Sir Matthew Beresford, had been in the habit of indulging his daughter to such a degree that rumour had it that she was never truly happy unless she was getting her own way. And only since the recent arrival of her half-brother, Matt Beresford, who had been obliged to give up a lucrative lifestyle in India to take up his estranged father's reins, had there been any noticeable improvement in her conduct.

Yet, despite Jessica's somewhat unpredictable behaviour, Stevenage doubted that there was a man alive who could resist such damnably appealing loveliness. Such kissable lips—would that he were given the opportunity!—the dearest little nose and those incredible green eyes set in the creamiest of complexions, the sum total of which was entrancingly framed in a dazzling halo of silvery blonde ringlets. And, as if all of that were not far more than any fellow could reasonably ask for, the saints above had also endowed the little beauty with the most curvaceous figure that young Stevenage had ever come across in the whole of his twenty-two years! His considered opinion had been that the occasional fractious outburst was a small price to pay for the privilege of being included amongst her favoured few.

Nevertheless, as he watched the shabby little gig bowl out of the stable yard, a pensive frown marred his handsome features and, in reply to Jessica's enthusiastic wave of farewell, the best he could manage was a half-hearted lift of his hand. He stood lost in thought for some minutes then, conscious that his duty to his injured sibling ought to be uppermost in his mind, he gave an impatient shrug of his shoulders and turned and retraced his steps into the inn.

'There now, Nicky,' declared Jessica warmly. 'I was quite right. You are managing the reins quite beautifully.'

Nicholas snorted. 'It was not my driving ability that I doubted, Jess!' he retorted. 'Matt has made sure that I can handle pretty well any carriage you might care to name. It's this mad idea of yours that I'm not keen on. I still don't see why we couldn't have stayed overnight with the others. We could have sent a messenger—'

'Oh, yes?' interrupted Jessica, with a withering glance. 'And had Imogen up half the night worrying herself to death about us, I shouldn't wonder. At least this way, she will be able to see for herself that we really are unhurt. And, what with Matt doing his level best to wrap her in cotton wool now that she is increasing, it simply will not do to have him flying off the handle!'

'Anyone would think that she was the first woman ever to bear a child!' muttered her brother.

'Now, be fair, Nicky,' returned Jessica complacently. 'You can't have forgotten that Matt's own mother died in childbirth!'

'Oh, lord! It had slipped my memory! How stupid of me. Sorry!' Glancing sideways, he gave her a rueful smile. 'I sometimes get the impression that you are starting to become almost human!'

Jessica laughed and a faint blush crept across her cheeks. 'I *do* try, you know,' she said quietly. 'Ever since that dreadful business with Wentworth, I have tried really hard to be more like Cousin Imo and behave as she and Matt would have me behave…' Her voice trailed away and her bright eyes clouded over as she cast her mind back to the previous September when Philip Wentworth, the estate gamekeeper, had all but succeeded in his attempt to abduct and seduce her. Had it not been for the timely actions of her newly acquired half-brother...! A cold shiver ran down her back as the never-to-be forgotten events of that dreadful day replayed themselves in her mind.

Mindful of his sister's discomfort, Nicholas reached across and took hold of his sister's hand.

'Well, I think that you've done amazingly well,' he sought to assure her. 'I scarcely recognised you when I came back from school at Christmas. Believe me, Matt would never have agreed to give you this Season if he hadn't thought that you had earned it.'

'He has been enormously good to us, hasn't he?' Jessica smiled and blinked away the tears that threatened. 'When he first turned up, I was really hateful to him, but after everything he's done for us all—working so hard to bring Thornfield back to scratch and then going to all that trouble to get Mama settled in Bath—I've grown enormously fond of him. It's not difficult to see why Imogen fell in love with him.' She gave a tremulous smile. 'As it happens, it has often crossed my mind that he is just the sort of man that I would choose to marry, some day!'

'I take leave to doubt that there are many like him,' chuckled her brother, returning his attention to his driving. 'Besides which, I rather had the impression that you had set your sights on a certain lieutenant.'

'Harry Stevenage!' Jessica let out a peal of laughter. 'Good heavens, no! He isn't nearly rich enough for my taste!' She shot a mischievous glance at her brother. 'You must know that I am on the lookout for a duke—or, at the very least, a belted earl!'

Having expected an immediate riposte for coming

out with the sort of remark that might well have been expected from the Jessica of old, she was surprised to discover that her brother seemed not to be listening to her. In fact, his attention seemed to be keenly focussed on the hedgerow just ahead of them. Looking about her, she was suddenly conscious of the fact that the narrow lane along which they were travelling was devoid of any other traffic.

Clutching at his arm, she whispered, 'What is it, Nicky? What's wrong?'

He shook his head. 'I'm not sure. I thought I saw—!'

The rest of his words were cut off as two villainous-looking individuals, each brandishing a stout stick, leapt out from behind a clump of bushes. Grabbing hold of the harness, the first man dragged the horse to a standstill, while his accomplice darted towards Jessica and threatened her with his cudgel.

'Yer purse, little missy, if ye please!' he growled, his free hand reaching out to clutch hold of her booted ankle.

At once, Nicholas was on his feet, beside himself with rage. 'Take your filthy hands off my sister!' he cried and, pulling the driving whip from its socket, he proceeded to lash out at the man on the gig's offside.

It did not take Jessica long to realise that, with this futile action, highly commendable though it might have been, her brother had put both their lives in consid-erable danger. Having quickly taken in the men's shabby attire, along with the fact that they carried make-shift weapons, it had occurred to her that, in all probability, the men's intent was merely to relieve their intended victims of any valuables they might be carrying and then to make themselves scarce. And, since she was more than willing to part with every single penny in her possession—as well as any other item of value that the men might have demanded—she would have been prepared to gamble that the easy acquisition of such an unexpectedly fulsome haul would have seen the two footpads very quickly on their way.

Tugging at Nicholas's coat-tails, she flung her bulging reticule at her tormentor, at the same time urging her brother to sit down and be quiet. But it was too late.

As the metal tip of the whip's leather thong struck him painfully on the cheekbone, the man who was at the horse's head uttered an angry snarl and, letting go of the harness, raised his stick and flew at Nicholas in a rage. His initial burst of confidence instantly collapsing, the boy recoiled in dread, lost his balance on the gig's narrow step and tumbled backwards into the roadway where he lay sprawled at the man's feet, entirely at his mercy.

Seconds ticked past as the thug stood glaring down at Jessica's now panic-stricken young brother and then, with a malicious grin on his face, he slowly raised his weapon in both hands, clearly intent upon inflicting some terrible punishment on the youth. Jessica's hands went to her mouth in horror but, unable to prevent the frightened whimper that escaped her lips, she closed her eyes, threw up a fervent prayer and prepared herself for the worst.

All of a sudden, a single shot rang out in the silence. The stick fell from the ruffian's hand as, letting out a howl of pain, he clutched at his bloodstained forearm. Then, without a backward glance, and followed closely by his equally terrified accomplice, he fled back in the direction from whence they had first appeared.

The sound of the two men crashing their way through the undergrowth was very quickly drowned out by the noise of fast-approaching hooves. Jessica, having almost fallen out of the carriage in her haste to reach her brother, sank to her knees at his side, begging him to speak to her. She barely registered the arrival of the mount's rider who, having leapt from his steed, was now lifting her, none too gently, to her feet and thrusting her to one side.

'Better let me see to him,' he advised curtly. 'He might have broken something.'

Jessica, who had been about to challenge the newcomer over his singularly high-handed manner, found herself hesitating. Although she could see only the back of the man's head from her present position, his attractively deep voice, whilst rather brusque, was well modulated and she could tell by the cut of his riding jacket—which fitted across his broad shoulders to perfection—that he appeared to be a gentleman of means. She bit back the stinging riposte that had been forming and regarded him with some interest.

Pulling off his gloves, the stranger knelt beside Nicholas's still-prone figure and began to run his hands over the boy's body. After several minutes, during which time Jessica clasped her hands together tightly, scarcely daring to take a breath, the man knelt back on his heels and uttered a satisfied grunt.

'No bones broken,' he professed cheerfully. 'My guess is that the lad has merely passed out—this should do the trick.' And, extracting a small brandy flask from his inside pocket, he gently prised Nicholas's lips apart and allowed a few drops of the spirit to trickle into the boy's mouth.

Her eyes wide with apprehension, Jessica edged closer in order to better her view. As far as she could see, there seemed to be no appreciable change in her brother's demeanour but then, quite suddenly, there came a slight choking sound and the boy's eyes flew open.

'W-wha's happening?' he croaked and, catching sight of his sister's anxious face, he would have tried to sit up had not the stranger placed a restraining hand upon his chest.

'Easy now, my boy. Gently does it.'

Jessica flew at once to her brother's side.

'Oh, Nicky, Nicky!' she gasped. 'Are you hurt?'

'Just about everywhere!' groaned Nicholas as, very gingerly, he forced his body into a sitting position and raised a hand to his throbbing head. 'What happened?' he queried, looking firstly towards his overjoyed sister and then up at their rescuer, who having risen, was holding out his hands to help the boy up.

'Your attackers made off,' was the man's terse reply.

Nicholas frowned and, his mind still somewhat befuddled, shook his head. 'I thought I heard a shot,' he faltered. 'But then—I suppose I must have passed out.'

After allowing the stranger to help him to his feet, Nicholas leant his trembling body against the side of the gig and, reaching out, took hold of his sister's hand. 'They didn't hurt you, did they, Jess?' he asked urgently. 'I'll never forgive myself—'

'No harm done, I promise you!' she returned, hurriedly patting his hand, then, after a moment's hesitation, she gave him an apologetic smile. 'Apart from the loss of all our money, that is,' she added ruefully.

'Oh, good,' he replied, clearly still in something of a daze. 'Hadn't we best get on our way, then?'

Then, taking a deep breath, he straightened his shoulders, gripped hold of the gig's side-rail and attempted to haul himself up on to the driving seat. Almost immediately, he felt himself swaying backwards and, had not a pair of powerful arms reached out and caught hold of him, he would surely have fallen to the ground once again.

'A little premature, perhaps?' suggested the stranger, with a sympathetic smile as, without apparent effort, he hoisted the boy on to the gig's seat. 'Hold tight, my lad. It looks as though we might have to secure you somehow. I must assume that your sister is capable of driving?'

Ignoring Jessica's gasp of protest, the man walked over to his horse and, after extracting a length of rope from the saddlebag, returned to Nicholas's side and calmly proceeded to strap the boy to the gig's backrest. Then, standing back, he surveyed his efforts.

'That should do.' He gave a satisfied nod then, turning to Jessica, he offered her his hand. 'Up you get, Miss Beresford. You need have no further fears of being set upon, I assure you—you will have my escort for the remainder of your journey.'

Fuming, but unable to find the words to express her indignation at the fellow's arrogant assumption that she would be unable to cope without his further assistance, Jessica could only do as she was bid. It was not until she was in her seat and had taken up the reins that the thought occurred to her that the man had addressed her by name.

'How do you suppose he knows who we are?' she muttered to Nicholas in a low voice, as she watched the tall stranger vault nimbly into his saddle and swing his mount round. 'Do you think he could be another felon—some sort of accomplice?'

'Odd sort of accomplice to go shooting his comrades,' returned her brother, who was feeling far from well. 'Don't be such a goose, Jess! The fellow has done us a good turn—though how the devil we are going to explain all this to Matt defies thinking about!' Then, clasping his hand to his throbbing head, he begged, 'Do let us get on!'

Chapter Two

For the first hundred yards or so, their escort remained behind the carriage, his clear grey eyes carefully scrutinising the terrain, both to the front and to the rear. Gradually, though, as the little party approached the more populated areas, the horseman drew closer and closer until, eventually, he was abreast of the gig. Then, after riding alongside in silence for some minutes, he spoke.

'Your brother is recovering from his shock, I trust?' he asked pleasantly.

'He appears to be doing very nicely, thank you, sir,' replied Jessica, without turning her head. Keeping her eyes firmly on the road ahead, she was pondering the man's remark. How was it that he knew her name and how could he have known that Nicholas was her brother? That this man—whoever he might be—seemed to be in possession of so much information about their circumstances concerned and puzzled her greatly.

But then, as the silence between them continued at length, Jessica's conscience began to smite her as, somewhat belatedly, it occurred to her that she had made no attempt to offer the man her gratitude for his timely intervention.

'I fear that we are greatly in your debt, sir,' she began primly, only to be interrupted by his smothered laugh. Swinging her head sideways, she glared at him. 'Have I said something to amuse you, sir?'

'Not at all, ma'am,' he returned promptly. 'I am glad that I was able to be of some service!'

Although his face was not turned in her direction, it was not difficult to see that it was creased in a wide grin. In the midst of her outrage, she was astonished to find herself thinking what a devilishly handsome creature he was when he smiled. Biting her lip in exasperation, she racked her brains to find a less stilted way of expressing her gratitude.

'I simply cannot imagine why those men should have chosen to waylay us,' she eventually managed. 'I should not have thought that this shabby carriage was the sort of vehicle that would lend itself to a hold-up!'

'It possibly had more to do with the way in which you were flashing your blunt, back at the Rose and Crown,' he offered.

'Flashing my...!' For a moment, Jessica was lost for words, but then, as a most disturbing thought entered her head, she found herself filled with a desperate need to vanquish her sudden suspicions.

'I take it, then,' she said carefully, 'that your arrival back there was not just some lucky coincidence?'

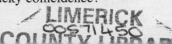

'Hardly!' was his astonishing reply. 'I was right behind you from the moment you left the inn!'

Her heart sank. 'W-why was that?' she asked, unable to prevent the tremble in her voice.

'Because of those two fellows,' he replied casually. 'I was aware that they had been watching you for some little while in the inn's stable yard and then, when I saw them make off through the back woods, it seemed pretty clear to me what they were about.'

A flicker of relief ran through her, but then, 'But why did you not see fit to warn us about them?' she demanded indignantly.

There was a moment's silence. 'I rather got the impression that you were not the sort of young lady who would take kindly to a piece of friendly advice from a total stranger,' he replied at last.

Now thoroughly affronted, Jessica snapped, 'What utter nonsense! If you knew that a felony was about to be committed, it was your duty to inform us!'

'Well, it is not exactly true to say that I *knew* they were up to no good,' he retorted, his hackles rising. 'Their furtive behaviour merely led me to believe they might well be—which is why I followed your carriage!'

'And then waited until they had attacked us!' was her withering retort.

Taking a deep breath, the man gave a brief nod. 'That was an unfortunate error on my part,' he admitted stiffly. 'I had not expected violence—their kind is, usually, only in it for the pickings. They like to terrify their victims into a quick surrender of their valuables and then make off, as fast as they can. Insofar as I have been led to believe, they tend to pick upon travellers who do not look as though they are able to take care of them-selves—such as your brother and yourself. I doubt that they were prepared for retaliation.'

Just as she herself had supposed at the time, thought Jessica ruefully. If only Nicky had kept quiet! But then, another thought flashed into her mind.

'You were perfectly content to see us robbed, then?' she flung at him.

His face darkened. 'If you will go round flourishing bundles of notes under people's noses,' he replied calmly, 'you can hardly complain when the inevitable occurs!'

Hurriedly recalling her efforts to persuade the gig's owner to part with his carriage, Jessica's cheeks reddened. Although she was bound to admit that there might be some slight glimmer of truth in what the man was saying, she was not at all happy to have received such a thorough set-down from him. With the excep-tion of her half-brother, Matt, the majority of men with whom she came into contact were usually so dazzled by her fairy-tale beauty that they were more inclined to grovel at her feet than find any fault with her beha-viour.

Having arrived in the capital some six weeks earlier, it had taken her no time at all to become the year's Toast of the Town. Under the aegis of Lady Sydenham—her cousin Imogen's godmother—she had been given entrée to all of the best houses, and now no fashionable gathering was considered complete if the lovely Miss Beresford was not in attendance—especially since her magnetic presence practically guaranteed that a good many of the available men-about-town would gladly forfeit a night at the gaming tables and put in an appearance, merely on the off-chance of a smile and a kind word from the beauty!

At first, having spent the previous year and a half desperately craving a Season in the capital, Jessica had revelled in all the attention that the *ton* saw fit to bestow upon her. However, the feverish excitement that she had felt at the onset was beginning to subside, only to be replaced by a kind of uninterested apathy. A great many of the most prestigious assemblies to which she had been invited had proved to be boring in the extreme and, even though she had already received at least a half a dozen proposals of marriage, she had been singularly unimpressed with every one of her intending suitors.

Gentlemen about town, it seemed to her, were very much of a muchness. They drank far too much, indulged in inexplicable sports like cock-fighting and bare-knuckle boxing and, when they weren't off to the fencing salons or the racecourse, they spent a good deal of their time in smoky gambling rooms or other questionable dens of iniquity. And, even when they did deign to turn up to some function or other, the obsequious insincerity with which they fawned over every single one of the affluent and unattached females present—regardless of their looks—seemed to suggest to Jessica that the majority of these coxcombs were merely seeking to palm themselves off on to some unsuspecting heiress, with an eye to lining their own pockets!

The failed abduction of the previous year had taught her an invaluable lesson regarding the wily behaviour of the predatory male and, thanks to her own valiant endeavours to model her conduct on that of her more decorous cousin Imogen, Jessica was now far less likely to be moved by mere sycophantic flattery.

Nevertheless, having had her radiant loveliness constantly remarked upon for practically the whole of her nineteen years—and despite all of her recent efforts to curb any repetition of the vulgar displays of vanity that had been all too common until Matt's arrival—it was hardly surprising that she should feel just a little piqued that their rescuer who, despite having spoken so few words to her throughout the entire journey, had managed to succeed in giving her the distinct impression that he was totally impervious to her appearance. In point of fact, his very indifference was making Jessica feel quite self-conscious—a most unusual state of affairs for the highly sought-after Miss Beresford!

Still deeply offended by the stranger's criticisms, it was with some considerable relief that she gradually became aware of the fact that the volume of traffic about them was beginning to increase and, as the carriage swung out of the King's Road into Kensington, she realised that they were at last approaching an area of which she was fairly cognisant.

Turning her face towards their escort, with the express intent of demolishing his pretentiousness with the full benefit of one of her most dazzling smiles, she said prettily, 'Since we seem to be nearing the park, sir, there is really no need for you to trouble yourself any further. I am very well acquainted with this part of town.'

'I have no that doubt you are, ma'am,' was his noncommittal reply. 'However, I believe that it behoves me to see you to your door.'

Had Jessica not been seated in a rocking gig, she would have stamped her foot, just as she had been frequently wont to do in one of her old furies. Instead, having spotted a narrow opening in the considerable crush of traffic ahead of them, she curled her fingers tightly about the reins and, giving them a quick flick, urged the horse forward, in the hopes of giving the stranger the slip.

The sudden lurching of the little gig caused Nicholas, who had been dozing on and off for most of the journey, to fling open his eyes in alarm. Whereupon he let out a warning gasp. 'Take care, Jess!'

Then, before she had time to realise what he was about, their escort had shot out a hand, caught hold of the left-hand rein and, with some considerable effort, had managed to haul the mare out of the path of a rapidly approaching curricle.

'Not a very clever manoeuvre, if I may say so,' he observed dryly, as the gig rocked to a standstill. 'Always best to keep out of the path of fast-moving traffic, I've found.'

Jessica, who was shaking from head to toe, was unable to discern whether the trembling was due to her pent-up fury or as a result of the near miss. She fixed the stranger with a look of such rancour that, in the normal way, would have had its recipient reeling back in dismay at its ferocity.

'How dare you, sir!' she ground out, her green eyes glittering dangerously. 'Let go of my rein this instant!'

Unperturbed, the man merely grinned, raising both of his hands to indicate that he no longer had control of her horse. 'Off you go, my girl!' he drawled. 'But do try to steer in a straight line, if you can possibly manage it!'

'I say, steady on, Jess!' murmured Nicholas as Jessica, teeth gritted, flicked angrily at the reins to signal the mare to walk on. 'This is no time to lose your rag—that's another good turn the chap's done us and that's a fact!'

Still fuming, his sister deigned not to reply. With a set face and a stiff back, she kept her eyes firmly fixed on the road in front of her and inched her way back into the fast-moving stream of traffic. Nicholas, having set about disentangling himself from the coils of rope that had held him upright, cast an anxious glance at her rigid expression and, recognising the warning signs, waited in breathless trepidation for the expected outburst which, to his intense surprise, failed to materialise.

The remainder of the journey was completed in total silence until, having reined in the mare outside the front entrance of the elegant Dover Street mansion currently occupied by the Beresford family, Jessica set the wheel brake and nudged her brother to get out of the gig.

For several seconds, she waited in expectation of the stranger dismounting in order to assist her to the ground. He, however, remained in his saddle and made no such move. Seething with frustration, she found herself obliged to shuffle awkwardly along the seat and summon Nicholas to hand her down.

No sooner had her feet reached the pavement than she turned towards the front steps and was just about to mount them when she heard the man call her brother's name.

'Master Beresford!'

Swinging round, she was just in time to see the rider

extracting a bulging package from his pocket. 'Here you are, young man! Catch!'

Jessica's astonished eyes followed the trajectory of the bundle as the startled youth made a valiant but vain attempt to grab it in its flight towards the steps. Having had no difficulty in recognising the item as her own missing reticule, she quickly sidestepped and caught the object neatly between her outstretched hands.

'My reticule' she exclaimed and hurriedly examined the interior of the crushed article. 'But all of the money is still here!'

A suspicious frown appeared on her face and she demanded to know how the rider had come to be into possession of her property.

He inclined his head. 'It would seem that your attacker dropped it in his haste to escape.'

Suddenly feeling very small and rather foolish, Jessica then found herself confronted with the inescapable fact that, no matter what her own private opinion in regard to this stranger, with his oh-so-toplofty condescension, might be, she was morally bound to express her gratitude for his assistance.

'I am very much obliged to you, sir,' she ground out, again making ready to climb the steps. 'Perhaps you would be so good as to remain with the gig while I acquaint my brother with the details of our unfortunate—escapade? He will, no doubt, wish to reward you for your efforts.'

'No reward is necessary, Miss Beresford,' replied the now widely grinning horseman, sweeping off his hat in the most grandiose manner. 'I am more than happy to have been of assistance, I assure you.'

Choosing to ignore this somewhat sardonic remark, Jessica flounced up the steps and tugged impatiently at the doorbell.

Their rescuer waited until the front door had opened to admit the couple, remaining absolutely motionless until, with a resounding thud, it closed behind them. Then, with an impatient shake of his head, he wheeled his mount around, ready to retrace his steps. Just as he was about to spur his horse into action, however, his attention was caught by a little flash of white on the step of the gig. Curious, he leant down to retrieve the object which, on closer inspection, proved to be Jessica's handkerchief. He deduced that it must have fallen from the pocket of her pelisse during her somewhat ungainly scramble from the gig, the memory of which brought a reluctant smile to his lips.

After staring down at the little scrap of lace for some moments, he gave a little grunt and was just about to toss it back into the carriage when, on a sudden impulse, he held it up to his nose, thoughtfully inhaling its delicate perfume. Then, with a short laugh, he tucked it into the inside pocket of his riding jacket and rode off in the direction of the park, without a backward glance.

'And you are telling me that during all that time, this fellow didn't even give you his name?' demanded Matt Beresford of his sister, after listening to her stumbling recital.

'Well—he may have,' owned Jessica, edging closer to her cousin Imogen, who was seated beside her on the sofa. 'There was so much confusion—I was worried that Nicky had hurt himself badly—then *he*—the man,

I mean—pushed me out of the way and, by the time we started off again, the opportunity didn't arise!'

'As a matter of fact,' interrupted Nicholas who, having had his head bathed and attended to by a sympathetic Imogen, was feeling much more the thing, 'I do seem to recall that he did introduce himself. It was when he was prodding me around feeling for broken bones and such, but I was in such a state that I'm afraid I failed to properly register much of what he was saying.'

He paused, frowning to himself. 'He did have a most unusual signet ring, though—I noticed it as he was putting his gloves back on—huge green thing it was—had a sort of dragon on it!'

'You really should have invited the gentleman in, Jessica,' said Imogen, shaking her head. 'It was very remiss of you. Now, unless he chooses to call to find out if you have recovered from your ordeal, it is most unlikely that we will ever be given the opportunity to thank him for coming to your rescue. If he had not turned up when he did, heaven only knows what might have happened! I do wish you had thought to stay at the inn and sent a messenger on. It would have saved so much trouble!'

'I'm awfully sorry, Imo,' replied her cousin. 'I really thought it was for the best. I didn't mean to upset you, I promise.'

'Just wait until I lay my hands on young Stevenage!' Matt ground out wrathfully. 'If he thinks for one moment that—'

'No, really, Matt!' interrupted Jessica in protest. 'Harry was not to blame—he did try to stop me, but I…'

Her voice faltered and her eyes dropped in confusion as Beresford's own swivelled angrily towards her.

'*You* did just as you always do—which is exactly what suits you! Well, Miss Cleverboots, I'll have you know that I have had quite enough—!'

He stopped as his wife reached out and laid her hand on his jacket sleeve.

'As long as they are safe, my love, that's really all that matters, isn't it?'

Staring down into her silver-grey eyes, Matt gave a reluctant smile and took her hand in his. 'I can't have you getting distressed, sweetheart. This sort of thing cannot be at all good for your condition!'

'Oh, really, Matt,' laughed Imogen, patting his hand. 'How many times must I tell you that I am not an invalid! I am a perfectly healthy young woman who happens to be expecting a baby!'

Unconvinced, Matt shook his head. 'I should have packed everything up and returned to Thornfield the minute you told me!' he groaned. 'Home is always the best place to be at such a time. There, at least, you would not have to put up with this sort of irresponsible upset!'

'Nonsense, my dear,' chided his wife gently. 'And miss the Conyghams' ball? It is said to be the event of the Season! Surely, you cannot be thinking of denying me the opportunity to show off that glorious confection of Madame Devy's that has just cost you such an exorbitant amount of money?' Her eyes twinkled up at him. 'Whilst it still fits, remember!'

With another reluctant grin, he bent his head and pressed his lips to her forehead.

'Well, so long as you promise to let me know the minute it all starts getting too much for you.'

She gave him a warm smile. 'You must know that I would never do anything that might harm either this child, or myself, Matt,' she returned quietly. 'I have already given you my word.'

Matt's lips twisted briefly for one moment then, with a quick nod, he turned away and strode back to his own seat on the other side of the fireplace.

'I'm really sorry, Matt,' said Jessica, stepping forward and catching hold of his hand just as he was about to sit down. 'I promise you that I was trying to avoid any upset—I don't want Imo getting distressed any more than you do! It was just meant to be a straight-forward ride home!'

He took a deep breath, 'Very well, Jess. I will say no more about it—apart from giving young Stevenage a piece of my mind, that is! You can hardly expect me to think him the most suitable escort for you if he is unable to control your outrageous behaviour!'

Jessica reddened. She was well aware that Harry Stevenage was as putty in her hands but, having grown rather fond of the young lieutenant, she did not care to think of him being chastised on her account.

'Please, Matt!' she begged her brother. 'Harry is not to blame for any of this! Had it not been for the fact that his mind was so distracted with Olivia's injuries, I am sure that he would have taken a much firmer line!' And, seeing Matt's expression soften, she added, encouragingly, 'He was simply splendid in the way he took charge of everything—quietened down the horses, sent for a doctor and procured rooms for both of the invalids—all in the space of barely an hour!'

'Well, at any event,' retorted Matt, partly appeased, 'it would seem that the lad's two years with the military have not been entirely wasted. I dare say it will do no harm to give him the benefit of the doubt—this time!'

Heaving a sigh of relief, Jessica sat down again, but then, noticing a deep frown upon Nicholas's face, she enquired anxiously if his head was still paining him.

'No, not really,' he muttered absently. 'I know it's there—somewhere in the back of my mind—almost on the very tip of my tongue.'

Staring at him in astonishment, she asked, 'What on earth are you talking about?'

'That fellow's name,' he replied, still frowning. 'I almost had it. Dryden or Brydon or—oh, botheration! It's gone again!'

'Haydn?' chorused Jessica and Imogen in unison, whilst Matt simultaneously offered 'Lydian or Layburn?' all of which suggestions Nicholas met with a vigorous shake of his head.

Whereupon, the next ten minutes or so were spent plying Nicholas with every conceivable version of any similar-sounding name that the three of them could call to mind until, finally, as the offerings became more and more nonsensical, Imogen and Jessica collapsed against each other in convulsions of laughter and begged their menfolk to desist.

'How about Reardon or Raven?' chortled Matt who, totally entranced by his wife's infectious gurgle, was loath to bring the unexpected merriment to a close.

Nicholas started to shake his head again, then he

stiffened and a faraway look came into his eyes. 'Raven?' he mused. 'Ryvern? Great heavens! That's it!' he exclaimed, sitting bolt upright.

'Ryvern?' chimed his audience, in chorus.

'No, not Ryvern!' was his gleeful reply. 'Wyvern! The fellow's name is Wyvern—hence the dragon on his ring, I suppose!' he added in triumph.

There was a long pause, then, 'Wyvern?' said Matt thoughtfully. 'I seem to remember that there was a Viscount Wyvern in my year at Oxford—Theodore Ashcroft by name—no, hang on—I heard that his father, the earl, had died, so I suppose Theo would have inherited the title. About my age, would you say?'

Uncertain as to the age of the stranger, Nicholas was obliged to admit that he had no idea, but Jessica, who had had greater opportunity to study their rescuer, gave a vehement shake of her head.

'Several years younger, I should have thought,' she declared. 'Midtwenties, possibly—and he certainly didn't strike me as aristocratic! Quite the contrary, if you want my opinion!'

'Nevertheless,' Matt pointed out, 'at least it gives us something to go on—no harm in making a few discreet enquiries. The least I can do is to thank the fellow for returning my delinquent sister to the bosom of her family!'

He ducked as a velvet cushion sailed over his head. 'Rotten shot!' he said, as a broad grin formed on his lips. 'Clearly, all those hours I spent trying to teach you to play cricket were a total waste of time!'

Chapter Three

Having deposited his hired mount at the nearest livery stables, the subject of their discussion, recently decommissioned Dragoon Major the Honourable Benedict Ashcroft, now Ninth Earl of Wyvern, set off up South Audley Street to walk the short distance to the family's Grosvenor Square mansion.

He had not gone far, however, when he heard himself hailed by a familiar voice.

'Ashcroft! I say! Over here, old chap!'

On the far side of the road, the driver of a very dashing curricle and pair was waving his whip at him in the most enthusiastic fashion. Instantly recognising his one-time comrade-in-arms, the Honourable Freddy Fitzallan, Wyvern, his face breaking into a broad smile, returned the salute with gusto and nimbly wove his way through the busy traffic to greet his old friend.

'By all that's wonderful!' grinned Fitzallan, leaning down to grasp Wyvern's outstretched hand. 'Last person I expected to see! Just got back, have you? Where are you off to? Hop up; I'll give you a lift.'

'Hardly worth your trouble, Freddy,' said Wyvern with a grin, hoisting himself up beside his friend, nevertheless. 'But I'm headed for Ashcroft House, if you are of a mind.'

Fitzallan whipped up his horses and, with considerable expertise, threaded his way back into the stream of vehicles.

'Dreadfully sorry to hear about poor old Theo, Ben,' he said, shooting a fleeting glance at his friend. 'Hard to believe someone as experienced as your brother could have been that careless with his weapon!' He paused for a moment, then added, with a slightly self-conscious air, 'S'pose we will all have to get into the habit of calling you Wyvern now!'

'So it would seem,' returned the new earl morosely. 'And the very last thing I could have wanted, as you must know!'

Fitzallan gave a sympathetic nod, then, clearing his throat, asked, 'When did you get back?'

'Managed to get a passage last night—got into Tilbury early this morning. Had to leave Berridge and Taverner to collect up my things and bring the horses and carriage over as best they could—I hired a hack and rode straight to Brentford. Thought it best to get the full details from the solicitor before I saw my grandmother.'

'If there's anything I can do to help, old chap, I hope you know that you have only to ask!'

'Point taken, Freddy,' said Wyvern, forcing a smile. 'But, unless you happen to have the odd thirty thousand going begging, it would appear that there's not a lot that anyone can do!'

Fitzallan let out a low whistle. 'Phew!' he gasped 'As

bad as that! I had heard the rumours, of course—difficult to avoid them, as you know—but I hadn't realised…'

He was silent for a moment, then, somewhat apologetically, went on, ''Fraid my pockets are to let, as usual. Had to borrow a score from Holt, only yesterday. Maybe he can help—pretty well loaded, dear old Simon, as you know!'

Shaking his head, Wyvern replied, 'I was joking, dear boy—wouldn't dream of asking either one of you. Apart from which, there would be little point, since I don't have the means to pay back a loan of that magnitude.'

Then, as briefly as possible, he outlined the bones of his earlier meeting with the family solicitor, carefully skating over the less savoury aspects of his deceased older sibling's downfall.

From the limited information that he had managed to cull from Humphreys, who had been the Ashcroft family's solicitor for a good many years, Wyvern had endeavoured to piece together something of his late brother's final days.

It appeared that, during the two years following the carriage accident in which his young wife and baby son had both lost their lives, the late Lord Wyvern had done his best to drown his sorrows in drink. Unfortunately, to the eventual detriment of Ashcroft Grange, the Wyverns' family seat in Middlesex, he had also spent a great many of his waking hours frittering away large sums of money at the gaming tables of one or other of the many gambling dens in the capital. Insofar as his younger brother had been able to establish, it would appear that not one person amongst the late earl's recently acquired circle of friends had felt himself either inclined or able to curtail Theo's reckless proclivities.

To make matters worse—if that were at all possible—Humphreys had then discovered that the late earl, having gambled away the bulk of his own not inconsiderable fortune, had begun to make significant inroads into the estate's ancient assets. In order to fund his spiralling obsession, he had systematically sold off a good many of the cherished silverware collections, along with a quantity of highly prized paintings, irreplaceable tapestries and other such items of value.

Barely able to meet the look of disbelief in his client's eyes, Humphreys had been obliged to steel himself in order to continue his recital of the sorry catalogue of the late earl's excesses, the sad truth of the matter being that, had it not been for the dedication of the small handful of staff who had stayed loyal to their rapidly declining young master, the once carefully husbanded and prosperous estate might well have run to seed. In addition to which, he revealed that Theodore had penned a list containing the names of his creditors, who were collectively owed an amount in excess of thirty thousand pounds—twenty-five thousand of which was in unpaid gambling debts!

As the enormity of his beloved brother's fall from grace had gradually began to force its way into Wyvern's shocked sensibilities, the reasons for Theo finally having elected to put a period to his life had become all too clear to his reluctant successor.

Nevertheless, as he now pointed out to Fitzallan,

who had digested his friend's halting narration in a frowning silence, the question still remained as to how the devil he might set about salvaging the situation?

'If what your man says is correct,' observed Fitzallan, carefully inching his way through the congestion of traffic on Grosvenor Street, 'it would seem that you have very little option left but to sell up and take what you can get out of the deal.'

'Oh, not you as well!' exclaimed Wyvern, affronted at his friend's casual dismissal of the estate that had been in the family's possession for nigh on eight generations. 'That was Humphreys's advice too, but the whole idea is unthinkable! I would sooner die!' But then, as the awful significance of these melodramatic words hit him, he let out a hollow laugh and added, 'I trust it won't come to that, of course!'

'Steady on, Ben, old thing!' protested Fitzallan. 'We have not *quite* reached point-non-plus. If we all put our heads together, we may yet come up with a solution. You might even find that her ladyship has the odd idea or two up her sleeve—she always used to keep her ear pretty close to the ground, as I recall.'

Wyvern attempted a grin. 'From what Humphreys tells me, Grandmama would seem to be as mettlesome as ever—still haring around the countryside as though she were no more than twenty-five!'

'Must be close to eighty now, I imagine?'

'Admits to sixty, I believe,' returned Wyvern, as Fitzallan's curricle swung into Grosvenor Square. 'You will come in and say "hello", of course—she always had a soft spot for you.'

Pulling out his timepiece, Fitzallan looked down and

shook his head ruefully. 'Some other time, if you will excuse me. Arranged to meet Holt at Brooks's—half an hour late already. P'raps you'll get the chance to look in on us later this evening?'

Promising that he would see what he could do, Wyvern leapt down from his perch, saluted his friend and mounted the shallow steps up to the front door of the family's Grosvenor Square residence, to which he shortly found himself admitted by his grandmother's elderly retainer.

'Good to see you back safely, your lordship,' beamed Jesmond, as he ushered Wyvern into the hall and signalled to a waiting footman to relieve him of his outdoor garments. 'Your luggage arrived this morning. Her ladyship has been expecting you hourly. You will find her in the red salon.'

Still unable to prevent the recoil of distaste that he felt at hearing himself addressed by what had been, until a mere two months previously, his older brother Theodore's title, the new earl strode across the hall to greet his grandmother, who was presently emerging from the doorway of the aforementioned salon.

'Benedict! My dearest boy—you have arrived at last!'

A tall, white-haired lady, now in her eighty-first year, Lady Lavinia Ashcroft, Dowager Countess of Wyvern, moved gracefully towards her grandson, exhibiting considerable agility for one of her advanced years. Unlike a good many of her peers, she disdained the prevailing fashion for the semi-transparent muslin afternoon dress and was elegantly clad in a simple but expertly cut round gown of black kerseymere, trimmed at the neck with a neat white ruff.

After kissing Wyvern soundly on both cheeks, she held him at arm's length, carefully scrutinising his ruggedly handsome face.

'You look tired, my boy. I shall have Mrs Winters prepare you a bath—but first, you must join me in a glass of brandy. Jesmond!'

Taking his arm, she allowed her grandson to escort her back into the red salon, so named because of the crimson silk wall hangings and curtains with which it had been furnished many years earlier. Smaller than any of the other reception rooms in the house, it was the Dowager Countess's favourite place to sit in the afternoons, due mainly to the fact that its window overlooked the busy London square, providing her with not only ample advance warning of any impending visitor but, perhaps more significantly, enabling her to keep her eye on her neighbours' comings and goings.

'You have seen Humphreys?' she enquired, as soon as Wyvern had taken his seat and Jesmond had left the room.

Wyvern nodded. 'I went to Brentford first thing, as soon as we docked. But it is just as you said in your letter—Theo does appear to have taken his own life.'

'Humphreys gave me to understand that your brother had left a letter for you. I trust that it contains some sort of explanation for his extraordinary behaviour of late?'

Extracting his brother's missive from his pocket, Wyvern passed it to her. 'Nothing of any consequence, I fear—apart from his apology. He was clearly very confused when he wrote it.'

Leaning back wearily, he ran his fingers through his crisp dark hair, mentally reviewing the singularly odd tenor of his brother's last words.

Ben, old chap, the note read, *Can't go on—got myself into an unholy mess—can't seem to sort it out—mine is yours now—too late for me. Save the Grange, I beg you—relying on you—remember where we used to play when we were lads—forgive me, Theo.*

His forehead puckered in a frown. 'I am still finding the whole affair almost impossible to comprehend. I was aware that Theo was pretty cut up after losing Sophia and young Edwin, of course, but I had no idea that he was in such a bad case. A fellow officer did hear a rumour that he was drinking heavily, but to learn that he has frittered away the entire family fortune on gambling and profligate living is unbelievable—especially when you consider that he was the one Father was wont to call "old sobersides"!'

Save for the sonorous ticking of the long-case clock in one corner, the red salon was silent until, suddenly conscious that his grandmother was waiting for him to continue, Wyvern, striving to keep his innermost feelings under control, took a deep breath.

'Nevertheless,' he managed eventually, 'it is to his credit that Theo seems to have stopped drinking long enough to recover his senses. But he was clearly not himself when he wrote that note—if everything is as bad as Humphreys has given me to understand, how could Theo possibly have expected me to put it all right?'

'I trust that you do not intend to fall into an emotional stew over this, my boy!' retorted the countess, eyeing her grandson sharply. 'Your brother proved himself to be a weakling and, in the end, it appears that he took the coward's way out, so let us have no more repining over the matter!'

'Hold hard, Grandmama!' protested Wyvern, altogether taken aback at the countess's apparent lack of sympathy towards his late brother. 'You can hardly expect me to agree with your view that Theo was a weakling. Any man might turn to drink after such a tragedy, especially if he holds himself responsible for the death of his family, as Theo clearly must have done—he was driving the carriage, after all! His suffering must have been very great—'

'Pish and tush!' interrupted his grandmother dismissively. 'He is not the first person in the world to have been bereaved and left to get on with life—nor will he be the last! I would remind you, young man, that I myself was left a widow at no more than twenty-two when your grandfather was tossed from his horse and broke his neck. Did *I* fall into a decline and take to drink, I ask you?'

Since this was clearly a rhetorical question, Wyvern shook his head and did not reply, knowing from past experience that to interrupt his grandmother when she was in full flood was a pointless exercise.

'No, I did not!' she went on. 'With an estate to run—as well as two young children to raise—I put aside my grief and tears, buckled down and got on with it, so please do not whimper to me about suffering. It is bad enough that your brother gave in to his demons, but to leave you to deal with the problems that he had created and then decided that he could not cope with, is simply the outside of enough!'

At her grandson's continued silence, she tossed back the remains of her drink and gave a dismissive shrug. 'Well, I have said my piece—you may get up and leave in a huff if you choose but, if you are the man that I take you for, you will pour us both another brandy and let us get down to the business of discussing how we may set about undoing the damage caused by Theodore's lack of self-discipline!'

Loath as he was to agree with his grandmother's harsh observations regarding his much-loved brother, Wyvern had to admit that she did, perhaps, have something of a point and if, in fact, the very perceptive old lady could come up with any useful ideas concerning the rescuing of Ashcroft Grange from its creditors, it would certainly be unwise of him to lock horns with her at this juncture.

'I take it that we have no wealthy relatives of whose existence I have been previously unaware?' he asked, as he refilled her glass and handed it to her, retrieving at the same time his brother's note, which the countess had carelessly tossed on to the drum table beside her seat.

'Sadly, no.' She chuckled, relieved to see that she had not dented his good humour. 'If your Aunt Fiona's begging letters are anything to go by, her Irish earl has even less than we have! No, dear boy, it seems to me that what we could really do with at the moment is a rich heiress on the lookout for a peerage!'

Wyvern stiffened. 'I had always supposed that I might have some little say in the matter of choosing a bride,' he demurred.

She peered at him suspiciously. 'You are not already promised, I trust?'

Regretfully setting aside the intrusive images regarding a certain little Parisian opera-dancer he had lately had in his keeping, Wyvern gave a short laugh.

'No such thing, I assure you! However, to return to the point, I am inclined to think it that it is fairly unlikely that even the most pushing of mothers would be willing to marry her daughter off to an absolute "down-and-out"—belted earl or no!'

'Nonsense, Benedict!' chided his grandmother. 'The Ashcroft name must still count for something in this country.'

'Not if what Humphreys has told me is anything to go by,' returned Wyvern bitterly.

'How dare the man!' exclaimed the countess, lifting her chin and drawing herself up to her full height. 'What has he been saying?'

Wyvern shrugged. 'Well, I certainly received the impression that the Ashcroft name alone no longer carries sufficient weight to get us any more credit with Coutts—Theo, apparently, having exhausted their goodwill! Fortunately, Humphreys has managed to persuade the partners not to press for immediate repayment. Unfortunately, there is still the matter of all the other creditors who, I have little doubt, will soon be baying at our door!'

Lady Lavinia sipped thoughtfully at her drink.

'Then it is clear that we will need to make a push right away, my boy,' she said, 'before the upper echelons get wind of the full extent of your brother's transgressions—they have been known to close ranks for far less serious demeanours!'

She paused, contemplating her grandson for a moment, then gave a decisive nod.

'We must set about arranging a soirée!'

'A soirée!' replied Wyvern, considerably taken aback. 'But we are in still in mourning!'

She shrugged. 'We do not have the time to consider all the social niceties, my boy. I was not thinking of a huge affair—just a few close friends, perhaps—simply to announce our re-entry into society. As for suitable bride material, we could do worse than start with Eulalia Capstick—she has been out for a couple of years now and still no takers! Or, better still, what about Felicity Draycott?'

Wyvern choked on his drink. 'Do I take it that you have already drawn up a list of suitable females?' he demanded in astonishment.

'Not as such,' replied the countess, with a haughty sniff. 'But I have always found that it does no harm to keep one's ear to the ground.'

'And might I be permitted to know the names of the rest of these illustrious females whom you have selected as suitable candidates for my hand?' asked Wyvern warily. 'If my memory serves me right, the dumpy Miss Capstick must have at least five Seasons under her belt. And, even though our family has been acquainted with the Draycotts since Felicity was in leading strings, having partnered the lady at dinner on more than one occasion in the past, I can assure you that she is totally without conversation!'

'Hardly a matter of the greatest consequence!' grunted Lady Lavinia, waving her hand dismissively. 'The gal comes with a dowry of fifty thousand pounds, as well as being sole heir to her father's estates—one of which, if you recall, borders the most westerly side of Ashcroft. It would be hard to hit upon a more satisfactory solution to our difficulties! In addition to which, rumour has it that she has been carrying the torch for you ever since you were at Cambridge!'

An expression of acute displeasure crossed Wyvern's face. 'If it's all the same to you,' he returned hurriedly, 'I would just as soon not further my acquaintance with Miss Draycott.'

Shaking her head, the countess rapped him sharply on the wrist with her fan. 'You are in no position to be overly particular, Benedict,' she said sharply. 'Gals who are both wealthy *and* comely tend to have their pick of the town's beaux! And, unfortunately for us, the market appears to have conjured up very few pretty faces this Season—apart from the Beresford chit, of course, but she—'

Wyvern's ears immediately pricked up. 'Beresford?' he asked, his eyes agleam with curiosity.

His grandmother shrugged an elegant shoulder. 'Jessica Beresford, current Belle of all the Balls!' she said carelessly. 'A cit's daughter, of course, but *he* was one of those nabobs who came back from India positively dripping in lard. I once met the man, Sir Matthew Beresford—dead now, so I'm informed—encroaching little nobody he was, especially after he got his knighthood! Married an Emily Herrington, then took her off to India, where she died giving birth to the gal's half-brother—who, I understand, is also Matthew by name.'

'Half-brother?' frowned Wyvern who, having found his attention all at once diverted by the most vivid memory of a pair of flashing green eyes, was desperately trying to keep up with his grandparent's mercurial change of direction.

Lady Lavinia nodded. 'The present Mr Beresford,' she told him. 'Seems the father would have nothing to do with the boy—blamed him for his wife's death or some such nonsense! Anyway, Sir Matthew married again, a Blanche Deveril—I am not familiar with the family—and *that* marriage produced a further two off-spring. Then, last year, *this* Mr Beresford turned up and laid claim to his dead father's estate, married his stepmother's niece and is now the Jessica chit's guardian!'

Pausing for breath, she cast an inquisitive glance in her grandson's direction, but then, having registered the riveted expression on his face, shook her head.

'Jessica Beresford is not for you, Benedict,' she said decisively. 'I am reliably informed that her half-brother has inherited the bulk of Sir Matthew's estate. The girl is worth a mere five thousand a year and, whilst such a sum may be sufficient to have half the town's swells beating a path to her front door, it is not nearly enough for our purpose!'

'Calm yourself, Grandmama,' returned Wyvern, with a wry grin. 'I assure you that I have no intention of joining the ranks of those ramshackle bucks! I have already had the dubious pleasure of meeting the young lady in question and find myself singularly disinclined to pursue the acquaintance.'

But then, having recalled his odd action regarding Jessica's handkerchief, he flushed slightly and, in order to redirect his grandmother's attention, queried, 'Who else do you have in mind for this grand scheme of yours?'

The countess's brow furrowed. 'Well, there are one or two other heiresses worthy of consideration, plus the usual smattering of rich widows, for instance—if you have no objection to an older woman?'

'From where I'm standing,' remarked Wyvern dryly,

'even the two-headed, bearded lady from Astley's Circus is beginning to sound quite plausible—provided that she has the necessary wherewithal, of course!'

'Now you are just being ridiculous,' sighed the dowager, then, glaring at her grandson, added, 'Do you mean to try to save the Grange or don't you?'

Wyvern ran his fingers distractedly through his crisp dark hair. 'I mean to do my best,' he replied stiffly. 'There are other avenues I might explore.'

'Such as?'

He shrugged. 'I will need to return to Ashcroft and take a look for myself—assess the damage and so on. It is possible that things may not be quite as bad as Humphreys has led me to believe—he has always been something of a doom merchant, as I recall!'

'Anything is possible, I suppose,' retorted his grandmother. 'Nevertheless, you must certainly go there as soon as possible—there are still several members of staff in residence. I dare say I might manage to rake up sufficient funds to pay them something of what they are owed.'

Wyvern froze. It had completely slipped his mind that the countess had already met the cost of his brother's funeral and other sundry expenses while awaiting his return from Paris, where he had been serving with the Army of Occupation. For several minutes he studied her closed expression then, making up his mind, he said diffidently, 'I suppose it would do no harm to pay a courtesy visit to the Draycotts—our families were on quite good terms at one time, as I recall.'

Her eyes softening, his grandmother looked across

at him and gave a brisk nod. 'That is exceedingly sensible of you, Benedict. Saving the estate is far more important than pandering to our own personal likes and dislikes—Ashcroft Grange has been in the family for over three hundred years. It was a hard struggle for me to keep it going sixty years ago and now it is your turn—you simply must not let it go without putting up some sort of a fight!'

Jumping to his feet and crossing the short space that separated them, Wyvern sat down beside his grandmother and grasped her hands.

'I promise you that I will do whatever it takes, dearest one,' he said, strengthening his resolve. 'Miss Felicity Draycott will find me to be everything a girl has ever dreamed of, you have my word!'

Chapter Four

Owing to several pressing business engagements, Matt Beresford had been temporarily obliged to shelve the matter of discovering the identity of his siblings' benefactor. He did, however, feel constrained to remonstrate with Lieutenant Stevenage when, three days later, that young man eventually returned to town.

On arriving at the Beresford residence, the lieutenant was shown straight away into the ground-floor study, where a stern-faced Beresford awaited him and, without further ceremony, confronted him with the series of disastrous events that had occurred following Jessica's defiant exit from the inn at Turnham Green.

'And now, sir, what have you to say for yourself?' demanded Matt, fixing the lieutenant with his most severe frown.

Stevenage's cheeks had grown pale with shock. 'I really must crave your pardon, Mr Beresford,' he stammered. 'I begged her not to attempt the journey, but she…'

'Has a mind of her own?' supplied Matt who, being well acquainted with Jessica's obstinate streak, was not entirely unsympathetic to the young man's plight.

A vivid flush then covered Stevenage's face but, squaring his shoulders and looking his host straight in the eye, he said, 'Nevertheless, sir, I hold myself entirely responsible for what happened and give you my word that, should such a situation ever occur again, Miss Beresford's welfare will be my primary concern.'

'Along with your sister's, I trust?' interposed Beresford dryly.

'Er—yes, but of course,' came Stevenage's hurried response. 'Both ladies would be of equal concern, naturally!'

Matt's lips began to twitch. 'And how is Miss Stevenage?' he asked, anxious to save the young man any further embarrassment. 'I trust that she suffered no great hurt?'

'Nothing of consequence, sir. I sent a message to my father and he came down with a carriage and took Olivia home—she is fine now, sir.' The lieutenant paused, eyed Matt nervously then, taking a deep breath, went on, 'I'm truly sorry about the landau, sir. I thought it best to remain at the inn until your coachman recovered, but then he refused to leave until the pole was fixed, which is why I have been out of town for so long—I would not care for you to think that I was fighting shy of facing you!'

There was such an earnest expression on the young lieutenant's face that it was all Matt could do to control the wide grin that threatened. During his short acquaintance with Stevenage, he had found him to be a most honourable young man and, prior to this recent contretemps, had seen no reason to put any obstacle in the way of his growing friendship with Jessica. Matt knew that it would be a good many years before the young man, at barely twenty-two years of age and at the very beginning of his military career, would find himself in any position to support a wife. And, although it was clear that Stevenage was, for the moment at any rate, besotted with his young half-sister, Beresford was reasonably sure that he was not the sort to take liberties. This, along with the fact that Stevenage had a sister of an age with Jessica, made him, as far as both Matt and Imogen were concerned, a safe escort and ideal companion for the girl.

'Your apology is accepted,' he grunted. 'I dare say you did the best you could, in the circumstances.' And, gesturing towards the tantalus on his desk, he offered Stevenage a glass of brandy. 'Luckily for all of us, none of you suffered any serious damage—but take it as a lesson, my boy!'

A few quick sips of the fiery spirit settled the young man's nerves sufficiently for him to pluck up sufficient courage to enquire whether he might be permitted to escort Jessica again, some time in the near future.

'I believe we have engaged a box at the Drury Lane this evening,' said Matt, after a moment's consideration. 'Perhaps you and your sister would care to join us?'

Although he was far from being an ardent devotee of the opera, Stevenage accepted his host's offer with alacrity, reasoning that it would be well worth sitting through a few hours of unintelligible caterwauling just for the pleasure of seeing Jessica again. Olivia, he felt certain, would be more than happy to accompany him.

* * *

When the siblings arrived at the theatre, however, he found Jessica strangely preoccupied. She seemed pleased to see both him and his sister again and even offered him a very pretty apology for ignoring his advice the other day. But then, apart from enquiring after Olivia's health, she seemed disinclined to say much at all and, by the time they had been shown to their box and settled themselves into their appointed seats, the performance was ready to begin. After that, although Stevenage made valiant attempts to catch her eye throughout the first act, the volume of sound issuing from the combined talents of the orchestra and chorus, coupled with the constant hubbub from the patrons in the cheaper seats in the gallery above, pretty well drowned out any real attempt at conversation. Heaving a sigh, and hoping for better luck in the interval, he tried to concentrate his attention on the stage but, after some few minutes, gave this up, having been unable to fathom out what the devil was going on!

As his frustration and boredom increased, his eyelids gradually drooped, then closed and, had not the act climaxed on a sudden, rousing crescendo, he might well have fallen asleep. Instantly on the alert, his eyes flew open and he was up on his feet almost before the curtains closed. Motioning to Nicholas, he was just about to suggest that both they and the two girls might use this opportunity to slip out into the corridor and stretch their legs for a few minutes, when he heard Jessica's excited whisper.

'Nicky! Nicky!' She was clutching at her brother's arm. 'Look over there! The third box from the stage! I'm certain that that's him!'

'Him—who?' Momentarily confused, Nicholas peered across the crowded auditorium. Then, as his eyes settled on the box his sister had indicated, his face cleared. 'By Jove, I believe you're right!' he exclaimed, and almost fell off his chair in his eagerness to reach his half-brother, in order to point out Jessica's discovery to him. 'It's that Wyvern fellow, Matt,' he cried jubilantly. 'Look! Over there! Ought we to go across and speak to him, do you suppose?'

Jessica's emerald eyes were alight with excitement and she could feel her heart beating at the most incredible rate. She had spent the past three days in hourly expectation of the stranger calling to enquire after their welfare. Why this had become such a matter of importance to her, she was at a loss to fathom, especially when she recalled the stranger's high-handed attitude towards her. Yet the very sight of him, sitting a mere twenty-five yards across from her, was causing her to experience a quite extraordinary fluttering in the pit of her stomach.

He was not alone. Seated to one side of him was a very elderly lady, who was one of the most formidable-looking females that Jessica had ever set eyes upon. She could not recollect having been introduced to such an aristocratic dowager at any of the many illustrious events she had attended and, since the lady was hardly the sort of person one could readily forget, she concluded that she, along with her escort, must be newcomers to town.

Sliding her eyes across to the second female in the box, she gave a gasp of dismay. Unless she was much mistaken, the man's other companion was Felicity

Draycott, one of a coterie of coolly elegant, but rather
haughty, damsels who had spent the greater part of
Jessica's time in town offering her the cold shoulder!
Not that this had bothered Jessica unduly, since she
had been enjoying herself far too much to pay a great
deal of attention to their disapproving glances. But,
why on earth such a devilishly handsome and elegantly
turned-out man would want to waste himself on such a
top-lofty companion she could not begin to fathom—
unless, of course, the Draycott female was some sort
of relative of his! Having decided that this was the only
reasonable conclusion that could be reached, her lips
began to curve, her eyes grew bright and, as she
watched Matt enter Wyvern's box, a shudder of excited
anticipation ran through her.

Stevenage, who had been observing her growing excitement, demanded to know what all the fuss was
about. 'Why all this sudden interest in Ben Ashcroft?'
he asked, somewhat tetchily.

'Ashcroft?' said Imogen, turning towards him, a
bewildered look on her face. 'I was given to understand
that the gentleman's name was Wyvern?'

Stevenage shrugged. 'Yes, well, since he's just inherited his brother's title, I suppose it would be more
proper to refer to him as Lord Wyvern,' he replied in-
differently. 'I met him when he was an officer with the
13th Light. Our units were quartered together when I
was in Paris last year. He's only just returned home.'
He paused momentarily then, turning back to Jessica,
he said, 'Funnily enough, he was at the Rose and Crown
the other day, when we were there—he'd stopped to
water his horse and have a bite to eat, so he told me.'

'At the Rose and Crown!' cried Jessica, in astonishment. 'I don't remember seeing him! And you say you spoke to him? Where was this?'

'In the taproom,' replied Stevenage, with a puzzled frown. 'After you and Nicky took off—why so much interest in the fellow?'

'He's only the chap who saved us from those two thugs!' exploded Nicholas. Then, as a sudden thought occurred to him, he added, 'I suppose it must have been you who told him who we were?'

Stevenage flushed, remembering that after Jessica and her brother had driven off, instead of returning directly to his sister as he had planned, he had stomped off into the taproom and tossed back quite a large quantity of brandy, in order to try to quell his feelings of helpless frustration.

'Possibly,' he replied warily. 'I don't actually recall the entire conversation.'

He did, however, have the most uncomfortable feeling that his exasperation at Jessica's having ignored his advice, coupled with the effects of imbibing a good deal more liquor than was his usual custom, might well have caused him to express his opinions about her cussedness rather more freely than propriety demanded.

'No sweat, Harry,' said Nicholas absently, his attention still on the box opposite. 'We just wondered how he came by the information—oh, look! They're shaking hands and Matt is leaving!'

In barely suppressed expectation, Jessica awaited the return of her brother, her mind awhirl with possibilities. Had he invited the stranger—no, Lord Wyvern, now, she reminded herself—to call on them?

Or, perhaps, to join them for dinner? She looked over at the earl's box and a little shiver of excitement ran through her as she saw that Wyvern, having returned to his seat, was now looking in their direction. He was even more handsome than she had remembered! Her eyes shone more brightly than ever and, cheeks dimpling, she beamed one of her most enchanting smiles across the auditorium.

When Beresford returned to their box, however, the information that he carried with him was hardly promising. Wyvern had, of course, been everything that he should be. Glad to meet an old acquaintance of his late brother, more than happy to have been of service to the two young travellers, and so on. He had thanked Beresford for his invitations and had assured him that he would do his best to call on the family at some time in the near future but, because of pressing business commitments, he was unable to say when that might be.

On the other side of the theatre, Wyvern, in spite of himself, found his gaze drawn to the box opposite. For some inexplicable reason, he found himself more than interested to register Jessica's reaction to her brother's announcement. He did not have long to wait. No sooner had the gist of Matt's words begun to sink in than the dazzling smile was dashed from her lips, only to be replaced by an expression of the most profound disappointment.

Wyvern's brow furrowed; after the girl's rather haughty treatment of him the other day, he could not understand why his negative response to Beresford's invitation should elicit such an extreme reaction from her. But then, he reasoned to himself, given what young

Stevenage had, inadvertently, let fall about the lovely Miss Beresford, coupled with the not entirely favourable impression that he himself had formed, it was not beyond the realms of fantasy to conclude that these highly exaggerated mannerisms were merely part of a well-practised routine on her part.

Having seen the astonishingly reckless manner in which she had flourished a bulky wad of banknotes under the stableman's nose—to the considerable interest of a good many onlookers—followed by her total disregard for both her brother's and Stevenage's counsel, it had come as no surprise to Wyvern to discover that Miss Beresford in person was even more pig-headed than he had been given to understand. Clearly used to having things go her way, and heaven help those who had the temerity to cross her!

Well, the little madam could bat her eyelashes at him until the cows came home, thought Wyvern, with a disdainful shrug, but if she really imagined that she could persuade *him* to join the ranks of all those young jackanapes who were dancing to her tune, she was about to discover how very wrong she was! The girl clearly need to be taught some sort of a lesson and, as his mind dwelt upon the various ways in which the condescending Miss Beresford might be brought to heel, it very soon occurred to Wyvern that, had he but had the time at his disposal, he would not have been at all disinclined to take on the job himself! Such a pleasant distraction could well prove to be most gratifying!

As the gas lamps in the auditorium were slowly lowered for the start of the second act, an introspective gleam came into his eyes and his lips curved in amusement as he contemplated the possibilities. That softly rounded figure—he could well imagine how that would feel in his arms! And those eyes! He would swear that a man might drown in those glorious pools and be only too glad to do so! A sudden clash of cymbals from the orchestra pit jolted him out of this agreeable reverie and thrust him rudely back to his senses. A deep frown puckered his brow. What, in the name of thunder, had got into him? As if he didn't have more than enough complications in his life already!

Having spent the past few days investigating the true state of affairs at Ashcroft Grange, he had discovered that, to his considerable relief, the situation was not nearly as hopeless as the solicitor, Humphreys, had led him to believe. Many valuable artefacts had disappeared, it was true, but Wyvern was soon to learn that the handful of dedicated servants still in residence had been more than anxious to restore the property to its former glory and had worked very hard to repair the damage that had been caused by his brother's incontinent associates.

Brigham, the elderly land agent, had informed his new master that there was still sufficient revenue coming in from the four tenant farmers to keep the estate ticking over for several months, given that nothing out of the way occurred in the meantime. This being so, Wyvern was reasonably confident that, for the moment, at any rate, the interest from what was left of his own small capital would just about cover the servants' wages and his own day-to-day expenses.

And, even though he had never felt the slightest inclination to involve himself in the running of the rambling estate, the intricate workings of which were still something of a mystery to him, these findings were of some comfort to him. Even more so to his grandmother, perhaps, who had spent the entire period of Wyvern's absence in a continual fret as to what news he would impart to her on his return from Brentford.

There still remained, however, the formidable dilemma of how to lay his hands on the prodigious amount of money needed to satisfy the late earl's creditors who, as soon as the news of Wyvern's arrival back in the capital had reached their ears, were already starting to clamour for satisfaction.

It was entirely as a result of his deep concern regarding this seemingly insurmountable problem that he had finally agreed to accompany his grandmother on a prearranged call to Draycott House that very morning.

His dark eyes slid over to the young lady who was seated at his right. With her hands folded primly into her lap, her whole attention appeared to be focussed on the stage below. Having spent the entire obligatory half-hour of the morning visit attempting to engage her in some sort of conversation, it had not taken him very long to realise that, since she had failed to express a single opinion on any of the many topics he had raised, Miss Draycott was apparently still quite incapable of forming one! In addition, she seemed to have developed the most disconcerting habit of demurely lowering her eyes and glancing to one side whenever she spoke, thus avoiding any direct confrontation. And, whilst any other man might find this coy mannerism rather appealing, to Wyvern it was starting to be a distinct irritation.

As a soft sigh escaped his lips, he felt the countess's hand on his arm. Turning to face her, he gave a rueful shake of his head, having decided that, despite all of the Draycotts' obvious wealth and background, he might well be forced to look elsewhere for his family's salvation.

Across the auditorium, the entire second half of the performance passed completely over Jessica's head, so stunned was she at Wyvern's rebuff. Had he walked into the box and slapped her across the face she could hardly have been more mortified. She bit hard on her lip to prevent the tears from forming. To think that she had been prepared—even eager, as she recalled in embarrassment—to put that first unfortunate encounter with Wyvern behind her and begin anew. After all, she reasoned, how could she possibly have known that the man who had come to their aid was an earl? He had not introduced himself properly and he certainly had not behaved as one might have expected a member of the aristocracy to behave. In fact, as she recalled, having failed to dismount in order to assist her from the carriage, the man had been singularly discourteous!

Straightening her shoulders, she furtively wiped away the single tear that had managed to find its way on to her cheek and vowed to put the beastly man out of her mind. It was hardly as though she was short of beaux, she reminded herself crossly. She could name more than a dozen hopefuls who would happily cut off their right arms just for one dance with her! But then, as a sudden vision of that rather unpleasant spectacle presented itself to her, she gave a little shudder and, conscious of Stevenage's anxious eyes upon her, she turned and bestowed such a sweet smile upon the young lieutenant that he was totally overcome.

Chapter Five

Wearily tossing aside yet another demand for immediate reimbursement of one of the many outstanding debts incurred by his brother, Wyvern leaned back in his chair. Closing his eyes, he raked his fingers through his thick, dark hair, endeavouring to make some sense of the seemingly hopeless mess that had been bequeathed to him.

Although he was reasonably confident in the knowledge that Brigham, the Grange's highly competent manager, was doing his best to return the estate to something of its former excellence, the hiring of the extra labour required had made considerable inroads into what was left of Wyvern's available funds. Added to which, the lavish affair that his grandmother had insisted upon throwing the following Friday looked set to deplete them even further. More than once this week already, a highly embarrassed Jesmond had been obliged to draw the earl's attention to the disturbing fact that several of the family's long-standing suppliers had taken to requesting cash payments for the innumerable items that Lady Lavinia had ordered to mark the family's re-entry into society. She, however, had been loftily unrepentant, having pointed out that it would hardly do to give their guests even the slightest hint that the family might be in some sort of financial difficulty.

With a resigned sigh, Wyvern rose to his feet and began to pace about the room, racking his brains to find some solution to the problem. No matter how offensive the idea was to him, it was becoming abundantly clear that he would have to apply for a loan of some sort— but to whom could he turn? He had not failed to register Humphreys's caution that Theo had outrun the patience of all the major banking facilities, so he was fairly sure that, even were he to approach them 'cap in hand', so to speak, it was highly improbable that any petition from himself would be likely to find favour amongst that closely-knit brotherhood either.

He was not unmindful of the fact that, should he care to request their assistance, he was extremely fortunate in that he had a great many acquaintances who would not hesitate to come to his rescue. Indeed, every day for the past week, his dearest friend, Sir Simon Holt, had been urgently pressing him to accept loans of quite ridiculous sums of money with no conditions attached. To add grist to his mill and, despite the earl's protests to the contrary, Holt had not hesitated to point out to his friend that, had it not been for Wyvern's quick action in the field at Waterloo, he himself would not have survived the battle.

Nevertheless, Wyvern was loath to avail himself of his friend's generous offer. Having seen other close friendships founder under similar well-meant circumstances and knowing that, as things stood at present, he had absolutely no hope of ever being able to repay such a loan, he could not bring himself to opt for a course that, in the end, could well jeopardise his long-term friendship with his ex-comrade-in-arms.

All of which led him to the only available alternative, highly distasteful though it might be! In the absence of any other salvation and since it was clear that the situation was beginning to grow somewhat desperate, it would seem that coupling his name with one or other of the heiresses on Lady Lavinia's list looked to be the only option left to him!

In spite of his long absence from town, he was sufficiently versed in the ways of its inhabitants to know that any received impression that a gentleman might soon be about to benefit from a sudden increase in his fortune, either through inheritance or by marriage, was enough to hold his creditors at bay. Indeed, given that a debtor's future prospects were deemed to be more or less cut and dried and of sufficiently generous proportions, a great many of those creditors were often inclined to press their client into borrowing even more money from them.

Several days had passed since the visit to the opera, during which time he had not only paid two morning visits to Felicity, but had also accompanied her to a musical evening given by one of her mother's acquaintances. Having cast his eyes over the few remaining names on his grandmother's list, he had been obliged to conclude that, despite her obvious drawbacks, it was clear that Sir Jonathan Draycott's daughter was the best of a very dismal bunch!

He had seldom allowed thoughts of marriage to

intrude on his carefree bachelor life, particularly after Theo and Sophie had secured the Ashcroft lineage by obligingly producing a son. But he was finding it hard to come to terms with the fact that he, who, scarcely six months previously, might have had the pick of the Season's tastiest offerings, now appeared to be considerably restricted as to choice!

As he cast his mind back over his not-unimpressive string of past conquests, he could not help but heave a deep sigh of regret. He then had to take himself severely to task, reminding himself that marrying for love, amongst persons of his rank and status, was hardly an option. Marriage, as far as members of the aristocracy were concerned, was simply a convenient method of increasing land assets whilst, at the same time, preserving the quality of long-established pedigrees. In this sense, Felicity Draycott, despite her lack of any discernible charisma, was perfectly acceptable and, in the general way, all that a countess needed to be. Added to which, since the lady—according to his grandmother—seemed to hold him in a certain amount of esteem and, it appeared, had turned down more than one prospective suitor during his prolonged absence, it was not unreasonable to assume that she would be willing to accept his proposal—if he could just bring himself to make the offer!

Nonetheless, the thought of having to spend the rest of his days—not to mention the nights, as he reminded himself with a wry grimace!—in such uninspiring company filled him with despair. The idea of finding himself part of that sad little company of disillusioned husbands who, with increasing regularity, chose to spend most of their lives in one club or another, or in the clandestine company of a series of other females, was too sickening to contemplate.

On returning to his desk, his attention was caught by a glint from the green glass paperweight in front of him. All at once, the recurring memory of a pair of sparkling green eyes invaded his thoughts. Now *there* was a girl who had no difficulty in expressing an opinion, he reflected, as his lips curved in a whimsical smile. Had he been a gambling man, he would have been prepared to lay odds that Jessica Beresford was the sort who would always give as good as she got! He suspected that life with that little spitfire would be anything but boring!

Sadly, however, any further contemplation of Miss Beresford's attributes was forestalled by a light tap on the door and the butler's subsequent entry, it having transpired that the late earl's manservant had just arrived in the house and was requesting an immediate audience with his new master.

'Cranwell?' frowned Wyvern, returning abruptly to his senses. 'Show him in at once, Jesmond! Whatever it is must be pretty important to have brought him all this way!'

As well as having served as valet to both Wyvern's father and brother, Cranwell was also the unfortunate servant who, having carried out the late earl's order to deliver that very puzzling letter into the hands of the solicitor, had returned to Ashcroft Grange to discover his young master's dead body slumped across the library desk. However, due to the man's unswerving loyalty to the family over the years—not to mention his advancing years—Wyvern had not yet had the heart to tell the elderly valet that his services were no longer needed. Instead, he had left Cranwell with instructions to put whatever remained of the late Lord Wyvern's personal effects into some sort of order. This being so, and given that it was barely three days since he himself had returned from Ashcroft, he was at a loss to understand what possible difficulty Cranwell could have encountered that had necessitated him undertaking such a wearisome journey to the capital.

Resuming his seat at the desk, he waited for Jesmond to return with the unexpected visitor. Then, casting an intent look at the elderly manservant, he enquired, kindly, 'Well, now, Cranwell! What great emergency has brought you all this way—even you cannot possibly have finished sorting out his late lordship's gear in such a short time, surely?'

A brief smile crossed the man's face and he shook his head. He had been with the family long enough to recognise when he was being roasted.

'I'm afraid not, your lordship,' he replied, in his usual staid accents. 'I still have plenty to occupy me in that respect. I am here on a rather more pressing matter—Mr Brigham was of the opinion that it needed to be brought to your notice immediately.'

His attention caught, Wyvern leaned forward. 'Well, out with it, man! What is so pressing that a letter would not have served?'

'We—ah…um— That is, Mr Brigham and Mr Kirmington and myself, sir— We felt that it would be more advisable to inform you directly, sir. The fact is, your lordship,' he burst out hurriedly, having perceived the growing impatience on Wyvern's face, 'we have reason to believe that the Grange has been broken into!'

'Broken into!' returned Wyvern, astounded. 'Burgled, do you mean?'

'Well, no, sir, not exactly,' came the man's hesitant reply. 'Things have been moved around—drawers tipped up and so on, but, as far as we can ascertain, nothing has been removed.' He paused, then added, almost apologetically, 'As you are aware, my lord, there is very little of value left to be taken and that, sir, is the reason I am here. We do believe, sir—ah…um— Mr Kirm—'

'Yes, yes, I know!' cut in Wyvern sharply. 'You and Brigham and the butler—for pity's sake, man—what the devil is it that you all believe?'

'We are all of the opinion that he— They— Whoever— Must have been searching for something, my lord. And, my lord, I would venture a guess that it must be something rather important. As far as we are able to establish, there seem to have been three separate attempts so far, in spite of all our efforts to secure the property!'

Wyvern was mystified. 'But all the doors and windows are kept locked at night, surely?'

'Of course, sir,' affirmed Cranwell. 'However, we now believe that entry must have been made by way of the pantry window, which, as you may recall, sir, is less than a foot square and has no lock. It was not until Cook complained to Mr Kirmington this very morning that a butter crock had been knocked off the windowsill and several items of food had gone missing, that Mr Kirmington, upon investigation, noticed that the window latch had been forced, leading us to the conclusion that this had been the means of entry.'

Pausing briefly in order to determine whether the frowning earl was still following his argument, he then ventured, 'Mr Brigham has subsequently repaired the damage to the window, your lordship, and has taken the precaution of fitting a padlock to the latch.'

Wyvern pursed his lips. 'And you say that these— break-ins, as you call them—have occurred on three separate occasions?'

Cranwell inclined his head. 'On each night since your departure, sir. On Monday, the library was ransacked—books pulled from the shelves and thrown about the place. On Tuesday, every single drawer and cupboard was emptied and the contents rummaged through and, last night, those few pictures that we still have left were lifted from the walls and their backings removed! Mr Brigham was of the opinion that, even though he is certain that he has foiled any further attempts to gain access, the matter should be brought to your attention without delay.' Shooting a questioning glance at his master, he added, 'Clearly someone in search of something, as I am sure your lordship would agree?'

'So it would seem,' acknowledged Wyvern, his brow puckering. Having spent the best part of his three-day sojourn at the Grange collecting every available scrap of paperwork he could lay his hands on, he was reasonably confident that nothing of moment could have been left behind. 'However, what does rather puzzle me is how all of this somewhat destructive activity could have occurred without any of you servants being aware of it!'

'Begging your lordship's pardon, sir,' returned Cranwell, nervously shifting his stance, 'but, in view of the fact that the house staff has been reduced to a mere half-dozen or so—not to mention the fact that male and female staff are housed in separate attic wings…' He flushed uncomfortably and his voice petered out.

'Point taken, Cranwell,' replied Wyvern heavily, as he called to mind the complicated warren of rooms, stairways and corridors that comprised the Grange, which was situated at the foot of a shallow escarpment, on the ridge of which could still be seen the ruins of what had once been the Cistercian monastery of Wyvern Abbey. Following his Act of Dissolution, Henry VIII had gifted the abbey, along with its considerable acreage of land, to Sir Cedric Ashcroft, in reward for his support during the previous year's rebellions. Sir Cedric, created First Earl of Wyvern, had plundered the buff-coloured limestone from the decaying monastery to make extensive alterations to what had been, originally, the Abbey's farmhouse. The present dwelling, due to successive earls having continued to alter, reshape and impose their own ideas on the original property, was now an impressive house, some four storeys high, winged on either side of its magnificent frontage by two lofty extensions.

Unfortunately, the building had grown into a structure of such rambling proportions that Wyvern was bound to concede that the idea of anyone situated in one of its attic rooms being able to hear intruders in another part of the house was, to say the least, somewhat unreasonable.

Rising to his feet, he tugged at the bell cord. 'You travelled up by the mail, I take it?' he asked the manservant.

Cranwell shook his head. 'No, my lord,' he replied. 'In view of the urgency of the situation, I took the liberty of hiring a chaise.'

'Very wise of you, Cranwell,' returned Wyvern. Then, allowing himself a slight smile, he added, encouragingly, 'It was perfectly correct of you to bring this matter to my attention. Jesmond will see that you are given some refreshments and, as soon as you are sufficiently rested, I shall accompany you back to the Grange. We must see if we cannot put a stop to all this nonsense!'

After he had delivered the weary but now considerably relieved Cranwell into the butler's competent hands, the frowning Wyvern returned to his seat at the desk.

Yet another problem to add to an already quite formidable list, he thought grimly, as he endeavoured to apply his mind to the question of who could have broken into Ashcroft Grange and, rather more to the point, for what could these intruders have been searching?

Chapter Six

Although Jessica made every effort to banish the
dilemma of Wyvern's indifference from her thoughts,
the highly provoking subject continued to plague her.

She found it hard to believe that the man could be
so high in the instep as to regard her family as beneath
his touch. Thanks to Imogen's godmother, Lady
Sydenham, having successfully paved the way for
them, the Beresford family had been extremely well
received by the *beau monde*. Imogen and Matt were
well liked, and Jessica herself, as she could hardly have
remained unaware, was extremely popular, not only
with most of the young men about town, but also with
quite a few of their female counterparts.

Back home in Kirton Priors, she had always reigned
supreme in the popularity stakes. Here in the capital of
the fashionable world, however, it had not taken her
very long to discover that holding such an undisputed
position in one's own small neighbourhood was, in
reality, of rather small consequence when one found

oneself surrounded by a not inconsiderable number of other very attractive young ladies. Consequently, she had taken Imogen's advice and had gone out of her way to make friends with many of her fellow debutantes— with the possible exception of the somewhat stuffy coterie to which Miss Felicity Draycott belonged!

All of which made Wyvern's complete lack of interest in seeking any sort of introduction very difficult for her to comprehend. Eventually, however, after having forced herself to review their first encounter, she was obliged to admit that her own conduct towards the helpful stranger had not been all that it might have been, in the circumstances. Moreover, the longer she thought about it, despite all arguments to the contrary, it became increasingly obvious to her that the reason she had behaved so badly at the time was that Wyvern had managed to discompose her in a way that few men of her acquaintance had ever succeeded in doing.

Throughout the whole of that miserable journey back to town, she could have sworn that she had felt his eyes burning into the back of her head. Added to which, that high-handed, matter-of-fact tone of voice he had insisted on employing had merely served to increase her annoyance and, at the same time, helped foster her conviction that he was, in reality, enjoying some sort of private joke at her expense! Not forgetting the fact that he had virtually accused her of being responsible for the entire fiasco! It was small wonder that she had allowed herself to become slightly riled, she thought resentfully.

But then, when she recalled the childish way in which she had flounced off into the house that evening, her cheeks grew quite hot and she found herself admitting that, in the light of that shocking display of bad manners, Wyvern's subsequent indifference was hardly surprising.

Nevertheless, she was at a loss to understand why his lordship's lack of interest should have put her into such a state of restlessness for, no matter how much she tried to avoid thinking about it, the vexing subject would persist in returning to disturb her peace. She had already lost a good many hours' sleep pondering over the problem, causing Imogen to remark about the dark shadows under her eyes.

'You are beginning to look quite peaky,' her cousin commented, anxiously studying Jessica's wan expression. 'Too many late nights, I fear! Perhaps we had better start turning down a few of these,' she added, motioning to the pile of invitations at her elbow.

Summoning up a smile, Jessica replied, 'No, please don't, Imo. I have a slight headache, that is all. A little walk in the garden will soon have me back to rights!'

Since her brother and cousin had gone to so much trouble in order to provide her with this Season in London, Jessica could not bring herself to confess to having discovered that her former excitement at the constant round of morning visits, musical evenings, assemblies, and the like, was beginning to pall.

In order to appease her cousin, she took a few turns around the garden, wondering what she could do to prevent her thoughts from wandering back to that relentlessly invasive dilemma. What she really needed, she thought despondently, was some sort of distraction—but what?

* * *

As it happened, Nicholas was soon to provide his sister with such a diversion when, shortly after breakfast, he announced his intention of visiting the British Museum, in order to view the recently installed pieces of marble that Lord Elgin had recovered from the Greek Parthenon.

Not that Jessica was especially fascinated by the sort of erudite topic that held her bookish brother spellbound but, having heard a good deal of gossip concerning these particular ancient relics, she had to own to a certain curiosity about them. She therefore informed her astonished brother that, provided that he had no objections, she would be glad to accompany him on his outing.

Since Matt found that, due to a prior engagement, he himself would be unable to escort the pair to their chosen destination, a note was sent round to Stevenage's quarters to enquire whether Harry and Olivia would care to join the proposed expedition.

Sadly, as it turned out, the young lieutenant's duties at the barracks prevented him from accompanying the youngsters. And, since Matt was reluctant to agree to them going off on their own, it was beginning to look as though their proposed jaunt was in danger of being axed. Nicholas, however, having reminded his brother that there were only a few more days left of his Easter break from school, was quick to point out that, if he did not go today, it was doubtful if another such opportunity would be likely to present itself.

Stifling any misgivings that he might have felt, Matt eventually agreed to put Cartwright and the chaise at their disposal.

'He will drop you off in Montague Place and return there to pick you up at a pre-arranged time,' he told Nicholas. 'However, you must promise me that you will be at the appointed place, sharp on the dot.' He hesitated, then looked the youngster squarely in the eye. 'I want no repetition of last week's fiasco, Nicky. I take it that I can rely on you to keep your sister in line?'

'You have my word, Matt,' his brother assured him then, with a slight grin, added, 'Although, I am inclined to think that even Jess would think twice before kicking up a fuss in the British Museum!'

'Don't you be too sure about that, my lad!' grunted Matt. 'I dare say Jess could cause havoc in the middle of Westminster Abbey, if she put her mind to it!'

Accordingly, at half-past one that same afternoon, Nicholas and Jessica were deposited at the gates of Montague House, which housed the collection of antiquities. Having judged that two hours should be more than enough time to study the sculptures, Nicholas would happily have settled upon three-thirty as the most suitable time for Cartwright to return to pick them up. Jessica, however, having suddenly remembered that the museum was situated within a short walking distance of the capital's most fashionable shopping centre, begged her brother to add another hour or so on to his timetable, in order that they might take a quick stroll along Oxford Street. Somewhat reluctantly, Nicholas acceded to her request and instructed the coachman to bring the carriage to the corner of St Giles Circus at five o'clock sharp. Then, taking his sister's arm, he hurried to join the eager throng of people making their way into the building.

Jessica's first thought, when confronted with the exhibition, was that a good deal of fuss seemed to have been made over what was, after all, little more than a lot of pieces of broken stonework. But then, as she followed her blissfully contented brother around the gallery, she found herself dwelling on how magnificent the ancient carvings must have looked in their original state, compared with how dreadfully disfigured most of them were now. By the time that Nicholas had drunk his fill of the works and expressed himself ready to leave, her eyes were quite moist.

'It's all so frightfully sad, don't you think?' she asked him, as she dabbed away her tears.

After eyeing his sister in some dismay, Nicholas glanced around apprehensively, fervently praying that no one else was near enough to witness her extraordinary behaviour. Hurriedly grabbing her by the elbow, he drew her towards the exit. If Jess was about to make a complete ass of herself, he thought, the sooner he got her out of the place, the better!

'What in heaven's name was that all about?' he demanded, as soon as they had quit the building.

'Surely you felt it too, Nicky?' gulped Jessica. 'It was all so very, very poignant. All those broken bits of statues—they seemed so pathetic lying there! I think his lordship should have left them where they belonged!'

'Don't be idiotic, Jess,' Nicholas remonstrated. 'Had it not been for Lord Elgin, they would have been completely destroyed! He saved them for posterity!'

His sister, however, was not to be placated. 'Better

to be destroyed than be put on display with your head and arms missing,' she riposted moodily and, thrusting her nose in the air, she started to walk away from him.

'Oh, do snap out of it, please, Jess,' he pleaded then, reaching out his hand in an effort to detain her, he suddenly remembered her earlier request. 'Come along now!' he cajoled her. 'If we hurry we will just have time to take a quick look at the shops in Oxford Street. You said you wanted to do that, remember?'

Jessica hesitated, then, having thought better of her actions, sheepishly tucked her fingers under her brother's arm, saying, 'I'm really sorry, Nicky—it was just the idea of them all being parcelled up and taken away from their homeland—I won't mention it again, I promise!'

'That's the girl!' returned Nicholas, and breathing a sigh of relief, ushered her across the road and into the crowded thoroughfare that was home to London's highly famed shopping centre.

Almost an hour later, however, he was beginning to regret his impulsive offer, for it was becoming increasingly difficult to prise his sister away from all the choice merchandise on display. Having caught sight of the time on a clock in the window of a jewellery store that they had just passed, he felt constrained to point out to Jessica that they had covered both sides of the entire length of the street and, unless they retraced their steps immediately, the chaise would be at St Giles Circus well before they got there.

'We have to leave right now, Jess,' he insisted. 'I gave Matt my word and I simply cannot let him down!'

Casting a last longing glance at a particularly ravishing pair of evening slippers, Jessica gave a regretful nod. 'You are quite right, Nicky—we had better get back—*oh, no!* Look, Nicky! Do something, quickly! You must stop them!'

Nicholas jerked his head in the direction of his sister's pointing finger.

At the corner of a nearby alley, a group of jeering urchins was in the act of pelting stones at a young baker's lad who seemed either unwilling or unable to defend himself. As he cringed away from the assault, the tray of pies he was attempting to balance on his head slid sideways and fell, scattering its contents on to the cobbled street. While one of his assailants pushed the unresisting youth to the ground and pinioned him with his foot, his jubilant accomplices immediately swooped upon the fodder and started to gather up as many of the fallen delicacies as their grubby little hands could hold.

Dragging her protesting brother behind her, Jessica flung herself into the mêlée, thrashing out at the nearest culprit and demanding that they leave the cowering youth alone.

It was the noisy group of curious onlookers that first caught Wyvern's attention as he drove past the spot in his curricle but then, on turning his head to ascertain the cause of all their merriment, his eyes grew wide and a gasp of disbelief fell from his lips.

At the mouth of the alleyway stood a furious-faced Jessica Beresford. She seemed bent on shaking the living daylights out of the small ragged boy whom she held in her clutches, to the accompaniment of ribald jeers and catcalls from the several highly amused bystanders! Her brother Nicholas, as Wyvern observed to his considerable dismay, was haring up the alley, apparently in hot pursuit of three other ragamuffins!

Jerking his carriage to a halt, Wyvern tossed the reins to his tiger and, resolutely ignoring the warning bells that were resounding inside his head, hopped smartly from his perch and shouldered his way through the small crowd.

Jessica, he discovered, had thrust the snivelling guttersnipe to one side and had now turned her attention to the baker's lad who was still cowering against the wall, his arms crossed in front of his face.

'Please don't be afraid,' she said gently, kneeling down at his side. 'I won't let them hurt you any more. I promise!'

She reached out a hand, in an attempt to soothe the stricken youth but, before she had time to register what was happening, she felt herself being yanked upright and set down firmly on her feet, in none too gentle a manner.

'You little idiot!' came a throaty growl from behind her. 'What the devil are you about?'

Scarlet-faced, Jessica spun round but, no sooner had her wrathful eyes encountered Wyvern's irate gaze, than the hot words of protest died on her lips. *Oh, not again!* she thought wretchedly, as her heart plummeted to her boots. *Why does it always have to be him?*

'I— I—' she began apprehensively, only to observe that Wyvern had already switched his attention to her brother, who had just that moment returned from his vain attempt to catch the young culprits.

'Is it totally beyond you to keep your sister under

control, young man?' he castigated the boy. 'If word of this sort of behaviour were to get out, your whole family would be made a laughing stock!'

Nicholas shrank back in apprehension, one look at Wyvern's infuriated countenance having warned him that any attempt on his part to justify his sister's actions would meet with nothing but derision. But she, having had time to regain some of her composure, jumped immediately to her brother's defence.

'Leave him alone!' she said angrily, thrusting herself between the two men. 'If you feel that you must shout at someone, then let it be me! My brother was only trying to help—which is more than you seem prepared to do!'

Wyvern, finding himself suddenly confronted with a pair of wide, blazing green eyes, felt as though he had been struck by a bolt of lightning. The effect was so overpowering that he could almost feel himself being drawn deep into their viridescent depths. His breath shuddered in his throat and, tearing his own eyes away from the source of his discomposure, he cast desperately about for some immediate diversion—anything that would help to eradicate the disquieting image from his mind.

His gaze immediately fell upon the fallen tray, surrounded by the broken remnants of several pies and, lastly, the trembling figure still huddled against the wall. A puzzled frown creased his brow. As far as he could tell, the lad did not appear to be injured in any way. *Why the devil had he not picked himself up?* he wondered irritably. Striding across, he tapped the youth on the shoulder.

'Up you get, lad,' he said, firmly. 'It can't be that bad, surely?'

'It's not the slightest use you talking to him in that tone of voice,' interposed Jessica irritably, pushing the earl to one side. 'He's petrified—and, given the circumstances, that's a fairly normal reaction from a boy of his sort.'

Wyvern, carefully avoiding any eye contact with her, echoed, 'A boy of his sort? How do you mean?'

Jessica stared at him, dumbfounded. 'Surely you can see…the lad is not…like the rest of us…he's…' Hesitating, her hand crept to her lips as she struggled to find suitable words that would most aptly fit the youth's condition.

'He is what we at home tend to call "an innocent",' said Nicholas, hurriedly stepping forward to support his sister. 'We grew up with one such as this—tall and immensely strong, but his mind, sadly, that of a three-year-old. Your lordship must see that we could not stand by and see the youngster taken advantage of!'

With a guilty start, Wyvern's eyes shot across to the boy and he at once realised that, had he but taken the time or trouble to observe him properly, he could not have failed to recognise that the lad's entire demeanour was clearly off kilter with what one might reasonably expect from such a strapping youth. In a pondering silence, the earl's gaze remained fixed upon the huddled figure as he struggled to find adequate words to excuse what he knew Jessica and her brother must regard as crass stupidity.

Since she was unable to gauge Wyvern's reaction, Jessica gave a defiant lift of her chin and, whisking her handkerchief from her reticule, knelt down in the debris at the boy's side and, murmuring gentle words of encouragement, proceeded to attend to the nasty-looking graze on his elbow.

Having lost interest in the proceedings, most of the crowd had, by now, moved on. A young flower girl, however, came forward and volunteered the information that the injured lad's name was Danny Pritchard and that his mother owned the pastry shop at the far end of the alleyway. Jerking her thumb over her shoulder, she added, 'That's 'er comin' down now!'

Three pairs of eyes swivelled in the direction in which the girl was pointing.

Hurrying towards them was a plump, distraught-faced little woman who, as soon as she had laid eyes on the boy, cast herself down on her knees at his side, and begged him to get to his feet.

'Now then, Danny! Up you get, and come along home with Mum,' she cajoled him but, although he raised his head and stared at her, the boy's eyes did not seem to hold any sign of recognition. His mother sat back on her heels, a despairing frown on her face. 'Looks like 'e's gone into one of 'is states,' she said helplessly. 'I hadn't oughter sent him out with them pies, but I'm that rushed today. If you could just 'elp me get 'im back on 'is feet, sir, I'm sure 'e'll soon come to.'

Glad to have been given something of an opportunity to redeem himself in some small way, Wyvern, stepping forward with alacrity, said, 'Leave him to me, ma'am.' Then, with an encouraging smile, he thrust his hands under the youth's armpits and hoisted him upright, almost losing his balance in the process. Steadying himself quickly, he was amazed to find that Danny's height was practically on a par with his own.

For several moments, the boy remained slumped in the earl's arms, making no visible effort to support himself, but then, gradually, as the sound of his mother's continual coaxing began to penetrate his befuddled brain, he began to straighten himself up. Eventually, he loosened himself from Wyvern's grip and, impatiently thrusting the earl away from him, he stretched out his hands and clutched hold of his mother, uttering a strange keening sound as he did so.

'That's right, Dannyboy,' nodded Mrs Pritchard as she reached up to apply the hem of her apron to his tear-stained cheeks. 'Now let's get you 'ome, shall we?'

At first, Danny seemed quite content to allow his mother to shepherd him homewards, but then, all of a sudden, he stopped, stood perfectly still and, thrusting his hand into his pocket, turned to face Jessica, holding out what appeared to be a large mother-of-pearl button.

'Pretty,' he said. 'Pretty lady.'

Jessica dropped her eyes and the colour rose in her cheeks.

'Oh, lawks, miss!' gasped the pie woman in dismay. ''E don't mean any offence! 'E's just wanting to give you one of 'is "treasures". It's 'is way of thanking you. I'd be that glad if you'd take it!'

In fascinated silence, Wyvern watched as Jessica, tears forming in her eyes, reached out and, taking hold of the button, carefully placed the token into her reticule.

'It is truly beautiful,' she said softly. 'I will treasure it always.'

The boy nodded. 'Pretty lady, pretty treasure.'

Then, taking his mother's arm, he urged her forward, saying, 'Lemonade, now.'

'I expect he will soon forget about all of this,' said Jessica, with a quivering smile.

'That's true enough, miss,' nodded Mrs Pritchard, now quite composed. 'It'll 'ave gone right out of 'is mind by the time we get back to our front door, you mark my words!' Then, with a quick glance up at Wyvern, she added, 'I'm that grateful for what you done, sir. There's not many who would've stopped to 'elp the lad—them little varmints want skinnin' alive, so they do!'

Flushing slightly, the embarrassed earl shook his head. 'The young lady is really the one who deserves your thanks,' he demurred and, taking Jessica's arm, he edged her forward. 'Miss Beresford waded in to your son's defence like a veritable gladiator! I am only too glad that I was not on the receiving end of her fury!'

Jessica shook her head and the colour rose in her cheeks as the pie-woman, having repeated her words of gratitude, took her son firmly by the arm and drew the shambling youth back up the alleyway.

Wyvern's gaze slowly slid across to Jessica's face. Her lips were trembling and her vivid green eyes were bright with unshed tears. His heart contracted and, before he was able to stop himself, he had reached out his hand and, taking hold of hers, gave it an encouraging squeeze. This unexpected act of kindness from one who, barely five minutes previously, had been so quick to condemn her behaviour, caused a ripple of pleasure to run through her. She stole a quick glance up at him and, having registered the warmth of his expression, her lips curved in a shy smile, the effect of which sent Wyvern's heart catapulting around his chest.

'You must be thinking me all kinds of a fool,' he began, as he reluctantly relinquished his hold. 'I do most humbly beg your—'

'Oh, no, sir!' Jessica interrupted him. 'I am sure that Nicky and I could not have managed on our own. The way you took charge was quite—!'

She stopped in mid-sentence, suddenly overcome by a curious mixture of confusion and embarrassment. *What on earth are you about?* she chastised herself. *Surely you cannot have forgotten that this is the man who has done his level best to avoid having anything to do with your family!* Then, straightening her shoulders, she took a deep breath and, in a somewhat shaky tone of voice, said, 'We are most grateful for your assistance, your lordship. However, I am sure that you will not wish to be detained any further—you must have a great many far more important matters that require your attention.'

'Well, possibly,' he acknowledged slowly, being somewhat taken aback at her sudden change of manner. 'Nevertheless, I trust that you will allow me the pleasure of escorting you back to your carriage—it is parked nearby, I imagine?'

'Unfortunately not, sir!' interposed Nicholas, giving his sister a pointed nudge. 'Our carriage is waiting for us down at St Giles Circus—which is almost a mile away!' Then, gesturing to the clock that was hanging above the doorway of a nearby chandlery, he added bitterly, 'We were supposed to be there at five o'clock sharp but, since there is no way we can get back there in less than seven minutes, it looks as though I must prepare myself for the most frightful wigging!'

'Bad luck,' commiserated the earl, with a sympathetic smile, and he was just about to bid them both 'good day' when a mischievous imp of an idea leapt into his brain. Then, with a challenging gleam in his eyes, he looked directly at Jessica and said, 'Although, if your sister is not averse to a slight squeeze, it is possible that I might manage to get you there in time to spare you that!'

'Oh, capital, sir!' breathed Nicholas, his eyes brightening. 'We'd be eternally grateful!'

'Miss Beresford?' queried Wyvern, a little smile twitching at the corners of his lips.

'Yes— No— That is— I mean, thank you, your lordship!' replied Jessica, doing her best to ignore the curious fluttering sensation in her stomach. 'If you are sure that it would be no trouble?'

'My pleasure entirely,' affirmed Wyvern softly. Then he confused her even further by smiling such a devastating smile at her that her heart seemed to be leaping about in all directions.

Less than two minutes later, she found herself squeezed tightly between the two men on the driving seat of Wyvern's curricle, whereupon the earl whipped up his horses and set the carriage off at a spanking pace down the crowded thoroughfare.

'I trust you are not finding this too uncomfortable, Miss Beresford?' asked the earl, with a quick glance in her direction.

'Not at all, sir,' she answered, her voice not quite steady. She was achingly aware of his muscular thigh pressing against her skirts and found, to her consternation, that this unusual sensation seemed to be conjuring up all manner of unladylike thoughts.

Wyvern, equally conscious of the warmth of her nearness, was doing his level best to banish several not dissimilar reflections of his own. However, since this was growing increasingly difficult, he frantically racked his brains to find some more mundane topic of conversation that might take his mind off his predicament.

'May I ask why you left your carriage at St Giles?' he inquired, in what he hoped was a nonchalant manner. When Jessica did not immediately reply, Nicholas leant forward, informing the earl that this was where they had arranged for their coachman to pick them up.

'We went to see the exhibition at the British Museum,' he explained. 'And, what with Oxford Street always being so dashed crowded, it seemed as good a spot as any for him to come back for us.' He jerked his head towards his sister. 'Jess wanted to look at the shops, you see! Although it wasn't as if we didn't have plenty of time, to begin with,' he then felt constrained to point out. 'But she spent such ages looking at fripperies and then, of course, we had to go and get involved in another one of her crusades—as if her blubbing all over the blessed marbles wasn't bad enough!'

Jessica shot a darkling look at her brother. 'I was *not* blubbing, as you call it,' she said stiffly. 'I was merely expressing my disapproval of the way in which some of the statues had been mishandled.'

'You disapprove of the exhibition?' asked Wyvern, his eyes gleaming with curiosity.

'It merely bothered me to see how badly damaged some of the exhibits were,' she replied quietly.

'But you did say that you thought they ought not to

have been brought here!' argued Nicholas, before letting out a low whistle of admiration as Wyvern neatly manoeuvred his vehicle between two heavily laden coal wagons.

'Well, your sister is not entirely alone there,' said Wyvern dryly, as he swung the curricle round the corner into St Giles Circus and pulled up with a flourish. 'And, if I may be permitted to say so, she is perfectly entitled to hold whatever opinion she wishes on the subject. Not everyone agrees with Elgin's decision to remove them from Greece! As a matter of fact, I, too, along with several of my friends, have been inclined to have reservations on the subject.' Pausing, he gestured to the opposite side of the street where, as they could see, the Beresford carriage was only just in the process of drawing to a halt. 'Excellent! Couldn't have timed it better. Five o'clock exactly!'

Then, leaping down from the perch, he lifted his arms and, placing his hands around Jessica's waist, swung her swiftly to the ground.

The shock of his unexpected action left her gasping for breath and, when he did not immediately remove his hands, a violent trembling started within her.

For a moment, as they stood staring into one another's eyes, time seemed to hang on a thread then, with an abrupt start, Wyvern released his hold and, stepping away from her, proclaimed, in his best theatrical manner, 'Your carriage awaits, my lady!'

'It was exceedingly kind of your lordship to go to so much trouble,' stammered Jessica. She was so distracted by the violent thumping of her heart that she was scarcely aware of Nicholas's insistent tugging at her sleeve, urgently begging her to make haste.

'No trouble at all, Miss Beresford,' replied Wyvern, with another of his devastating smiles and then, to add to her confusion, he took hold of her hand and lifting her fingertips to his lips, murmured softly, 'I assure you that it was an absolute pleasure.'

At this somewhat flamboyant gesture, the merest hint of doubt began to worm its way into Jessica's mind and, suddenly convinced that Wyvern was again bent on amusing himself at her expense, she made ready to snatch her fingers away from his grasp. But no sooner had her eyes flown up to challenge him, than she realised that, far from laughing at her, Wyvern's expression was full of warmth and—to her growing bewilderment—some other sentiment that she could not readily identify, but which seemed to be causing her heart to behave in the most unruly manner.

Reluctantly withdrawing her hand from his, she bent her knee in a swift curtsy, before bidding him a final farewell. Then, without a backward glance, she tucked her hand into her brother's arm and allowed him to escort her across the busy road and into the waiting carriage.

'Damn! Damn! and thrice damn!' cursed Wyvern, as he watched the Beresfords' carriage disappear into the distance.

'Problem, guv?' chirped his tiger, hopping up on to his perch, as Wyvern edged his vehicle back into the stream of traffic.

'Problem, indeed, Berry,' replied Wyvern, with a heavy sigh. *And not as though I didn't already have more than my fair share of those!* he thought ruefully. *Although, I suppose if I had a grain of sense, I could steer clear of this one, without too much trouble!*

Flicking his reins, he retraced his journey back down Oxford Street and thence to St James Street, which was to have been his intended destination, had he not allowed himself to be sidetracked by a pair of emerald-green eyes! And all without so much as the batting of a single eyelash, he was obliged to concede. Indeed, if this afternoon's events were anything to go by, it was beginning to look as if he had done the fair Miss Beresford something of an injustice. Selfishness was hardly an epithet that one could apply to such exceptional behaviour—stubborn, yes, and wilful, without a doubt! He shook his head, taking no pleasure in recalling that his original opinion of the girl had been based upon mere hearsay and, even less to his credit, upon the disgruntled words of a slightly intoxicated would-be suitor!

Nevertheless, as he swiftly reminded himself, to further the acquaintanceship in any way would be deucedly unwise of him—given the extraordinary and somewhat disquieting sensations that had played havoc with his usual casual urbanity. His lips twisted in a wry smile. Only a year ago, he might have had little hesitation in throwing his cap into Jessica Beresford's ring! After all, in those far-off, pleasure-filled days, he had been what society was wont to call 'a good catch' and, had he been of a mind to do so, could have taken his pick of any one of the never-ending parade of hopeful young débutantes being brought forward for his attention. All to no avail, however, for despite all of his grandmother's words of wisdom, Wyvern had always been of the opinion that some sort of meaningful relationship was the cornerstone to a successful marriage.

And, no matter that the Polite World might regard Felicity Draycott as a model of perfection, it had not taken him long to realise that even a single night spent in the bed of that remote, unresponsive female was likely to be more than enough to cool any man's ardour, let alone that of a truly red-blooded male such as he! He was beginning to suspect that the begetting of the necessary heir to his estate might prove to be a great deal more of an ordeal than a pleasure!

Wyvern had always been a man of strong passions, full of vigour and determination: a bruising rider, an excellent marksman, his swordsmanship second to none although, as some of his army comrades had often been wont to remark, he was sometimes inclined to be a little on the hot-headed side!

Nevertheless, his innate good sense was more than enough to counsel him that, since, apart from his earldom, he had nothing but a crumbling old mansion and a mountain of debt to offer any prospective bride, marriage to Felicity Draycott looked to be his only escape from the dreadful coil that his brother had bequeathed to him! And, no matter how distasteful the idea might be, the sooner he could bring himself to start paying serious court to her, the sooner his problems would be solved—those of a financial nature, at any rate, he amended grimly.

Chapter Seven

'And no further attempts at any break-ins, while you were there?' asked Sir Simon, as soon as Wyvern had rounded off his brief account of his visit to the family estate.

'Not at the Grange,' replied the earl with a brisk shake of his head. 'But, oddly enough, the minute I got back to Ashcroft House, I was informed by the butler that, only last night, one of the footmen had chased off a pair of would-be intruders! Trouble is,' he added, tossing back his drink, 'I haven't the faintest idea what these villains—whoever they may be—are after!'

He and Holt, along with Fitzallan, had ensconced themselves in a secluded corner of the smoking room at White's, currently their preferred choice of venue.

'Must have known that you were away,' observed Fitzallan, as he signalled to the barman to bring another bottle. 'They certainly seem pretty determined to get their hands on this mysterious document!'

'Document?' frowned Wyvern. 'What makes you think it's a document they're after?'

'Should have thought that it was blindingly obvious, old chap!' responded Fitzallan, with a pained expression on his chubby face. 'Ain't as if you'd be likely to find much else stuffed inside the frame of a painting, now is it?'

'I would be inclined to agree with you,' said Sir Simon, nodding thoughtfully. 'Had it not been for the fact that Ben has been through every bit of Theo's paperwork.'

'With the proverbial fine-tooth comb!' put in Wyvern, gloomily.

'And he didn't leave you with so much as a hint of what these fellows might be searching for?'

Shaking his head, Wyvern reached into his inside pocket and drew out his notecase. 'Apart from a pile of unpaid bills and dunning letters, this is all he left me,' he said, as he extracted the piece of paper containing his brother's final message. 'See for yourselves. It's just a load of disconnected foolishness. It's clear that he was at his wit's end!'

Unfolding the missive, he laid in on the table, evening out the creases with the tips of his fingers.

His two friends stared down at the letter in silence, then Sir Simon, picking it up carefully between his thumb and forefinger, held it up to the light, turned it over to check the back then finally, to both his companions' utter bewilderment, he lifted the paper up to his nose and carefully sniffed at it.

'Just checking,' he retorted, having registered their incredulous expressions. 'Lemon juice, you know— invisible ink—just needed to be sure!'

Replacing the letter on to the table, he leaned back

in his chair and shook his head. 'I'm afraid I'm as stumped as you are, Ben, old chap!' he admitted.

'Well, well, well!' came a voice from the doorway of the room. 'If it ain't the new earl himself! Your servant, Wyvern! May we join you?'

Wyvern froze. Scooping up his brother's note and thrusting it back into his notecase, he settled himself more comfortably in his chair before saying, 'If you're after your money, Hazlett, you'll just have to wait your turn!'

The newcomer, one Viscount Digby Hazlett, was a tall, slim-built man in his mid-thirties, with pale blue eyes and lanky brown hair. An ugly scar, running from his left cheekbone down to his chin, marred his once-handsome features. Rumour had it that Hazlett had received this injury in a sword duel some five years previously but, since all trace of the other combatant—who was reputed to have been the younger son of Lord Aylsham—had inexplicably vanished into thin air, the mystery remained unsolved. The general consensus was that the fight had occurred as a result of young Jack Stavely having taken violent exception to some remark or other that Hazlett was supposed to have made concerning the reputation of a certain young lady whom Stavely had held in high regard. Given Stavely's sudden disappearance, however, nothing of this legend had ever been confirmed. It had always been supposed that the young man, wrongly under the impression that he had killed his opponent, had fled the country, the gallows currently being the punishment for such a heinous crime. Whatever the truth of the matter, it was an indisputable fact that, since that fateful night, not a single attempt to contact his family had ever been made by, or on behalf of, the young renegade. And, although society had been very careful not to point the finger of suspicion at Hazlett, his name had quickly been removed from a significant number of calling-card lists.

Ignoring the undercurrent of scorn in Wyvern's tone, the viscount merely raised his eyebrows and affected a pained expression. 'My dear Wyvern!' he drawled. 'Who mentioned money? Far be it from me to kick a man when he's down! As I understand it, you're about as strapped for cash as old Theo was before he stuck his spoon in the wall!'

'Steady on, Hazlett!' protested Fitzallan, eyeing the silent Wyvern anxiously.

Knowing the earl's temperament as well as he did, it would have come as no surprise to him to see Wyvern suddenly leap to his feet and plant his fist right in the middle of Hazlett's mocking countenance. 'It's damned bad form to make remarks like that! You have Ben's word that you will get your money—can't you just leave it at that?'

'No problem, old bean,' murmured the viscount, settling himself into a chair at a nearby table and signalling to his podgy-faced companion, Viscount Cedric Stockwell, to do likewise. 'I'm in no hurry, I assure you. Just wanted to express my sorrow at your loss and to wish you all the best in your endeavours.'

Wyvern's eyes narrowed in suspicion. 'What endeavours might those be, then?' he enquired as he reached for his glass.

He had been too long acquainted with the notorious viscount to be taken in by the man's dubious attestations of good will. Besides which, since he was uncomfortably conscious of the fact that Hazlett held a good many of Theo's promissory notes and could, if he so desired, demand restitution at any time, he had decided that it would probably do no harm to humour him.

Having signalled the barman to bring a bottle, Hazlett waited until the man had departed then, after pouring both his companion and himself generous servings, he quaffed back a good half of the contents of his glass before announcing, 'Well, from what I've heard, you're hoping that Draycott's fortune's going to solve your problems!' And, pulling a large lace-edged handkerchief out of his pocket, he proceeded to dab the drops of moisture at the corners of his lips. 'Won't work, you know. Been tried before!'

Despite the barely concealed snort of laughter from Stockwell, followed by Fitzallan's muttered expletive, Wyvern's face remained impassive.

'Care to place a wager on that?' interposed Sir Simon casually, as he reached across the table for the brandy bottle and proceeded to fill his glass. 'I'll lay you a pony that Wyvern clears all of his brother's debts long before the Season comes to a close!'

Hazlett stiffened and his eyes narrowed. 'How's that, then?' he enquired, shooting a piercing look at his quarry. 'Come into an unexpected fortune, have you?'

His eyes flashing from one to the other, the frowning Hazlett studied the three men at the table but then, his face clearing, he threw back his head and laughed outright.

'By Jove!' he guffawed. 'Then it's true! You *are* thinking of setting your cap at the fair Felicity—fat chance *you'll* have! She's not in the market for a husband!'

'Come off it, Hazlett!' retorted Fitzallan, his grin widening. 'Touch of the old "sour grapes" there, if I am not mistaken! Doubt if there are many folk around who ain't acquainted with the fact that Miss Draycott turned you down flat!'

Hazlett flinched. 'That might well be so,' he ground out, a deep flush covering his face. 'But I'll have you know that I fared no worse than a good many others before me! Your precious friend here is in for something of a shock if he is basing his hopes of survival in that quarter!'

With this, he tossed off the remainder of his drink, rose to his feet and, after executing a cursory bow, strode off in the direction of the exit, with his loyal henchman hard on his heels.

'There's someone who won't be happy until he sees me in the Fleet,' sighed Wyvern, reaching for his glass and taking a reflective sip of its contents. 'How Theo ever stood the man's company, I shall never understand!'

The three men were silent for some minutes, each of them involved in his own thoughts until Fitzallan, with a sudden frown, looked across at Sir Simon and said, 'You seem pretty sure that Miss Draycott is going to accept Ben's offer—how come?'

'No such thing, I swear!' laughed his friend. 'Just thought it wouldn't do any harm to get the rumour going—Ceddy Stockwell's not known for keeping choice bits of gossip to himself. Might help to keep the brokers from the door for a little while longer and give Ben a bit of a breathing space.'

Much moved by his friends' show of solidarity, it was a minute or two before Wyvern could trust himself to voice his gratitude. 'You are the best of fellows,' he said heavily. 'And I am indebted to you both for such a vote of confidence—despite the fact that I still cannot quite bring myself up to the mark!'

'You surely don't suppose that the lady is going to turn you down?' asked Sir Simon, eying his friend keenly.

'Apparently not—if I'm to believe my grandmother,' replied Wyvern with a short laugh. He was finding that he did not altogether care to discuss such an unpalatable matter, even with such close friends. 'It's simply that I cannot quite get my head around the idea of marrying someone just to get my hands on her father's fortune! I'm ashamed to admit that I've always had a rather poor opinion of the sort of chap who is prepared to take such a course. In fact, the very thought of actually joining those ranks is a pretty bitter pill for me to swallow!'

'Amen to that!' chimed in Fitzallan, in total agreement with the earl's sentiments.

Sir Simon, however, was slowly shaking his head.

'There is absolutely no reason for you to feel that way, Ben!' he expostulated. 'It surely can't have escaped your notice that people of our sort seldom marry for anything other than money—or land—or some equally power-driven urge! I would say that you have found yourself an entirely suitable match! The Draycotts have the money and the Ashcrofts have the land *plus* the all-important title! Provided that you don't actually dislike the girl, of course, I dare say that the two of you will rub along together quite happily!'

'I had always rather hoped to do slightly better than

simply "rub along" with any wife I chose!' returned Wyvern, with a grimace. 'Nevertheless, Simon, I do take your point and it is quite clear that I will just have to learn to swallow my pride and "screw my courage to the sticking place", as the old saying goes!'

'That's the spirit, old chap!' acknowledged Sir Simon, clapping him on the back. 'You've never been one for letting the side down and, since it would seem that the lady is yours for the asking, the sooner you get on with it, the better you will feel.'

'Tomorrow might be as good a time as any, I suppose,' returned Wyvern with a self-conscious shrug. 'It would certainly add the icing to my grandmother's cake if I were to announce my engagement in the middle of her festivities tomorrow evening.' He raised a questioning eyebrow. 'I take it that you *will* both be attending? Usual faces and pretty tame stuff, I know, but I would appreciate your support, if you've nothing else on hand.'

'Cut line, Ben, old chap!' protested Sir Simon, in astonishment. 'Haven't the three of us always gone into battle together? Where else would we be at such a time?'

Showing every sign of being hailed an absolute triumph, the Dowager's soirée was in full swing. Thanks to her ladyship's wide circle of illustrious acquaintances, it appeared that everyone who was anyone was desirous of attending, if only to have his or her presence marked. Wyvern had lost count of the number of luminaries who had elected to call in and extend their good wishes. He had been delighted to welcome his former commander, the great Duke of Wellington who, along with a number of high-ranking officers, had spent several minutes in conversation with both himself and his grandmother. Even the ageing Prince Regent, accompanied by his current set of sycophantic hangers-on, had condescended to put in a brief but, nevertheless, very visible appearance. All in all, Lady Lavinia was well satisfied with the results of her endeavours to bring the Ashcroft family back into the limelight and, had not Wyvern been in such a fierce struggle with his conscience over the impending marriage proposal, he might also have declared the evening a success.

As it was, any pleasure that he might have garnered from the occasion was heavily marred by his friends' frequent and unwelcome reminders of his earlier undertaking.

'My advice is to strike while the iron's hot!' urged Fitzallan. 'The more you stop to think about it, the more difficult it will be!'

'In the normal way, I would have been inclined to agree with you,' Sir Simon muttered, as he pressed himself up against a pillar to allow a rather large matron to edge her way past the group. 'Sadly, it would appear that the chances of Ben getting the lady to one side in this almighty crush might prove nigh on impossible!'

'Not what one might call the ideal set of surroundings!' nodded Wyvern, with a pensive frown. 'I can hardly shout my offer at her!'

'Nevertheless,' pointed out Sir Simon, 'there's nothing to stop you having a quick word with Draycott himself— arrange a suitable interview—that sort of thing?'

'Give me another day's grace, in any event,' returned the earl, with a heartfelt sigh of relief. 'I'd better do it now, then, before I'm given a chance to change my mind!'

'Good man!' said Sir Simon, while Fitzallan gave a fervent nod and clapped Wyvern on the back.

Although his heart was in his boots, it was with a strangely detached air that Wyvern threaded his way through the thronging mass to the far corner of the ballroom, where he found the Draycott party in conversation with a group of their friends. Having already stood up for the requisite two dances with Felicity, he knew that there was no danger of her imagining that he would press her for a third, so he simply acknowledged her presence with a smile and a swift bow and, turning to her father, asked if he would be good enough to spare him a moment of his time.

'Indeed, sir!' rejoined the baronet, his eyes brightening, as though he had every reason to know what was about to follow. And, taking Wyvern's arm, he drew him towards a more secluded corner of the room.

'Now then, my boy. And what may I do for you?' he enquired, his bracingly jovial tone of voice causing the earl to wince in distaste.

'I had it in mind to call on you tomorrow morning, sir,' said Wyvern, endeavouring to still the tremor in his voice. 'Will you be available—at around eleven o'clock, say?'

Sir Jonathan drew a deep breath and gave a satisfied nod. 'But of course! Of course, my boy! Point taken! Say no more! Eleven tomorrow it shall be then!'

Hardly able to believe that he was finally on the verge of committing himself, Wyvern inclined his head and, in something of a daze, was in the process of returning to his anxious comrades when a sudden flurry of excitement over by the room's threshold claimed his attention.

Craning his neck, he peered over the heads of the crowd in order to acquaint himself with the identity of what he could only suppose must be yet another illustrious dignitary who had chosen to grace the gathering with his or her presence. As his eyes lit on the party at the doorway, his heart did a double somersault and every vestige of breath seemed to have been knocked from his body.

There, along with her brother Matt and cousin Imogen, stood Jessica Beresford, looking unbelievably lovely in a gown of shimmering silver gauze that seemed to cling to every faultless curve of her body; her pale blonde hair, caught back with a diamond-studded filigree tiara, fell about her creamy shoulders in a profusion of shining ringlets. Around her neck she wore a delicate silver chain bearing a single, flawless diamond, which nestled provocatively in the cleft between the rising mounds of her perfectly formed breasts.

For several moments, due to his inability to take a full breath, Wyvern stood rooted to the spot, watching his grandmother greet the newcomers and usher them into the room. An involuntary groan escaped his lips when he realised that Jessica seemed to be paying little attention to the various high-born guests to whom the Dowager was introducing the little group. Instead, her bright eyes were keenly searching around the room— as though she was looking for someone. Fairly certain that it was him for whom she was seeking, Wyvern gritted his teeth in dismay and stepped back hurriedly, hoping to make it to one of the side doors before she could spot him, thereby avoiding the necessity of having to acknowledge her presence.

Having barely recovered from a grim contemplation of the unwelcome fate that the morrow held in store for him, the very last thing Wyvern needed at this moment was to find himself anywhere in the vicinity of the captivating Jessica Beresford and her oh-so-compelling green eyes, for he was only too aware that, in his present highly vulnerable state, it would be well nigh impossible for him to conceal his growing desire for her.

Reaching the relative safety of the doorway that led into a side passage, he shot a quick look over his shoulder to ascertain that he was still unobserved. Unfortunately for him, just at that same moment, the movement of the dancers on the floor left a clear space between the keen-eyed Jessica and himself. Briefly raising one hand in recognition, she beamed a smile at him and, before he could determine what she was about, she had separated herself from her party and was making her way towards him.

Clenching his teeth in consternation, he ducked out of the door and hurried down the passageway, having assumed that Jessica would remain in the ballroom with her family. At the sound of the door re-opening behind him, however, his stomach clenched and he spun round in alarm, only to witness Jessica peering round the edge of the doorway, frantically signalling him with her fan.

Grasping the handle of the nearest door, he flung it

open and shot inside, slamming it shut behind him, fully confident that the girl would hardly be so foolish as to enter the room after him. After a moment or two, as the doorknob rattled and started to turn, his anxiety turned to dismay and he felt a flush of anger rising; his eyes narrowed and his fists clenched at his sides. What the deuce could she be thinking? Had she no sense at all? Surely she could not be so naïve as to be unaware that she was about to walk straight into one of the most compromising positions in which it was possible for a young lady to find herself? All at once, it came to him that saving the headstrong Jessica Beresford from herself seemed to be turning into somewhat of an unlooked-for habit with him. He took a deep breath and stepped way from the door just as it began to open.

'Your lordship?' came a hesitant whisper and Jessica, her hand still on the doorknob, inched tentatively into view.

Flinging out his hand, Wyvern grasped her roughly around the wrist and dragged her into the room, kicking the door shut behind him.

Jessica's eyes widened in confusion and she attempted to free herself from his grip.

'My lord!' she protested. 'Please let me go! You should not—!'

The rest of her words were silenced as Wyvern hauled her towards him and clamped his free hand over her mouth. He was beside himself with fury.

'Are there no brains at all inside that pretty little head of yours?' he rasped. 'Are you mad or just plain stupid? Have you no thought for your reputation?'

Ignoring Jessica's vigorous shaking of the head and

her frantic gestures towards the door, he wrapped his arms around her and drew her close to his chest. She squirmed furiously in his hold and, as he felt the movement of her threshing legs against his own, a shiver of arousal ran through him. Unable to contain himself, he bent his head to her upturned face.

'Or was this the *real* reason that you followed me here?' he demanded hoarsely as, disregarding the concerned expression in her eyes, he lowered his mouth to hers. But, even as their lips touched, he felt a sharp rap on the side of his face.

His hand on his cheek, he thrust himself away from her and stared down at her in something of a daze. Dear God! What in hell's name was he doing?

The look on Jessica's lovely face was something to behold. Her viridescent eyes were flashing with righteous indignation and her hand, still upraised, held what was left of her ivory fan, its delicate sticks now shattered beyond repair.

Swallowing hard, he put out a hand, as if to defend himself. 'You need not expect me to apologise!' he said bitterly, as he watched her march to the doorway and fling open the door. 'You led me to believe—you should not have followed me in here! What was I supposed to think?'

'I take leave to point out that you are the one who is at fault on this occasion, my lord!' came Jessica's swift rejoinder. Flinging up her hand she pointed at the be-ribboned posy of flowers that was hanging on the outside of the door, clearly indicating the room's intended function. Then, as a mischievous glint suddenly filled her eyes and a gurgle of laughter threatened to overcome her, she laid her head on one side and enquired sweetly, 'Unless, of course, your lordship is in the habit of frequenting the ladies' retiring rooms?'

No sooner had the sense of her words begun to penetrate his conscious than Wyvern felt his stomach clench in dismay. He staggered backwards, his eyes flicking wildly around the small salon until, having taken in the dressing table, along with its conglomeration of hairbrushes, the powder pots and papers of pins, the assortment of female garments draped over the chairs and, most telling of all, the corner screen that concealed the commode, a dull flush spread across his face. Clutching at his cravat, which all of a sudden was beginning to feel much too tight, he stepped hurriedly towards the door, intent upon making as speedy an exit as dignity would allow.

'Your pardon, ma'am,' he croaked, not daring to look the now highly amused Jessica in the eyes.

But then, as the sound of female voices drifted down the passageway outside, Wyvern grew pale and retreated from the doorway in alarm. It was impossible to conceive the scandal that would ensue if he were to be discovered here with Jessica Beresford! Any likelihood of a union between the Draycotts and the Ashcrofts would be demolished in a trice! In mute appeal, he cast her a despairing look. In an instant, the self-righteous smile flew from her lips and, grabbing the dumbfounded earl by the hand, she thrust him towards the nearby corner of the room.

'Get down!' she hissed and, before he had time to consider his options, she had dragged one of the highbacked sofas crosswise in front of him. Hastily grabbing one of the papers of pins from the basket on the dressing table, she flung herself down upon the sofa, whereupon she proceeded to pull up her skirt, ripping several inches of the flounce away from its hem.

As two ladies pushed open the door and entered the salon, Wyvern felt the hairs on the back of his neck beginning to rise. He had the distinct feeling that, in allowing himself to be so easily coerced into this ludicrous situation, he had merely leapt out of the proverbial frying pan straight into what was like to be a veritable inferno!

The first of the newcomers, the Honourable Mrs Fortesque-Jones, nodded a pleasant greeting to Jessica and settled herself on the stool in front of the dressing table, where she proceeded to effect repairs to her topknot, several coils of which had disengaged themselves from the feathered concoction to which they had been attached. Her companion, Lady Blackmore, after flicking a powder puff over her florid cheeks, then commenced to wander aimlessly about the room, peering short-sightedly through her lorgnette at the various pictures on the walls and making unfavourable comments as to the skill of the artists. Jessica, apparently intent upon pinning up the damage to her gown, could only pray that neither of the ladies would deem it necessary to disappear behind the screen in order to relieve herself!

She could not begin to understand how she had managed to get herself into this situation. To have followed Wyvern into the passage was unforgivable, she knew, but she had merely wanted to ask him not to mention the Oxford Street incident. And then, having seen him disappear into the ladies' tiring room, she had felt bound to inform him of his mistake. He had, after all, come to *her* rescue twice already. How was she to know that he would grab hold of her in such a violent manner? She raised the tips of her fingers to her mouth, recalling the delicious sensation that had run through her in that fleeting moment when his lips had pressed against hers and wondered how it would have been if she had allowed him to continue. Only the sudden shocking memory of that other dreadful occasion with Wentworth had brought her to her senses and given her the strength and courage to strike Wyvern with her fan. Jabbing disconsolately at her hem, she wished that the women would make haste with their toilette, so that she could release Wyvern and get back to the ballroom before her disappearance was remarked upon.

'I hear Draycott is expecting young Wyvern to make an offer any day now,' said Mrs Fortesque-Jones, as she patted her completed hairdo back into place.

'And *I*, for my part, am surprised that Sir Jonathan has seen fit to encourage such a match,' returned Lady Blackmore tersely. 'Word is that the Ashcrofts are pretty well under the hatches! It's my guess that this evening's do is some sort of last-ditch stand!'

Jessica flinched as the pin she was weaving into her hem found the tip of her finger instead. Wyvern and Felicity Draycott? A silent sigh escaped her lips and her heart sank. It would seem that she still had a good deal to learn about the strange ways of the opposite sex.

Wyvern, crouched uncomfortably between the rear of the spindle-legged sofa and a large copper urn containing a potted palm, closed his eyes in despair. As if being in imminent danger of having his presence discovered in the ladies' tiring room were not punishment enough for his precipitate actions, it seemed that he was now about to suffer the added ignominy of having his character shredded in front of Jessica Beresford.

The arrival of yet another female into the salon, however, saved his blushes.

'So this is where you've been hiding, Jess—I've been looking for you everywhere!'

The newcomer was none other than Imogen Beresford, looking decidedly exasperated as, sitting herself down beside her cousin, she surveyed Jessica's botched handiwork in some dismay. 'Oh, my goodness! Your lovely gown! Why on earth did you not call for me to help you?'

'I'm so sorry, Imo,' prevaricated her cousin. 'It was difficult to reach you in the crush.'

Imogen gave a decisive shake of her head. 'You had best leave it to Blanche to deal with,' she said. 'Failing which, we will have to return it to Madame Devy to have it remade—how on earth did you come to rip it so badly?'

'I—I think someone must have trodden on it,' Jessica, her colour heightening, was forced to dissemble. 'The ballroom was so crowded—I just felt it tearing. Neither you nor Matt were anywhere to be seen, so I—I thought I had better come along here and see if I could fix it myself.'

With a brisk nod, Imogen stood up and held out her hand. 'Well, we have no time to worry about it now. We must hurry. We will have to return home for you to change before we go on the Ilchesters—you know we are promised to them later this evening.'

A worried frown furrowed Jessica's brow. 'But I have not yet paid my respects to her ladyship,' she protested, as her cousin drew her towards the door.

'Matt has already made our excuses, my dear. He has collected our cloaks and has called for the carriage. Do come along, Jess, you know how he hates to keep Cartwright waiting.'

The pair exited the room and started back up the passageway. Jessica, racking her brains to think of some way to let Wyvern know when the coast was clear, was in the process of pulling on her gloves when, after hurriedly stuffing the second of the pair into her reticule, she came to a sudden halt.

'Oh, my glove!' she cried. 'I must have left it on the sofa—I shan't be a minute! Do go on—I'll catch you up!'

And, before Imogen could remonstrate with her, she had turned tail and sped back towards the retiring room where, to her considerable relief, she met up with the two former occupants who were just on the point of leaving. Allowing them to get well out of earshot before she spoke, she tiptoed to the sofa and called softly, 'Make haste, my lord. You have no time to lose!'

Then, without waiting to see if the earl had understood her instruction, she scurried back along the passage, intent upon creating some sort of diversion, should she chance to encounter any other female who might have chosen just that moment to pay a visit to the ladies' salon.

Chapter Eight

Shortly before eleven o'clock the following morning, Wyvern constrained himself to climb the flight of steps that led up to the front door of the Draycott's London residence in Mount Street. No sooner had he given the bell-pull a single peremptory tug than the door opened and he was ushered into the spacious hallway, where a waiting footman speedily relieved him of his hat and gloves.

Motioning the earl to follow him, the Draycott's butler led the way to his master's study, passing the closed door of what Wyvern vaguely recalled as being the breakfast parlour and through which could be clearly discerned the sounds of barely suppressed feminine chatter. A shiver of guilt ran through him when he realised that the supposed objective of this morning's visit could well be common currency throughout the household. Indeed, it would come as no surprise to him to learn that Miss Draycott and her mother were, at this very moment, ensconced within that parlour impatiently awaiting the expected summons from the baronet. The thought of which, in view of his actual intentions, was enough to make Wyvern's blood run cold.

'Come in, come in, my boy!' declared Draycott, springing to his feet the moment the door was opened, waving the butler away without giving him the opportunity to announce the startled earl.

'Sit down, sit down my boy,' continued Sir Jonathan in the most jovial manner and, indicating the tray of glasses and decanters on a nearby table, added, 'You will take a drink, of course?'

Feeling greatly in the need for some fortification, Wyvern accepted a brandy and sat down on one of the high-backed leather chairs straddling the fireplace. Having poured himself a tumbler of whisky, the baronet took the chair opposite. After tossing back a goodly mouthful of the amber liquid, he smacked his lips in enjoyment and, placing his glass back on the table, leaned forward, his hands clasped on his knees.

'Now, then, my boy,' he beamed. 'No need for prevarication between us, surely? We both know why you are here, so what say we get the bones of the business over and done with?'

'It was very good of you to see me at such short notice,' began Wyvern cautiously. Although he had rehearsed this speech over and over again in his mind during the past few hours, saying the words out loud in the cold light of day seemed, somehow, far more nerveracking than he had expected.

'Nonsense! Nonsense!' said Sir Jonathan, playfully tapping the side of his nose. 'An absolute pleasure, I assure you! In fact, it don't hurt to tell you that Lady Draycott is quite beside herself with the good news!'

'The very fact of which makes my present task all the harder, sir, I fear,' returned Wyvern, drawing in a deep breath.

A puzzled frown on his face, Draycott stared at his visitor. 'I'm afraid I don't quite follow…?'

Mentally gritting his teeth, Wyvern pressed on with his self-appointed ordeal. 'It would seem that there has been a good deal of mounting speculation regarding any intentions that I may have in regard to Miss Draycott, Sir Jonathan,' he said, striving to still the tremor in his voice. 'The reason that I sought this interview was in an attempt to clarify this situation.' Pausing, he then looked directly into his host's eyes, saying, 'I am here to tell you, sir, that I cannot find it in me to petition you for your daughter's hand in marriage!'

'W-what are you saying, sir!'

Starting to his feet, Draycott pulled a large pocket-handkerchief from the pocket of his velvet smoking jacket and proceeded to mop the beads of sweat that were forming on his forehead.

'In consequence of our two families' long-term acquaintanceship,' Wyvern went on quietly, 'and, whilst I will always hold Felicity in the highest regard, the deep affection that I have always considered essential to the success of a marriage is, I am sorry to say, sadly lacking on my part. My feelings for Miss Draycott are as a friend—a close friend, it is true—but not as a prospective wife. That being so, I can only offer you my most sincere apologies if my recent attentions have given either of you cause to assume otherwise.'

Walking hesitantly over to his desk, Draycott stood absently drumming his fingers on the desk's leather surface. Then, turning, he made his way back to the fire-place, picked up his glass and tossed the remainder of its contents down before plonking himself back into his seat.

Draycott studied the earl in silence for some moments then, pursing his lips, he grunted, 'Your lordship can hardly have been unaware that, for some time, my daughter has been in daily anticipation of a proposal of marriage from you!' And, with a nervous glance towards the door, he added, in a rather more wheedling tone of voice, 'Possibly the knowledge that the girl comes with a dowry of fifty thousand pounds might go some way towards helping to promote the sort of affection you speak of?'

Wyvern stiffened. 'In my opinion, sir,' he returned curtly, 'any man who petitioned for your daughter's hand merely on the grounds of her large fortune would be doing her a great disservice. And I, for my part, could not contemplate such an abhorrent course of action. As her father, sir, you must surely agree that Felicity deserves far better than a marriage of convenience!'

'Humph!' retorted Draycott, his scowl deepening. 'Can't see that sort of argument going down particularly well with her ladyship!'

'Then I fear I must crave both her ladyship's and your most humble pardon, sir,' interrupted Wyvern, as he rose swiftly to his feet. 'I beg that you will convey my deepest regrets to Miss Draycott for any distress that I might—quite unintentionally, I do assure you—have caused her. And now, sir, since my presence is clearly somewhat superfluous, perhaps you will be good enough to excuse me?'

Then, without waiting for Draycott to summon a servant to show him out, the earl executed a swift bow, left the room and made his own way back to the entrance hall. Passing the breakfast parlour, however, he could hardly fail to remark the now rather pregnant silence that emitted from within.

Nevertheless, no sooner had the Draycotts' front door thudded shut behind him than Wyvern's formerly depressed spirits suddenly began to rise and it was with a considerably lighter frame of mind that he descended the steps to the pavement. For he knew that, despite having just forfeited his one chance of reversing the Ashcroft family's straitened circumstances, any suggestion of him coupling his name with Felicity Draycott had been rendered totally out of the question—ever since that brief but heart-pounding moment when he had held Jessica Beresford in his arms.

A rueful smile tugged at his lips as he recalled the series of events that had led him to this unassailable conclusion. Having based his entire opinion of the highly discomposing Miss Beresford upon the words of a disgruntled would-be suitor—and an inebriated one at that—he had been somewhat unprepared to discover how very mistaken he had been about her. Indeed, having already marked her unaffectedly compassionate attitude to the young simpleton's misfortunes in the Oxford Street scuffle, Miss Beresford's actions on the previous evening had only served to verify the earl's growing belief that she was not nearly as self-centred as Stevenage had given him to suppose. In fact, had he been a gambling man, Wyvern would have been prepared to lay odds that no other female of his acquaintance would have gone to such extraordinary lengths to attempt to extricate him from what could so easily have turned into the biggest scandal of the Season!

Added to which, he took no pleasure in reminding himself that the whole ghastly nightmare had been brought about by his own crass stupidity! That Jessica Beresford had been able to muster such presence of mind in the circumstances was quite remarkable and, in view of the highly reprehensible discourtesy he had shown her, her subsequent performance, culminating in the voluntary destruction of a very expensive evening gown, had been even more astonishing!

He fingered the barely perceptible graze on his cheek, a tangible memento of Jessica's breathless struggle in his arms—a struggle that he now felt might well have been more concerned with her endeavours to point out his error in entering the wrong room rather than a violent protest against his embrace! Having reached that conclusion, it was somewhat disheartening to realise that the likelihood of finding himself in a position to test out this theory at any time in the immediate future was looking somewhat remote!

No sooner had he escaped from his enforced confinement on the previous evening, Wyvern had hastened to the ballroom, in search of his benefactress, but Jessica had been nowhere to be seen. He had quickly sought out his grandmother, to enquire of the Beresfords' whereabouts, only to learn that the family had paid their respects and departed some few minutes earlier.

'Although, why you should need to concern yourself with their comings and goings, I cannot begin to comprehend,' the dowager had remarked, after casting a suspicious look at his crestfallen expression. 'I thought that we had already agreed that the girl is not for you.' Then, before he had been able to summon up a suitable reply, she had turned the subject to the scratch on his cheek, questioning him as to its origin.

Having been unaware, until that moment, that Jessica's spirited retaliation had left any visible mark, Wyvern had had to think quickly. 'It's of no consequence,' he had replied. 'I stumbled against one of your blessed palm trees—the crush in here is quite overwhelming!'

'Yes, isn't it just!' returned his grandmother gleefully. 'It looks likely to be the biggest of the Season!'

She had then drifted off with a trio of elderly admirers, leaving Wyvern to the mercy of Holt and Fitzallan, who had spent much of the previous half-hour or so in search of their missing comrade. In response to their queries regarding his prolonged absence from the room, he had had to resort to telling them that he had been called away to deal with a slight domestic crisis. Since this was not really so far from the truth, he had not felt too badly about this mild distortion. Unfortunately, however, since Fitzallan had then chosen to rib him about the mark on his face, suggesting that he looked as though he had come off worst in a bout of fisticuffs, it had then been necessary to repeat his earlier falsehood. Although both men had accepted this somewhat unlikely explanation without comment, Wyvern, having intercepted the questioning look that had passed between his two friends, had received the distinct impression that neither of them had been totally convinced.

The remainder of the evening had passed in something of a blur, as far as Wyvern had been concerned. He had stood up for every dance, each with a different partner, and had caused his two friends considerable merriment by choosing to escort one of his grandmother's elderly acquaintances into supper. This he had done in an attempt to avoid any accusations of partiality. Only when the front door had finally closed upon the last of the guests to leave had he allowed his guard to drop.

But now, as he strode through Berkeley Gardens in the late morning sunshine, he felt surprisingly lighthearted, despite the impending threat of ruin! Giving his coat pocket a little pat, as if to reassure himself that the slim box he had acquired on his way to the Draycotts' residence was still intact, his lips curved in a contented smile. He had spent most of the early hours persuading himself that there was nothing to prevent him paying a courtesy visit to the Beresfords. Having missed them on the previous evening, he had, by now, convinced himself that it would be perfectly in keeping for him to call and express his regrets. That done, he was certain that he would find some way of handing Jessica the small package. Strolling through the gates of the gardens, he crossed the busy thoroughfare, skirting nimbly between the gaps in the traffic.

Chapter Nine

'Jess seems rather quiet lately,' murmured Imogen as she held up her needle to the light the more easily to thread it. She was contentedly involved in the happy pursuit of making matinée jackets for her unborn child. 'Have you noticed anything odd about her, Matt?'

'Odd?' Frowning, her husband lowered his newspaper. 'What devilry has the little imp been up to now?'

Imogen shook her head. 'Nothing I can put my finger on. It's just that she always seems…sort of…*preoccupied*…is the best way I can describe it.'

Matt raised an eyebrow. 'She was perfectly happy at the Ilchesters last evening—danced every dance, at any rate.'

'True,' nodded Imogen, laying down the tiny garment on which she had been working. 'It just struck me that she seems somehow *less* than her usual ebullient self of late. I did wonder whether we were accepting too many invitations, but she herself has assured me that this is not so.'

'Just so long as *you* are not accepting too many invitations, my love,' grimaced Matt, as he leant towards her and clasped her hand. 'Conyngham's ball or no, I won't have you tiring yourself out just to suit young Jessica's moods!'

Blowing him a kiss, his smiling wife pressed his fingers. 'If that's some sort of roundabout way you have of insinuating that I am starting to look hagged…' Her words tailed off as Matt leapt on to the sofa beside her and threw his arms around her.

'Mind the needle!' she cautioned laughingly, as he tossed aside her sewing and pulled her towards him.

'A fig for the blessed needle!' he growled, bending his lips to her brow. 'You are more beautiful now than you have ever been—and that's saying a great deal!'

This very pleasant interlude might well have continued had not the click of the door latch alerted the two of them to their senses. Groaning softly, Matt withdrew his arm from her shoulder and edged himself a respectable distance away from his blushing wife as she bent down to retrieve her discarded handiwork.

'Pardon me for interrupting you turtle doves,' came Nicholas's soft chuckle as he crossed the room towards them. 'Just thought I'd mention that Mrs Clover has finished my packing and I am off to Hatchard's to pick up a couple of books that I ordered. Is there anything I can get you while I'm out?'

'Oh, yes, please, Nicky!' exclaimed Imogen, rummaging in her workbox. 'I do need some more of this satin trimming—if you would be so good?'

'Oh, lor'!' Nicholas's face fell. 'I suppose that means a haberdasher's—I'd rather not, if you don't mind—that sort of thing is more Jess's territory than mine.' He hesitated. 'I'll go and ask her if she fancies a stroll—she's only mooning around in the drawing room.'

'It's really of no consequence,' protested his cousin with a laugh, but Nicholas had already departed in search of his sister.

Jessica, having spent most of the morning trying to find some occupation that would prevent her thoughts from straying to the previous evening's débâcle, was more than happy to agree to accompany her brother on his shopping spree.

She had slept barely a wink after getting home from the Ilchesters' party, the entire event having impinged upon her conscious scarcely at all. She was aware that she must have danced, but could not have said with whom, since the faces of her partners had passed before her in a complete blur, her mind having been fully occupied in trying to make some sense of her own rather outrageous behaviour concerning Lord Wyvern.

Although she had, for the most part, recovered from the shock of Wentworth's attempted seduction and had thrown herself wholeheartedly into the non-stop merry-go-round of her long-awaited London Season, she had been very careful not to allow her natural flirtatiousness to overcome her better judgement. In addition, she had gone out of her way to make sure that not one of her numerous admirers should gain the impression that she might favour him above his peers. In point of fact and, contrary to what might have been supposed, she had not come to London to capture a husband.

The failed abduction of the previous autumn had

taught her, amongst other things, to be far less free with her favours, especially after Matt and Imogen had taken her to visit another of Wentworth's many victims— pretty little Rosie Juggins, the fourteen-year-old daughter of the local innkeeper. Having met and spoken to Rosie a good many times in the past, the sight of the girl's swollen belly had thoroughly shaken Jessica, so much so that she had taken it upon herself to make regular visits to the girl, bearing such gifts as boxes of crystallised fruit or chocolates, in the vain hope that one or other of these delicacies might tempt Rosie's almost non-existent appetite. In the event, Rosie's baby had not survived what had turned out to be a particularly harrowing birth, causing its formerly happy-go-lucky mother to sink into a deep depression, the outcome of which had left her caring neither for her own appearance nor the opinions of others.

The rapidity of Rosie's downward spiral into squalor and misery had, more than anything else, convinced the once devil-may-care Jessica that it was necessary for young women to be constantly on guard against finding themselves in situations where their virtue might be compromised. How galling, then, to have to admit to herself that not only had she failed to guard against such a circumstance occurring, but, to her eternal shame, she had actually thrown herself head first into what might easily be described as a lion's den!

Fortunately for Jessica's peace of mind, since the most persistent and vivid recollections of the events that had followed her precipitate action the previous evening were having the effect of making her head ache rather badly, her brother's suggestion of a breath of fresh air could not, from her point of view, have come at a more auspicious time.

No sooner had the pair of them arrived at the draper's shop on Berkeley Street, however, than it became abundantly clear that, given the large press of customers striving to attract the attention of one of the assistants, it would be quite some time before they might expect to be served.

'Look here, Jess,' ventured Nicholas, in some exasperation, having been obliged to step out of yet another matron's impatient prowess towards the rear of the store, 'how about if I nip down to Piccadilly while you're waiting? I can't see you getting served for a good half-hour—I can be there and back in half that time!'

'I dare say you're right.' His sister sighed, her mind still occupied with her current problem. 'You get off to Hatchard's and I'll carry on here.'

'Right you are, then!' agreed Nicholas, deftly elbowing his way back towards the door. 'Don't you leave without me—I shan't be more than two ticks!'

As luck would have it, Jessica's blonde loveliness had already caught the eye of one of the store's harassed assistants and, ignoring the protests and objections from the many other customers who had prior claims to his aid, he beckoned her forwards and asked her how he might be of service.

Thus it was that, barely five minutes after Nicholas had departed on his own errand, Jessica found herself back at the store's threshold with five yards of satin trimmings tucked safely inside her reticule. Knowing that there must be at least twenty-five minutes or so still to go until her brother returned to escort her home, she was somewhat uncertain as to whether she should stand alone in the street waiting for him or attempt to walk the short distance back to Dover Street on her own—well aware that either action would be frowned upon in certain sections of society.

Having crossed over from Berkeley Square Gardens, Wyvern was still heavily engrossed in contemplating the various ways in which he might go about securing one or two private moments with Jessica. He was just in the process of passing the haberdasher's when the very subject of his reverie stepped out of the shop's doorway, looking heart-stoppingly alluring in her pale green muslin gown and matching straw bonnet and, from his point of view, far prettier than any picture he had ever had the good fortune to lay his eyes upon!

'Your lordship!' she stammered, stepping hurriedly to one side in order to avoid the inevitable collision.

'A thousand apologies, Miss Beresford!' declared the delighted earl, his eyes gleaming with pleasure as he swept off his beaver with one hand while reaching out the other to steady her. 'My head was in the clouds, I fear—too many late nights, one must suppose!'

A becoming flush covered Jessica's cheeks as he raised her unresisting fingers to his lips. 'I hear that her ladyship's gathering was a great success,' was all she was able to manage in the circumstances. 'I—we—were obliged to take our leave a little earlier than expected. Er—I trust that you were able to extricate yourself without further difficulty?'

'All thanks to your good offices,' he replied with a

wide grin. 'Although, I have to confess that it was some little time before I found myself able to stand totally upright! I must make a point of… *Hey, you there! Steady on, I say!'*

This last exclamation was hurled at the backs of two coarse-looking ruffians who, caring nothing for the comfort of the other pedestrians on the sidewalk, had rudely thrust their way through the crowd, cannoned into several bystanders, including Wyvern himself, and made off across the road before anyone was able to apprehend them.

'Ill-mannered oafs!'

Shaking his fist at the disappearing pair, the earl turned back to Jessica, only to discover, to his dismay, that she was in the process of helping an ageing matron to her feet—clearly another victim of the two jackanapes' discourtesy.

Never one to scorn an opportunity when it was staring him in the face, Wyvern scooped up the packages that the lady had dropped and, indicating the tearooms situated a little further up the street, declared, 'The poor thing is as white as a sheet—probably could do with a cup of tea—I'll go on ahead and find us a table.'

And, before Jessica had the wits to summon up a reply, he had strode off and disappeared into Gunter's tearooms. Although her natural instinct rebelled at the high-handed manner in which he had bade her follow his instructions, her better self was quick to realise that the casualty, whoever she was, was in no state to be abandoned.

Placing her hand under the older woman's elbow,

she shepherded her through the entrance to the tearooms and, discovering that Wyvern had already secured a table next to a window seat, she carefully settled the somewhat confused female on to its cushioned bench, alongside her salvaged collection of packages. Gentle probing by both Jessica and the earl soon ascertained that the only real damage that had befallen the well-padded matron seemed to be the unpardonable insult to her dignity. However, after several moments spent in giving considerable vent to her ruffled feelings, the lady managed to collect herself sufficiently to inform her hosts that her name was Mrs Barrowman and that she kept house for a 'young gentleman' just around the corner in Half Moon Street.

Further attempts at polite conversation by both Jessica and the earl soon elicited the fact that their unexpected guest was extremely hard of hearing, the circumstance of which Wyvern was not slow to realise could be very much to his advantage. Quickly summoning a waiter, he murmured his requirements, which were met with a nod and a respectful bow. The tea things were no sooner on the table when, to Mrs Barrowman's delight and astonishment, a cake-stand containing a plentiful selection of the establishment's most mouth-watering delicacies was set before her, along with Wyvern's smiling recommendation that she should 'try to put the whole unfortunate incident out of her mind'.

'A cup of strong, sweet tea will soon buck you up,' he said cheerfully, as he pulled out a chair for Jessica. 'And I dare say one or two of Mr Gunter's famous pastries might not come amiss?'

'I really shouldn't be here,' began Jessica, casting a nervous look at the clock on the wall, as she set about pouring the tea. 'I promised Nicky that I would wait for him in the haberdasher's—he was obliged to go to Hatchard's to pick up some books.'

'No need to worry,' persuaded Wyvern, inching the cake-stand even closer to their guest with a smiling nod. 'We should be able to see him quite clearly through the window when he passes.' He leaned forward and lowered his voice. 'As a matter of fact, I was hoping for a chance to speak with you. I was actually on my way to call—I have something for you.'

At Jessica's questioning look, he delved into his coat pocket and surreptitiously drew out the packet he had been carrying. He slid it across the table. 'It's as near a match as I could find,' he said, with a diffident smile.

Her curiosity getting the better of her, Jessica undid the paper wrapping and opened the slim box. 'But I cannot possibly accept this!' she gasped, staring in amazement at the delicate ivory fan nestling within its wrappings—an almost exact replica of the one she had damaged on the previous evening!

'But of course you can accept it,' Wyvern assured her firmly. 'It is not a gift, merely a replacement.'

'But where did you find it?' Jessica wanted to know. '*Vernis Martin* fans are incredibly hard to come by— and how on earth did you know what to look for?'

Nonchalantly raising one elegant shoulder, the earl gave a satisfied grin. 'It wasn't difficult,' he said. 'I simply retrieved yours from the waste basket in the corner of the room, then set about obtaining a copy.' He omitted to tell her that, in the two-and-a-half hours prior to his visit to the Draycotts', he had visited more than a dozen jewellers and accessory shops in his search for a replacement. Nor did he mention that the very scarcity of such fans had obliged him to lay out twenty-five guineas to secure the one that Jessica held so reverently in her hands. Nevertheless, as far as Wyvern, in his present light-hearted mood, was concerned, just to bask in Jessica's delighted surprise was more than sufficient compensation for his frantic trawl through the streets of Mayfair.

'It is by way of thanks for your sterling efforts last evening,' he murmured *sotto voce*, not entirely convinced that Mrs Barrowman was as deaf as she appeared but, after a quick glance over to the settle, he was relieved to observe that their guest seemed to be fully occupied in working her way through Mr Gunter's plates of sweetmeats. Added to which, she had fished out a much-thumbed copy of the *Lady's Monthly Museum* from one of her bags and appeared to be deep in perusal of the juicy titbits of gossip therein.

A slight flush crept up Jessica's cheeks, as she wondered to *which* of her efforts his lordship might be referring, since the result of her affronted retaliation was still vaguely in evidence upon his face. She, too, cast a surreptitious peek at their guest, before saying, 'I'm sorry if I hurt you—it was such a shock, you see!'

A slow grin started to spread across Wyvern's features. 'Well, you can hardly blame me for thinking that you were following me,' he said softly.

'Oh, but I was!' came Jessica's astonishingly frank reply. 'That is—I *did* try to catch up with you before you left the ballroom, but you dashed off so quickly—

and I did so want to make sure that I spoke to you before Matt and Imo got to you!'

She chewed at her bottom lip, a highly provocative action that had the effect of causing several not unpleasant spasms to shoot through Wyvern's lower abdomen. Then, taking a deep breath, she continued, 'I know I should have stopped at the doorway but, when I saw you disappearing into the—well, *you* know—it occurred to me that you must have made a mistake, so I just kept going!'

'And thank God you did!' he replied fervently, marvelling at the way her long sooty lashes framed her amazingly beautiful eyes.

'Well, you may think so,' she remonstrated. 'But I hardly expected to be—clutched at—'

'For which I apologise unreservedly!' he cut in hurriedly, regretting only that the kiss had finished before it had really begun. Barely time to taste her lips really. Except that he had—just—and therein lay his downfall.

There was a moment's silence, then they both spoke simultaneously.

'Were you really running away from me?'

'What was it you wanted to speak to me about?'

A tentative pause followed, the seconds ticking by as each of them waited for the other to continue. Then, 'Do go on,' they chorused, in unison.

Jessica's hand crept up to her lips as a little gurgle of laughter escaped, soon to be joined by the earl's deeper chuckle.

He watched in silence as she dipped into her reticule and brought out a lace-edged handkerchief with which to dab at the tears of laughter that had gathered in her eyes. Beneath the table, he clenched his hands tightly together, in an effort to prevent himself reaching across to perform the service for her. Racking his brains for some subject that would tear his thoughts away from the increasingly tantalising images that were beginning to crowd his head, he said, 'I have to commend your quick thinking with that sofa manoeuvre. Spur of the moment, was it?'

She shook her head, still smiling. 'Dredged up from my wicked past, I fear. My cousin Imogen and I were frequently obliged to resort to that very ruse when we were hiding from our governess—we were very young at the time, of course!' she added, in her own defence.

'And the boy,' he asked, 'the one your brother referred to as the "innocent"—did he also participate in your childhood games?'

'Jake? Oh, no! Jake is the son of our cook.' Her smile disappeared and she cast another nervous look at the wall clock. 'I really ought to be going—Nicky will surely be back at any minute!'

'Not yet, surely?' he protested. 'We have been here barely fifteen minutes—he will hardly have had time to get to Hatchard's, let alone return!'

Seeing her hesitate, he pressed her, 'Tell me about Jake—did he die?'

'Die?' Her eyes widened. 'Oh, no! He and his mother went to live with my mama in Bath.'

'You are, clearly, very fond of the lad.'

'Yes, I am,' replied Jessica, swallowing the sudden lump that had developed in her throat. 'As a matter of fact, I owe him a great deal—possibly my life!'

A little frown crept over Wyvern's brow as, almost

without thinking, he reached across the table and laid his hand on hers. 'Can you tell me?' he asked quietly.

With Imogen's words of warning still clearly imprinted upon her brain, Jessica gave a little shake of her head. Due to Matt's having gone to a good deal of trouble and expense, the frightful events of the previous autumn—insofar as her name had been concerned—had not been made common currency. Wentworth had been tried and found guilty of the attempted murder of her half-brother and had been duly transported. Jessica's involvement in the matter had remained a well-kept secret known only to her immediate family and to Matt's close friend David Seymour who, along with his new wife Barbara, had long since returned to his home in Mysore. Therefore, in spite of an almost overwhelming compulsion to confide in the earl, she was sufficiently sensible to remember to keep her counsel.

'Suffice to say that I was a good deal more headstrong in those days than I am now,' she said, reluctantly removing her hands from Wyvern's warm clasp and reaching for her gloves. 'I really ought to be going. I'm sure Nicky will be back within minutes.'

He shook his head. 'Do please stay and finish your tea. I have been keeping my eye on the passing traffic and I assure you that your brother could not have escaped my notice.' Grasping at straws, he added, 'You are new to London, I take it? How are you enjoying your first Season?'

'My *only* Season, sir!' she replied, with an amused smile. 'I doubt if my brother will be prevailed upon to spend any more time in the capital once we return to

Lincolnshire—he enjoys life at Thornfield too much. Of course, I am most grateful to him for agreeing to bringing us all. I had pestered him so much—poor man—that he was finally obliged to give in.'

'And you?' he pressed her. 'Do you miss the countryside?'

A rather wistful expression crossed her face and she gave a slight nod. 'Oddly enough I do,' she returned. 'Although I had not supposed that I would feel this way, I have to admit that I shall not be entirely sorry when the time comes for us to return home. The air is so much cleaner and the woods and fields will be full of violets and primroses just now.' She paused for a moment, then added, 'But, all things considered, although I have been having the most wonderful time, I find that it is the constant racket that I most dislike. The sounds of the countryside are much gentler on the ear, do you not think?'

'Less intrusive, certainly,' he nodded smilingly then, after a slight pause, continued, 'You mentioned earlier that there was something that you wished to speak to me about?'

'Oh, it was nothing really,' she replied, dimpling. 'I simply wanted to ask you not to say anything about the—incident—in Oxford Street the other day. Nicky and I agreed that it would be better if we did not mention it to our brother.'

'You had no need to concern yourself,' he said gently. 'I would not have referred to the matter, in any event.'

A guilty blush covered her cheeks. 'I had not really supposed that you would—but I just needed to be sure for Nicky's sake. He returns to his school on Monday and it would hardly be fair to have him leave under a cloud—the whole affair was all my fault, after all!'

'Oh, come now!' protested the earl. 'You can hardly be blamed for going to that poor lad's rescue! As I recall, there were no offers of assistance from that crowd of bystanders and—as for myself!' He grimaced in recollection. 'I fear I put up a pretty poor show. In my opinion, you are to be congratulated.'

'You are too kind, my lord,' returned Jessica, with another dimpling smile that set Wyvern's heart turning frantic somersaults. 'As it happens, I was more than glad of your help—although,' she added mischievously, 'I have to say that you do seem to be making somewhat of a habit of coming to my aid!'

Wyvern's eyes gleamed appreciatively. 'I would say that last night's magnificent efforts on your part leave us pretty well all square.' He grinned, steadfastly ignoring all the warning bells that were ringing in his ears. 'That's not to say you may not count on my assistance in any future—'

The rest of his light-hearted banter was interrupted by the sound of Mrs Barrowman, who was bustling about in the process of gathering up her belongings and preparing to depart, having reluctantly reached the conclusion that it was time for her to put an end to this very welcome respite from her daily chores.

'Thank you so much for coming to my rescue,' she said, her beaming smile encompassing the pair of them. 'And for my delicious tea, of course!' And, as the disconcerted Wyvern scrambled to his feet and inclined his head, she went on, 'I have had such a nice little rest, sir, and am most obliged to you—and to your good lady wife, of course!' she added, directing a courteous bob towards her somewhat taken-aback young hostess.

Jessica could not forbear from shooting a mischievous glance at Wyvern and, no sooner had she registered his manful efforts to restrain the twitch of his lips, than a bubble of laughter started to rise in her chest and she was obliged to burrow into her reticule in search of her handkerchief.

For several moments, the two of them stood smilingly watching their unlooked-for guest exit the tearoom. Then, giving herself a mental shake, Jessica turned to the earl and held out her hand.

'I dare say you must have a hundred and one things to do, my lord,' she said, in her very best drawing-room accents. 'I cannot imagine what is keeping my brother, but I really must be on my way now.'

'Yes, of course,' replied Wyvern, swallowing his disappointment at the unwelcome curtailment of what had looked to be developing into a most promising tête-à-tête. 'If you would just allow me to settle the bill, I will be happy to escort you back to Ringfords.'

Beckoning to a nearby waiter, he thrust his hand into his left-side hip pocket, feeling for his notecase. Stiffening suddenly, he transferred his attention to the opposite side, whereupon a look of consternation crept over his face.

'Good God!' he announced, as he collapsed back into his seat in dismay. 'I've been robbed—those thieving little tykes must have picked my pocket!'

'But that's dreadful!' exclaimed Jessica, as she, too, lowered herself back into her seat. 'You must send for the constable immediately!'

'Much too late, I fear.' Wyvern gave a rueful grin. 'Serves me right for not paying attention, I dare say!'

As Jessica saw his pensive expression, her eyes softened. 'Were you carrying a great deal of money, sir?' she asked.

'Hardly any, I'm relieved to say,' he returned somewhat brusquely, fishing inside his waistcoat pocket for a half-sovereign and tossing it to the waiting assistant. 'The notecase was practically empty!'

'Well, at least there is a certain amount of comfort to be gained from that!' said Jessica brightly, in an effort to console the earl but then, as the seconds ticked by and Wyvern's contemplative silence continued, it struck her that, perhaps, his notecase had contained something of far greater import than money.

'It is clear that the matter is causing you some distress, my lord,' she said hesitantly. 'Is there anything I can do to help?'

For a moment, he stared at her across the table, seeming neither to see nor to hear her, but then a slight shudder ran through him and a deep sadness appeared in his eyes. 'The notecase contained my brother's final letter to me,' he said, his lips twisting in a poor attempt at a smile. 'It is of no real importance—I have his words by heart.'

'Then I beg that you commit them to paper at once, sir!' she urged him. 'Before they slip away entirely— as they surely will!'

'There is little danger of me forgetting them,' he replied, with a vehement shake of his head and, closing his eyes, he began to recite softly, '"Ben, old chap, can't go on—got myself into an unholy mess—can't seem to sort it out—mine is yours now—too late for me…'" At this point, his voice wavered and, as the import of his brother's words flew into his mind, he stopped, once again aware of the terrible weight of his responsibilities.

What in the name of providence can I be thinking of? he chastised himself, rising hurriedly to his feet. Having carelessly thrown away the one chance that he had been given to secure his family heritage, here he was, sitting casually supping tea and doing his level best to ingratiate himself with a girl to whom he could no more pay court than fly to the moon! Added to which was the unpalatable fact that he had yet to contend with his grandmother's shocked incredulity when word of this morning's débâcle at the Draycotts' reached her ears—notwithstanding the certain ribald disbelief of his two colleagues!

Without further ado, he helped the somewhat bewildered Jessica to her feet and ushered her hurriedly out of the tearoom on to the pavement. And then, to add to her confusion, he let go of her arm and, leaving her to follow in his wake, set up such a pace back towards the haberdasher's that she had the utmost difficulty in keeping up with him.

She had not failed to register his anguish during his attempted recitation of his brother's words, which had given her some understanding as to why he had been so unusually distressed at having a virtually empty notecase stolen. It was clear that the lost memento had been of great sentimental value to him and she tried hard to conjure up some suitable words of comfort to a man who was, as she constantly had to keep reminding herself, still little more than a stranger. As yet, no obvious solution presented itself to this difficulty and, since she was, at the moment, having enough trouble endeavouring to match her pace with his hurried stride, she was obliged to set the matter aside and concentrate her efforts on not losing sight of his tall figure in the press of people on the pavement.

On reaching Ringfords, Wyvern halted, frowningly scanning the street in both directions but of young Master Beresford there was no sign. The earl, by this time, had recovered sufficient of his composure to venture the remark that he trusted that the unexpected delay with the missing notecase had not caused them to fail to spot Nicky's return from Hatchard's.

'We cannot have missed him!' he expostulated. 'He would not go on without you, surely?'

One look at the earl's intimidating frown was enough to curb Jessica's immediate desire to defend her young brother, so she simply shook her head. At this unexpected lack of response from one who he had discovered was usually more than ready to speak her mind, Wyvern looked down and, catching sight of her pained expression, he could not prevent his lips from twitching in a rueful smile.

'My dear Miss Beresford,' he said, reaching out to take her hand. 'I cannot apologise enough! It would appear that the loss of my notecase has had the added effect of addling my wits. I pray that you will find it in your heart to forgive such a shocking display of bad manners?'

Her eyes softening, Jessica gave him a tremulous smile. 'You have every reason to be out of sorts, my lord,' she assured him. 'I only wish that there was something I could do to lessen your hurt.'

As Wyvern wryly returned her smile and thanked her for her concern, he could not help but reflect that the simple act of her throwing herself headlong into his arms and fastening her tempting lips upon his would certainly go a long way towards alleviating the ache in his heart, even if only temporarily but, wisely, he kept these highly appealing thoughts to himself.

Since neither of them could think of anything further to add to the conversation, there followed several moments of slightly awkward silence while they stood waiting for the wayward Nicky to make an appearance; Wyvern reluctantly turned his mind towards constructing some sort of acceptable explanation of the morning's events for his anxious grandparent.

Jessica, however, chose the respite to mull over the extraordinary turn of events that had just occurred. Deliberating on the late earl's odd use of words in the letter to his brother, she could not help being curious at the term *mine is yours now*. Was the writer intending to indicate that all of his possessions were now Wyvern's, a somewhat unnecessary stipulation in a last message, she thought, since it was obvious that his younger brother would stand to inherit everything at the late earl's death—including his debts, she knew, having overheard parts of an earlier conversation between Matt and her cousin Imogen.

'How perfectly stupid to expect the poor fellow to pay off all his brother's gambling debts!' Imogen had protested, Matt having imparted to her some of the current rumours regarding Wyvern's financial difficulties.

'Not so, my love,' her husband had retorted.

'Gambling debts always take precedence over any other—it's a question of honour.'

'Oh, lord!' Imogen had sighed, shaking her head in exasperation. 'When it comes to you gentlemen and your inexplicable code of honour, we ladies can do nothing other than have the sense to give in gracefully.'

'And you know full well that you wouldn't have it any other way!' Matt had laughed, gently ruffling his wife's new short and highly becoming hairstyle. 'Lovelace has it to a tee—*"I could not love you, Dear, so much, loved I not honour more"*—extremely well put, I've always thought!'

At the time, Jessica had considered the whole concept of love and honour to be a somewhat romantic ideal, best kept between the pages of the novels that she and her cousin so enjoyed reading. And what any of it might have to do with the late earl's message to his brother was beyond her comprehension. Nonetheless, even though she was not best pleased at having to stand like some sort of mute next to the tight-lipped Wyvern, while silently cursing her own brother's abysmal lack of time keeping, that curious phraseology from the earl's missing letter would keep invading her thoughts. ''Mine is yours,' she murmured, half-aloud.

'I beg your pardon?' intruded Wyvern's startled voice.

At the earl's unexpected disruption to her deliberations, Jessica's eyes flew up to meet his and, almost without thinking, she asked, 'The mine—what sort of a mine is it?'

His forehead creased in a puzzled frown. 'Mine?' he said. 'I'm afraid I don't follow you.'

'I was wondering about your brother's mine!' she

admitted, her cheeks pink with embarrassment. 'The one he said was now yours! Is it a coal mine—a tin mine? What sort of mine is it?'

For a moment, he stared down at her, uncomprehending. Then, in an instant, his frown vanished and the beginnings of a smile appeared. 'Oh, I see!' he said, shaking his head. 'No, no. You have misunderstood. Theo was merely telling me—'

Suddenly he stopped and an odd expression came over his face. 'Good grief!' he gasped, clutching at his brow. 'I wonder if—dear Lord—I believe you may be in the right! How can none of us have thought of such a thing? My dear girl, you are an absolute genius!'

And, suddenly overcome with a curious mixture of realisation and excitement, he reached towards her and, regardless of the curious stares of the passers-by, would have pulled her into his arms, had not the sudden appearance of the long-overdue Master Beresford halted him in his tracks.

'Terribly sorry, Sis!' exclaimed the boy breathlessly. 'Met a chap from college and got chatting—didn't notice the time.' And, inclining his head respectfully towards the earl, he added, 'Thanks for keeping an eye on my sad romp of a sister, my lord—I had the most dreadful visions of her starting back without me!'

Wyvern, his former ebullience having fizzled away like a damp squib, felt a small spurt of anger run through him but, on catching the warning look in Jessica's eyes, unmistakably daring him to react to Nicky's rather unchivalrous jest, he forced some semblance of a smile to his lips and replied, 'The pleasure was mine entirely, I assure you!'

Nicholas gave a satisfied nod and then, taking hold of his sister's arm, lightheartedly suggested that they had better be on their way back home before Matt sent out a search party after them.

Doffing his beaver, Wyvern bowed and bade the siblings a polite 'good afternoon', his eyes following the pair as they made their way through the busy streets. And, despite the fact that all he could distinguish of Jessica was the bobbing, green-beribboned crown of her chipstraw bonnet, he did not alter his stance until well past the moment that the two siblings had turned the corner into Dover Street and disappeared from his view. Then, with a stifled oath, he crammed his own hat back on his head, turned swiftly on his heel and strode off in the opposite direction, towards his Grosvenor Square residence and whatever reception might await him there.

Chapter Ten

For as far back as her memory could take her, Felicity Draycott had been harbouring a secret passion for one or other of the Ashcroft brothers. Having spent most of the summer months of her solitary childhood sequestered at her father's country estate near Heston, in Middlesex, she had been given ample opportunity to observe the happy-go-lucky independence of the handsome pair.

In the first instance, it had been Theo who had captured her heart when, at twelve years of age, the elder of the two boys had come upon Sir Jonathan's then four-year-old daughter sitting on the bottom step of the Grange's sweeping central staircase, sobbing her heart out. The occasion, which she could perfectly well recall, had been one of the many extravagant social gatherings that the Ashcrofts had been wont to hold in those far-off days before the boys' mother had died. Various local families would be invited to attend these alfresco receptions and, after partaking of a sumptuous repast, whilst the adults might choose to rest in the shade of the Grange's magnificent chestnut trees or wander at will through the ground's extensive gardens, the younger members of the group would be left to enjoy themselves as they saw fit.

Due to the sprawling, almost labyrinthine construction of the Ashcrofts' family home, it went without saying that the favoured pastime among the older children would be 'hide-and-go-seek' and it would not be long before a dozen or so youngsters could be heard scampering up and down the three staircases and in and out of a seemingly inexhaustible number of cubby holes, in search of suitable places in which they might secrete themselves.

At the time, Felicity, having been the youngest member of that particular set of children, had been left to her own devices and ignored by the others, not one of whom had proved willing to encumber his- or herself with a small girl scarcely out of leading-strings. Theo, however, who on the occasion in question had been elected 'seeker', had taken pity on the sadly forsaken youngster and, after hoisting her on to his shoulders, piggy-back style, had not only carried her with him to search out the rest of the group, but had also allowed her to accompany him for the remainder of the activity.

Thereafter, Felicity had carried a torch for the young viscount, revelling in such moments as when he had abandoned his own game to teach her the rudiments of croquet and, when she had reached her early teens, had occasionally sought her out to partner him in one of the country dances that were part of the usual entertainment at any local house party. The arrival of the beautiful Lady Sophia Goodwin on the scene, however, had very quickly had the effect of crumbling Felicity's youthful dreams of becoming Theo's countess into the dust. Furthermore, no sooner had the beloved hero of her childhood, now Eighth Earl of Wyvern, betrothed himself to Sophia than Felicity had immediately, and unfalteringly, transferred all her hopes and affections to his younger sibling, where, for the past five years, they had remained firmly entrenched. As long as Benedict remained single, she had constantly assured herself, there was every hope that she would eventually capture his attention, which, to her abounding joy, following the newly ennobled earl's recent return from Paris, she finally seemed to have succeeded in doing.

Accordingly, it was with a gasp of horrified disbelief that she had leapt to her feet, as the ominous thud of the Mount Street front door had proclaimed the curtailment of the earl's interview with her father, without bringing about the anticipated and much longed-for proposal. Flinging herself to the window in a flurry of consternation, she had observed Wyvern striding purposefully up the street. With her mother close on her heels, she had burst into her father's study, demanding an immediate explanation for the earl's precipitate departure.

Upon hearing Sir Jonathan's rather garbled version of Wyvern's refusal to apply for her hand, Felicity, ignoring her mother's shocked protests and other attempts to restrain her, had made for the front door where, calling for her maid to accompany her, she had snatched up her gloves and reticule, thrust on her bonnet and dashed out of the house in pursuit. Her intention had been to try to intercept the earl, in order to assure him that she did not consider the deep affection of which he had spoken to be at all necessary, as well as to point out to him the many advantages that a match between them would bring. Being the out-and-out gentleman that he was, he would be bound to hear her out and surely feel obliged to escort her home, thus allowing her at least one more chance to press her case!

Heedlessly and in the most undignified manner, she had fought her way through the milling crowds of promenaders quite happily intent upon enjoying their customary Saturday morning stroll in and around Berkeley Square. Then, pink-faced and panting with anxiety, she had arrived at the square's Berkeley Street gateway, just in time to observe Wyvern disappearing into Gunter's tearooms, with Jessica Beresford, accompanied by an elderly woman who Felicity could only suppose must be the girl's abigail, following hard on his heels.

Both angry and disconsolate that her hastily planned confrontation of the earl had failed to materialise, Felicity had then, to her maid's utter astonishment, spent some ten minutes or more strolling back and forth past Gunter's windows, peering through the small panes of glass at the unsuspecting group within. Thus, she had witnessed Wyvern presentation of a most expensive gift to Jessica and, as if to add insult to injury, his tender holding of the little madam's hand!

Dejectedly trudging back to Mount Street, she had found herself with more than enough time to bring to mind the events of the previous evening and, having suddenly recalled Wyvern's puzzling and somewhat hasty retreat from the ballroom at just about the same time as the Beresford party had entered, a pensive frown had furrowed her brow. And then, to add even more fuel to her quickly mounting suspicions, she distinctly remembered having heard Imogen Beresford making anxious enquiries as to her young cousin's whereabouts. The earl, as Felicity also recalled, had appeared somewhat out of sorts when, some time later, he had eventually returned to the ballroom and had then spent the remainder of the evening looking decidedly preoccupied. At the time, however, since her father had only just that moment informed her of Wyvern's desire to meet with him on the morrow, as well as congratulating her on the likely result of that appointment, she had merely supposed that it was probably his slight apprehension over the impending interview that had been the cause of the earl's distracted manner. Now, however, having had time to consider the matter, and bearing in mind Wyvern's subsequent behaviour, she could only suppose that he and the Beresford girl had, in reality, been engaged in some sort of furtive assignation— probably to arrange a further meeting this morning! And, no sooner had this thought occurred to her than a hot resentment towards Jessica had very quickly followed. *The little flirt just has to have every man she sets eyes upon,* she had fumed, *and, it is all due to her that Wyvern changed his mind—making me a laughing-stock into the bargain!* Dispiritedly mounting the steps to her front door, she had then set her mind to considering the various ways in which she might get even with her rival.

Meanwhile, Nicholas, having finally turned up to escort his sister back to their Dover Street residence, was eagerly acquainting her with all the details of his unexpected reunion with his school colleague. 'And, as it turns out,' he grandly informed her, 'Ramsey's people are sending him back to Rugby on Monday in their own carriage and *he* has invited me to travel up with him!'

Endeavouring to smile and nod in all the right places, his less-than-interested sister had far too many things on her mind to pay more than the vaguest attention to his effusive descriptions of the, no doubt, highly worthy Ramsey's academic abilities. Instead, she set her mind to unravelling her own quandary in regard to the highly perplexing Lord Wyvern. Surely, it could not be right, she told herself, that a man who, according to rumour, was almost betrothed to one woman should continually look at another in *such* a way! She was quite positive that she had not imagined either the suggestive twinkle or the depth of emotion in his eyes. Even now, the thought of both sent delicious shivers up her spine and she was obliged to turn her head away from her brother, lest he should catch sight of the sudden blush that coloured her cheeks. With a sinking heart, she wondered if it were possible that she had allowed herself to be taken in by yet another handsome rake's plausible attentions. Wyvern had attempted to kiss her, after all, she reasoned—hardly the behaviour of a true gentleman—especially when she was a young, single female and a guest in his house! His actions, in that respect, had scarcely differed from those of the hateful Philip Wentworth's, who had cleverly won her confidence by professing to have her interests at heart. But Wentworth's performance, as had been revealed, had been all to do with getting his hands on her late father's money and property. The Earl of Wyvern could hardly have any such motive for trying to prolong the interlude in Gunter's tearooms, let alone keeping hold of her hands much longer than polite society dictated. And yet, despite seeming to be paying her far more attention than simple courtesy demanded, he had still not made the slightest effort to call at the house to pay his respects. Jessica let out a sigh. The whole issue was so very frustrating and, seemingly, quite beyond her powers to comprehend. To make matters worse, if that were at all possible, there was no way of determining if or when she would ever be given either the opportunity—or the necessary courage, she was bound to concede!—to confront the infuriating man with the dilemma he had bequeathed her!

'Buck up, Jess,' came Nicholas's bracing tones. 'If you walk any slower we won't get home until dinner time!'

Jessica gave a startled jolt, having been quite unaware that her deep introspection had had the effect of reducing her steps almost to a standstill. Hurriedly increasing her pace, she abandoned her deliberations and endeavoured to concentrate her mind on her brother's highly improbable descriptions of his school friend's sporting skills.

Upon their arrival back at Dover Street, they were greeted with the news that they had only just missed a most crestfallen Harry Stevenage. The young lieutenant, so Imogen informed them, had called round to bid the family a sad farewell, owing to the fact that both he and his unit were about to be dispatched to Newcastle, in the far north of the country, making it doubtful that he would return to London before the close of the Season.

'He did say that he will, almost certainly, be paying his usual visit to his godfather in the autumn and commissioned me to tell you,' added Imogen, with a smiling nod in Jessica's direction, 'that he would be most obliged if you could find it in your heart to drop him the occasional line.'

'Yes, of course,' was Jessica's somewhat disconsolate reply, it very quickly having occurred to her that, with both of her 'respectable' escorts off on their travels, the relative freedom that she had enjoyed for the past few weeks looked to have reached its conclusion. In the light of last year's unsavoury incident, she was well aware that Matt was hardly likely to be in favour of his young sister wandering around the capital on her own and, as for allowing her to go off with any gentlemen escorts, other than those whom he had himself personally and thoroughly vetted, she knew that this was equally out of the question!

She groaned inwardly, visualising the coming days filled with circumspect shopping trips with either Clara, her maid, at her side or, worse still, one of the footmen at her heels!

Chapter Eleven

'Well, old chap,' said Sir Simon, leaning back in his armchair. 'I cannot honestly say that I'm surprised—it was clear that your heart wasn't really in it!'

'Took some courage, though,' interjected Fitzallan, shooting an admiring glance at his friend. 'Wouldn't have cared to be in your shoes if old Draycott had turned nasty!'

'As a matter of fact,' cut in Wyvern hastily, 'since his lordship finally resorted to trying to appeal to my baser nature, I cannot help but feel that both he and his good lady would welcome me back with open arms, should I be prepared to resume my attentions to their daughter. Which, in the circumstances, would be pretty shabby of me, as I am sure you will agree.' Pausing, he heaved a deep sigh, then added, somewhat shamefacedly, 'Nevertheless—should push come to shove…!'

The three comrades were ensconced in the comfortable sitting room of Holt's set of chambers in Albany, whither a much-deflated Wyvern had fled some hours earlier, still smarting from Lady Lavinia's reproachful lambasting. His friends, whilst equally disconcerted at the earl's unexpected volte-face, had continued to be, just as he had expected, rather more supportive than his grandparent, having elected to hear him out without undue criticism.

'Correct me if I'm wrong, dear boy,' murmured Sir Simon, as he leant forward to replenish their glasses, 'but, since I was actually under the impression that "push" had already come to "shove", I am beginning to get the feeling that there must be something that you are not telling us. Cough up, there's a good chap!'

'Well, there *is* something,' returned Wyvern hesitantly. 'The trouble is that I have not yet managed to convince myself that—even if what I surmise does turn out to be the case—there is any likelihood of it making any real difference!'

A frowning Fitzallan put down his glass and stared at Holt in dismay, exclaiming, 'What the devil is the dear fellow rambling on about? Damned if I could make either head or tail of that, how about you? Seems to me that this whole rotten business is beginning to affect the boy's brain!'

But Sir Simon, who had been studying Wyvern's expression, held up his finger and shook his head. 'Cut line, Freddie!' he protested. 'I'm sure Ben is doing his best!'

Shooting his older friend a grateful grin, Wyvern took a deep breath. 'The thing is,' he continued, 'I found out—at least,' he then emended hurriedly, a slight flush rising in his cheeks, 'I had it pointed out to me—that the use of the word "mine" in Theo's note did not necessarily mean "possession"—it might possibly refer to an actual mine—as in *coal* or *tin* or whatever!'

There was a moment's silence as his two companions digested his words.

Then, 'By crikey, he's right!' Fitzallan let out a low whistle. 'P'raps old Theo owned a coal mine somewhere or other—decent revenue from that would certainly go some way towards solving your problem, Ben, old chap!'

'Perhaps I might take another quick look at Theo's note?' said Sir Simon, glancing at the earl in some curiosity, since he had not failed to register his friend's unexpected moment of confusion. 'I cannot quite recall the actual phrase.'

'Gone for good, I'm sorry to say,' returned Wyvern bitterly. 'A couple of ruffians barged into me this morning and filched my notecase. But the wording is still perfectly clear in my mind—"mine is yours now"— that's what he wrote. When I first read it, it made no sense but now, well…' his brow wrinkled '…now I'm almost convinced that he was trying to tell me something—something that he didn't want anyone else to get wise to!'

'I have to admit that that does sound quite plausible,' said Sir Simon, nodding in agreement but then, as something else occurred to him, he paused for a moment before asking, somewhat apologetically, 'Not that it is really any of my business, of course, but would you mind telling me whether you have discussed the contents of your brother's note with persons other than Lady Lavinia and your solicitor?'

'Apart from Freddie and yourself, you mean?' responded Wyvern, taken aback. 'No! Certainly not—why would you ask that?'

'It was simply that you mentioned that "someone" had pointed out the possibility that the word "mine" meant something other than we had all supposed,' countered Sir Simon gently. 'Which led me to wonder…?' He stopped, waiting for Wyvern's response.

The earl stared at him for a moment, then, with a rueful grin, he grunted, 'Hoist by my own petard, by God—it would appear that you two fellows know me better than my own mother!'

And then, being careful to omit all but the most salient points of his meeting with Jessica, he described how it was she, in fact, who had led him to his present conclusion.

'Tea with the Beresford chit, by Jove!' gasped Fitzallan, eyeing Wyvern in awe. 'You lucky beggar! They say that brother of hers keeps her on a pretty tight leash—I have it on good authority that he has refused permission for her to go driving with at least three different fellows that he didn't like the look of!'

'Clearly not as tight a leash as he possibly imagines, if what Ben tells us is anything to go by!' laughed Holt, but, on glancing over to the earl and registering his friend's somewhat bellicose expression, his smile disappeared and a startled look came into his eyes. Tentatively sipping his cognac, he mused on the matter and could only hope that he had drawn the wrong conclusion from his observations.

Having no desire to enter into enter any sort of ribald discussion examining Jessica's obvious attributes, Wyvern sought to steer his friends back to the original topic.

'How would one go about establishing the existence of such a mine—let alone its ownership—I wonder?' he interjected slowly. 'Like looking for the proverbial needle in the haystack, it seems to me!'

Returning his thoughts to the subject in hand, Sir Simon gave a quick nod. 'It would help if we knew what sort of mine we were looking for,' he said. 'Pity about Theo's letter—if we had been able to study it more thoroughly we might have come up with a few more clues.'

'Damned bad luck, that going missing!' mused Fitzallan. 'Couldn't have anything to do with the other business, I suppose?'

'How do you mean?' asked Wyvern, perplexed.

'Well, you know,' returned Fitzallan, with an embarrassed shrug. 'People searching for documents and so on—bit of a coincidence you having your pocket picked, if you ask me!'

'You mean you think the whole affair was done intentionally, then?' said the earl, in astonishment. 'But who would possibly know where I kept Theo's letter—apart from ourselves, that is?'

There were several moments' silence, as the three friends deliberated this point then, to his two companions' amazement, Sir Simon suddenly leapt to his feet and, punching the air in exultation, exclaimed, 'By all that's holy! I believe I have it!'

'Well, spit it out, for God's sake!' begged Wyvern, his eyes alight in expectation. 'The suspense is killing us!'

Taking a deep breath, Sir Simon regained his seat and, leaning forward, said, 'Who else knew the whereabouts of your brother's note, you asked? Well, I'll tell you! Both Digby Hazlett and Cedric Stockwell knew—because they were watching when you tucked it back into your notecase yesterday afternoon!'

'But they weren't to know what the paper was,' demurred Fitzallan, with a puzzled frown. 'And, it could hardly have been either of them who picked Ben's pocket, 'cos he would have recognised them!'

'Yes, I realise that, Flannelhead!' retorted Holt. 'They would hardly have set about burgling either the Grange or Ashcroft House themselves either, would they? My guess is that one or other of them—my money is on Hazlett—paid a couple of young ruffians to do the dirty work!'

'Hazlett!' frowned Wyvern. 'Why on earth would he…?'

'Well, it's clear that he is up to something,' declared his now highly animated comrade. 'You said so yourself! Theo owed him a great deal of money, yet he has made no attempt to dun you for any of it—made a point of saying so, in fact! And *why*, I ask you?' He paused, studying his colleagues' expectant expressions. 'Because, in my opinion, the fellow is after far more valuable pickings!' he finished exultantly.

'Like Theo's mine, you mean?' cried Fitzallan, now party to Sir Simon's excitement. 'P'raps it's a diamond mine!' His eyes glowed. 'Now that really would be something!'

'Now just hang on a minute, the pair of you!' protested Wyvern, who was still trying to make sense of Holt's words. 'Hazlett didn't actually read the letter—how would he know about any mine—even suppose the thing actually exists?'

'That's the whole point, dear boy!' returned Sir Simon patiently. 'It's my belief that he already knows *of* its existence but, like ourselves, he either has no idea of its whereabouts or—and this is far more likely—he needs some sort of *document of ownership* to get his hands on it—hence the break-ins and the pocket-picking!'

'He thinks that I have this document?'

'Well, he possibly did,' Sir Simon was bound to concede. 'But, if, as I suspect, he now has Theo's note, he has probably realised that you are just as much in the dark as he is and is marking time until you make your next move!'

'My next move?' said the earl, shaking his head in bewilderment. 'And what might that be, oh great and wondrous oracle?'

'Well, I might just have a suggestion there,' put in Fitzallan warily, with an indignant scowl at Sir Simon. 'Cousin of mine has connections at Lloyds—they keep some sort of register of ships and all manner of other things—he might be able to point us in the right direction—worth a try, at least, don't you think?'

'Good man!' nodded Wyvern, rising to his feet. 'Let's go visit this cousin of yours. Nothing like striking while the iron's hot, as the saying goes!'

'Well, I dare say we can try,' replied Fitzallan, reluctantly vacating his comfortable chair. 'But who knows where dear old Charlie will be at this time of day— probably tucked up nicely in the arms of his light o' love, if he has any sense!' Then, reaching for his hat and gloves, he added, 'But we can look in at Boodle's, if you've a mind—that's his usual haunt!'

* * *

Several hours and gentlemen's clubs later, however, the three comrades were still no nearer to tracking down Fitzallan's elusive cousin and, after another fruitless search in yet another tavern, Wyvern voted that they called it a halt for the night. After some deliberation, it was decided that it might be more sensible to allow Fitzallan to seek out his cousin independently, after which he could acquaint his friends with any useful information that he might be able to procure.

Although Wyvern's once-acute powers of observation were not quite as sharp as they had been back in his days of military service, they were still sufficiently well honed to have rendered him with the distinct feeling that, for some little time now, someone had been dogging their footsteps. After mulling over the matter for a few moments, it soon occurred to him that the three of them sticking so closely together made for an excellent target, should any sort of attack be imminent. Gently nudging Sir Simon in the ribs, he jerked his head to the party's rear.

'Picked him out half an hour ago,' murmured the grinning Holt. 'Better split up, don't you think?'

In unspoken agreement, the trio crossed over St James Street and made its way into Piccadilly, where the comrades said their farewells and went their separate ways: Holt to his set of chambers in Vigo Street, Fitzallan to his family mansion on the corner of Clarges Street and Wyvern walking the further distance back to Grosvenor Square.

The shadow, as the earl was very soon to apprehend, had chosen to ignore his two erstwhile companions and follow him, which, in the light of Sir Simon's earlier deductions, seemed to make perfect sense. Just to check that he was correct in his assumptions, Wyvern, deciding to give the insolent devil a bit of a run for his money, devised the most circuitous route that it was possible to take to get to Ashcroft House, changing direction at practically every junction and even, on at least two occasions, retracing his steps completely.

At this early hour of the morning, it being Sunday, the streets were relatively quiet and, apart from having to side-step the occasional inebriated reveller, Wyvern found himself with more than enough time to indulge in several flights of fancy.

At the time, Fitzallan's comment regarding diamond mines had brought a disbelieving smile to his face but now, as he let his imagination run wild, it was perfectly simple to conjure up a vision of pots—nay, buckets—full of the sparkling stones and, in his mind's eye, he could almost feel them trickling through his fingers as he plunged his hands into their midst. What could he not do with such largesse, he ruminated, his mind already building castles in the air! Pay off all Theo's outstanding debts, without question—especially that despicable cad Hazlett's—and, rather more to the point, it would enable him to present himself at Number Twenty-Four Dover Street in the fairly certain knowledge that, however tight a leash Matt Beresford chose to keep his sister on, *his* suit would be received with open arms. Mere earls might come two-a-penny these days, he grinned to himself, but abundantly wealthy earls on the look out for a bride were very thin on the ground!

During the previous eight of his twenty-six years, Wyvern had grown sufficiently confident of his own masculinity to consider himself well up to scratch in the art of interpretation, when it came to the various signs and signals given off by members of the female species. Nevertheless, nothing in his past dealings with the fairer sex had prepared him for the thunderbolt that had hit him when confronted with the delectable Jessica Beresford in full warpaint, this having proved to be an entirely new sensation to him, shaking him to the very core of his being. Even so, he was not insensible to the fact that, if the acquaintanceship were to prosper—in the face of her tender years and undoubted innocence—he would need to proceed with caution. He doubted that she had even the vaguest idea of the effect that her loveliness had upon the male of the species. Nonetheless, from the few tantalising signals that he had received, it was but a short step to convincing himself that Jessica would welcome his courtship. A courtship that, he promised himself with an optimistic grin, would be a *very* short one—conducted with all the usual due deference and regard, of course—at least until the joining of hands was over. He then allowed his imagination to run riot, in a somewhat premature anticipation of the many pleasurable activities that might follow the ceremony—vivid images of which were soon to send rippling shudders of exhilaration running through his body.

Regrettably, the sudden spattering of rain on his cheeks, heralding another blustery April shower, proved to be more than enough to cool his ardour and, making a quick dash up the steps of his Grosvenor Square mansion, Wyvern was reluctantly obliged to abandon his futile dreams of love and riches to the cold light of day. Before rapping on the door, however, he allowed himself the small luxury of raising one hand in a farewell salute to his pursuer, his eyes glinting with mischievous satisfaction as the fellow made a hurried, but vain, attempt to conceal himself amongst the sodden bushes in the Square's central garden.

Chapter Twelve

When no further news of his supposedly impending betrothal reached her ears, Jessica lived in daily expectation of a visit from the earl. Her days, now that both Stevenage and Nicholas had gone their separate ways, were just as she had supposed—morning calls to various of Imogen's rather dreary elderly relatives, and afternoons spent kicking her heels while her cousin rested, in preparation for the evening's festivities, with which Jessica grew more and more disenchanted as the Season progressed into May.

But Wyvern did not call and, to add to her disappointment, he failed to put in an appearance at any of the events that she attended during the week following their chance meeting outside Ringfords. Ever since that encounter, Jessica had been able to think of few things other than the astounding effect that the mischievous glint in Wyvern's eyes had had upon her heartbeat and how difficult she had found it to breathe properly when his hand had covered hers. But, most discomposing of all, perhaps, was how the slightest recall of that transitory kiss in the ladies' room was apt to send quite extraordinary sensations rampaging throughout her entire body!

She was quite at a loss to understand how to deal with this disturbing quandary and could not help wishing that she had a close friend with whom she could share her confidences. For, subsequent to her foolish and headstrong behaviour of the previous summer, and although she loved Imogen dearly, Jessica now found herself unable to summon up sufficient courage to discuss with her cousin a problem that she might well construe as being of a rather similar nature. Unfortunately, apart from her innocent, if somewhat furtive, assignations with Philip Wentworth—prior to his abduction and attempted assault—her only real experience with members of the opposite sex had been totally platonic. Moreover, since the failed abduction, Matt had been more than usually protective towards her for, being the sort of man who took his responsibilities very seriously, he was determined that no further occurrences of that sort should be allowed to blight her life.

To begin with, Jessica had been only too glad to comply with her brother's wishes, accepting that he had her best interests at heart but, gradually, as she had started to regain her confidence, his excessive solicitude for her safety was beginning to pall. Now that her two tame escorts had vacated the capital, Matt, to her lasting indignation and embarrassment, had been quite obdurate in his refusal to allow her to continue riding in the park, unless accompanied by his wife and himself. But, since Imogen's condition now prevented her from participating in that pleasurable activity, he too had chosen to abandon his own daily ride in favour of the occasional afternoon carriage-drive, given that it fitted in with the family's other engagements. It was true-that several of her most dedicated beaux had continued to keep up their pressure to petition him for permission to take her up in their carriages but Matt, being not entirely unfamiliar with the devious mentality of the concupiscent male—a facet of his past history that he was hardly likely to share with his young half-sister!—had found himself less than willing to deliver her into the hands of a relative stranger.

Jessica's increasing listlessness did, on occasion, cause Imogen a certain amount of concern but, wrapped up in her own little world of sublime self-contentedness, her cousin was not, perhaps, as observant as had previously been her wont.

Mindful of her beloved husband's deep-seated dread of losing her to childbirth and, although she was very happy to dance the occasional waltz with him—if only to remind herself of their irregular courtship—Imogen usually chose to sit out the more energetic country dances and reels, preferring to spend her evenings in spirited conversation with the group of other young matrons to whom she had attached herself. In this way, since Matt had stipulated that her partners should always return Jessica to his wife's side at the completion of each set of dances, it was no trouble for Imogen to keep a watchful eye on her cousin, should Beresford opt to remove himself from the relentless chattering of her female friends into the relative quiet of the card room, in the company of one or other of his own acquaintances.

On the Friday evening following the tea-shop incident, the Beresfords were engaged to attend Lady Henderson's supper dance, a fairly staid event at which, whilst she had few expectations of the earl putting in an appearance, Jessica still followed her recently developed custom of keeping several spaces on her dance-card in the avid hope that he might just do so. Having rejoined her cousin, after a rather halting progress through a cotillion with a rather bashful partner, whose familiarity with the dance's somewhat complicated figures and changes had turned out to be rather limited, Jessica, thankful for the temporary cessation, slumped back into her seat, wishing that she had taken advantage of Imogen's earlier suggestion that they might cry off this soirée.

But then, as her restless eyes flicked backwards and forwards across the crowded room, she suddenly froze and her heart seemed to thunder to a halt, before rapidly gathering pace to beat at more than twice its normal speed.

For there, at the doorway, looking directly at her, stood Wyvern, his handsome face wearing a slightly pensive frown. Then, to her growing delight, after pausing for a moment to murmur a few words into the ear of one of the two friends who accompanied him, he began to make his way over to her corner of the room.

'Good evening, Mrs Beresford,' he began, with a respectful bow to Imogen. 'Ben Ashcroft, at your service, ma'am. I believe your husband was acquainted with my late brother?'

Offering him her hand, a smiling Imogen nodded. 'So Mr Beresford has mentioned, your lordship, but he,

I must inform you, is in the card room, should you wish to speak with him.'

'Later, perhaps,' he replied, doing his utmost to ignore the expectant look on Jessica's face. 'I was hoping I might persuade you to take a turn about the room with me?'

Imogen's smile deepened. 'It is most kind of you, my lord,' she replied. 'But, if you will excuse me, I prefer not to dance this evening. However, if your lordship is short of a partner, I believe that my cousin Jessica still has one or two free spaces on her card.'

Inclining his head, Wyvern then turned towards Jessica, carefully avoiding her eyes. 'Then, perhaps Miss Beresford would care to do me the honour—this next is to be a waltz, if I am not mistaken?'

At her breathless nod, the earl reached out his hand and drew the somewhat dazed Jessica to her feet and led her across to the rather inadequate rectangle that had been set aside for the dancing.

'I trust that I was correct in assuming that you would prefer that I did not approach you directly?' he enquired, as he slipped his arm around her waist.

'W-why, yes, thank you, your lordship,' came Jessica's shaky reply. After all the empty days of waiting and wondering, to suddenly find herself standing so close to the object of her recent dreams seemed to be having the most peculiar effect on her ability to think straight. 'I—I had not thought it necessary to mention our…er…previous…acquaintance-ship!'

From Wyvern's point of view, having finally been unable to resist the temptation of seeking Jessica out, his oft-imagined bliss at the idea of holding her in his arms was proving, in reality, to be more akin to some sort of exquisite torture.

Taking a deep breath to steady his nerves, he swung her deftly into the compelling movement of the dance and, achingly aware of the soft warmth of her body beneath his fingertips, he sent up an ardent prayer that the day would soon dawn when he would find himself in a position to confess his love for her.

Almost mesmerised by the lithe expertise with which Wyvern steered her into a reverse turn, Jessica's momentary flash of panic was quickly forgotten. Relaxing, she gladly succumbed to the confident pressure of his hands and soon they were whirling and swaying across the floor, their steps in perfect time with the giddy, lilting rhythm of the music, and their hearts beating as one. Together they glided, as if on air, oblivious to the other dancers as they drifted into Love's wonderland, thrilling to each other's touch and wishing that the dance would never end.

Inevitably and all too soon, the music drew to a close and, after swinging the flushed and panting Jessica into a final flourishing twirl, the earl brought her, reluctantly, to a standstill.

'Not nearly long enough, by half,' he groaned, his voice husky with emotion. 'I suppose it is too much to hope that you have another free space on your card?'

Her heart plummeting to her toes, Jessica gave a regretful shake of her head. 'Sadly not, my lord,' she replied. 'Had you arrived sooner, I would have been more than happy to accommodate you.'

A wry grimace crossed the earl's face as, tucking her

hand into the crook of his arm, he led her slowly back towards her seat. 'I fear that my time has been fully occupied these last few days.'

A spark of excitement flew into her eyes. 'Did you manage to solve the mystery of the mine?' she asked eagerly. 'Was it, in fact, a coal mine, as I had supposed?'

'I now have little doubt that a mine of some sort does exist,' he told her. 'Thanks to your remarkable perspicacity. Unfortunately, I have not, as yet, managed to track down its whereabouts.' He paused and, standing quite still, swung her round to face him, the longing in his eyes quite plain to see. 'But, you may be sure that when I do, sweetheart, you will be the very first to know!'

Then, having handed the stunned and somewhat confused Jessica back into her seat and expressed his thanks to both Imogen and herself, he bowed, turned sharply on his heel and, without a backward glance, made for the room's exit.

'What a very pleasant young man,' observed Imogen, as the door swung closed behind him. 'I did hear a rumour to the effect that he was about to become attached to Felicity Draycott, but nothing seems to have come of it. You should consider yourself honoured, Jess, for his lordship only danced the one dance and now seems to have departed!'

'Well, yes, that is true,' stammered her flame-faced cousin. 'But, don't forget that *you* were the one he asked in the first place—he merely settled for me because you practically obliged him to!'

'Well, if the expression on his face when he was

steering you round the floor was anything to go by,' laughed Imogen, 'I would say that he certainly seemed to be looking rather pleased with himself! In fact, I shouldn't be at all surprised if his approaching me first wasn't just some elaborate ploy to get you to dance with him!'

Luckily, at this point, came the peal of the supper bell and, with it, Matt's return, relieving Jessica of the need to repudiate her cousin's all too astute observation. Instead, as she gathered up her belongings and followed the pair into the refreshment room, she bent her mind to the somewhat perplexing matter of Wyvern's final statement.

That he had been endeavouring to convey something to her had been abundantly clear, but what it might have been she could not even begin to hazard a guess. Both the look in his eyes and his final tender epithet had shaken her to the very core of her being, but then he had departed without allowing her either the time or the opportunity to question him further. The heady euphoria she had felt at being in his arms at last had very soon evaporated, to be replaced by feelings of uncertainty and frustration, leaving her thoughts in such turmoil that she no longer had any idea what to believe. *Was the exasperating man merely toying with her affections?* she wondered bleakly, as she joined her companions at the supper table. *Or, could it be possible that his intentions were sincere? And, if so, when might a further opportunity arise wherein she might put his hinted-at fondness to the test?*

On the other side of the room, positioned behind a piece of ivy-clad trelliswork, stood Felicity Draycott, her face contorted with jealous rage. Having been obliged to sit out the last several dances herself, due to

the sparsity of acceptable offers, she had been beset by
fury at the sight of Wyvern tenderly shepherding the
Beresford girl around the floor. That he had refrained
from attending any other of the week's events was insult
enough, after his hurtful slight of Saturday morning, but
then, to have had the gall to show up at this one for the
express purpose of dancing with his secret paramour
was far more than Felicity could endure.

'His lordship seems to have transferred his alle-
giance in a somewhat cavalier manner, wouldn't you
say, Miss Draycott?' purred a soft voice in her ear.

Startled, she jerked back and found herself looking
up into the scarred features of Viscount Hazlett. She
stared at him in distaste, never having liked him since
his previous year's presumptuous attempts to coerce
her into accepting his unwanted proposal of marriage.

'I have no wish to converse with you, sir,' she said
haughtily, and would have moved away had not his
hand on her arm prevented her.

'Now that is a pity,' he countered, as a knowing grin
puckered the skin on his damaged cheek. 'And here was
I thinking that I could have the very answer to your little
problem.'

'What problem?' she flashed back, affronted. 'I have
no problems that can possibly be any concern of yours!'

'Ah, but it seems that you do, my dear,' replied the
viscount, tightening his hold as she attempted to extract
her hand from his grip. 'Unless I am very much
mistaken, it would appear that a certain young beauty
is causing a great deal of turmoil within the breast of one
who, only last week, I am reliably informed, was on the
verge of offering his hand to your own charming self.'

Her attention was caught and she ceased her rather futile struggle. 'Do not be impertinent, sir,' she returned, keeping her voice low, for fear of causing an unpleasant scene. 'I gave you my answer last year and I promise you that I am not about to change my mind!'

'Then let me assure you that I have no intention of propositioning you again on that score,' he riposted, an angry glint in his eye. 'I merely thought to serve you a good turn in regard to the little problem I mentioned earlier!'

'And what,' asked Felicity, with a certain amount of asperity, 'can you possibly imagine that you could do about that particular matter?'

'Aha!' He chuckled. 'So you are, at least, prepared to hear me out?'

She shrugged, her eyes once again scouring the room in the forlorn hope that Wyvern might have returned. 'If you have something to say, then kindly say it—I cannot stay here all evening!'

'As a matter of fact,' he said, stroking her hand, which was still in his possession, 'I do have a plan of sorts that will help your cause, although it will require a certain amount of co-operation from your good self!'

'In what respect?' she returned guardedly, somewhat nervous lest she should be seen in conversation with a man whose reputation, as she was well aware, was far from spotless.

'It merely requires that you befriend the young lady in question and get into the habit of taking her about with you.'

'Befriend her!' Felicity let out a shrill laugh, causing one or two of the assembled company within earshot to turn their heads in her direction. 'If you know anything at all about my feelings for her, you must know that she is the last person on earth that I would want to befriend!'

'We cannot expect to reap until we have sown,' continued Hazlett patiently. 'Taking Miss Beresford into your circle is merely part of the wider design I have in mind—for which it is necessary that you gain her confidence.'

'I suppose that I could do that if I were to put my mind to it,' returned Felicity, considering. 'Although I find myself hard pressed to understand how it could be of any possible benefit to me!'

'I promise you that it will all become clear eventually, my dear,' soothed the viscount, as another attempt at a smile brought his jagged scar once more into prominence. 'And, to further that end,' he went on, ignoring the look of repugnance that had appeared on Felicity's face, 'it would also help me in my quest to assist you, if you were to find yourself willing to supply me with certain information.'

'What sort of information?' came her guarded reply.

'Am I correct in thinking that you spent a good deal of your childhood on the Ashcroft estate?'

At Felicity's cautious nod, Hazlett then set about questioning her in regard to the two brothers' habits and, in particular, their favourite childhood haunts; when she reproachfully protested that, since she had been far too young to be included in their boyish pursuits, she had no idea of the manner in which they might have occupied themselves, the viscount grew quite angry and pressed her to try to remember.

'Well, I believe that they climbed trees, boated on the lake—the sorts of thing that all boys do, I imagine,' she retaliated crossly, quite at a loss as to why these trivial matters seemed to be of such importance to the viscount. 'Although, as it happens, I do seem to recall that they spent a good deal of their time up in the ruins of the abbey—building camps and so on!'

At this last, Hazlett's eyes lit up in interest. 'The abbey?' he asked her. 'Are you sure of that?'

'Well, as sure as I can be,' replied Felicity, with a dis-affected shrug. 'You must remember that both boys were so much older than myself—and, as a small girl, I could hardly have expected to be invited to join them in their rough-and-tumble pastimes!'

For several moments, the viscount stared down at her without speaking, presumably weighing up whether or not there was any real substance in what, as far as Felicity was concerned, had been her own rather trifling contribution to his queries. After waiting in vain for some explanation as to his rather odd manner of questioning, Felicity lost patience with him.

'I fail to see what any of that has to do with your proposal that I should strike up a friendly relationship with the Beresford female!' she flung at him. 'And, unless you are prepared to explain to me immediately, I intend to have nothing further to do with your foolish machinations. Kindly let go of my hand and take yourself off!'

'Calm yourself, dear lady, I beg of you!' returned Hazlett, with a low chuckle. 'Have I not told you that all would become clear eventually? Since I am about to relieve you of a—how shall I put it?—unwanted thorn in your side, it occurs to me that the less you know of any arrangements I might make, in regard to the aforesaid, the better. In this way, should any of those plans misfire, you could, quite truthfully, claim to have known nothing about the matter! You really must just learn to respect my judgement in the case, my dear Miss Draycott! I assure you that, eventually, everything will turn out for the best.'

'I trust that these "arrangements" you speak of do not involve damaging Miss Beresford in any way!' countered Felicity nervously. 'I would not care for you to think that I condone violence of any sort! I merely wished for Wyvern to cease his mooning after her—the girl has so many other beaux to choose from, after all is said and done!'

Hazlett gave another of his unsettling smiles, sending a shudder of revulsion running down Felicity's spine, leaving her wishing, more than ever, that she had not been so unwise as to voice her innermost thoughts to him. Impatiently freeing her hand from his hold, she would have turned away from him had he not blocked her pathway.

'Just be sure that you play your part, Miss Draycott,' he said, now with a clear hint of menace in his voice. 'You would not wish our little conversation to become common currency, I'll be bound!'

Then, with a mocking bow, the viscount stepped back to allow her to proceed. 'Do not fail me,' he murmured softly, as, trembling with uneasiness, she stumbled past him towards the safety of the ladies' retiring room. 'Mark me well—I shall be in touch!'

Following Wyvern's precipitate departure, the Hendersons' supper dance, from Jessica's point of view at least, was proving to be even more tedious than before. The four-piece musical ensemble seemed to be unable to keep time with one another and one of the violinists was decidedly flat which, she thought to herself, was exactly as she herself felt at this moment. To add to her annoyance, Richard Howlett, her most recent partner, had trodden on her slipper, his clumsy great foot practically severing the pretty silver rosette that embellished its top.

Lifting the hem of her pale-blue sarsenet evening gown a few inches to inspect the damage, Jessica was not sure whether to laugh or cry. Her lovely new slippers were almost ruined, to be sure, but at least a visit to the retiring room, to attempt some sort of hasty repair, would provide a much-wanted respite from the heat and incessant chatter.

'Oh, my goodness!' exclaimed Imogen, having surveyed her cousin's predicament. 'How very unfortunate. The rosette is hanging on by the merest thread—we must make haste to cut it off, lest you trip and fall over!'

She made as if to rise, but Jessica pressed her back into her seat. 'You stay there,' she said firmly. 'The retiring room is just across the hall—I can manage perfectly well myself—I shan't be more than a few minutes.'

And, taking great care not to trip on the trailing ornamentation, she made her way across the floor to the nearest doorway whilst, at the same time, harbouring a secret hope that Wyvern might not, as she had previously assumed, have actually left the building. Perhaps she would bump into him in the corridor, she thought breathlessly. Pushing open the heavy oak door in eager anticipation of his being there, waiting for her, with a full and plausible explanation of his odd behaviour of late, she stepped into the passage.

Sadly, it was not to be. Several individuals were milling about in the hallway, but Wyvern was not amongst them. With a self-conscious shrug and much lowering of spirit, Jessica let herself into the ladies' retiring room, a wistful smile curving her lips as she cast her mind back to that other never-to-be-forgotten occasion.

Any further thoughts regarding that memorable incident, however, were soon to be dashed from her mind, as the unmistakable sound of copious weeping met her ears. Looking around the room for the source of the distress, her eyes lit upon the corner screen behind which, it was now quite evident, some unfortunate female was crying her eyes out.

Closing the door with as little noise as she could manage, she stepped forward and softly enquired whether she might be of any assistance. At the sound of her voice, the unknown lady broke into a fresh torrent of tears.

'You will make yourself ill if you continue in that manner,' warned Jessica, tapping on the screen. 'Please come out and let me help you!'

The crying stopped, to be followed by a loud sniff and a few lesser snuffling sounds then, 'Do you have a handkerchief I could borrow?' came a plaintive voice. 'Mine is no longer serving any useful purpose!'

Jessica held her breath in surprise. That voice, she was almost certain, belonged to none other than Felicity Draycott! What on earth could have happened to the girl to cause her such anguish? Then, diving into her reticule, she pulled out a neatly folded scrap of linen and, raising her arm, tossed it over the top of the screen. 'Now, do come out from behind the screen before someone else comes in,' she urged the now-silent sufferer. 'I am sure you will feel better if you splash your eyes with some of this cool water here in the jug.'

With Jessica's handkerchief to her eyes and her face averted, Felicity crept into view. 'You have been most kind,' she began, but then, as she registered the identity of the person who had come to her aid, her face crumpled in dismay and she began on another bout of weeping. 'Oh, no!' she wailed. 'Not you! This is more than I can bear!'

Although she was somewhat taken aback at the older girl's reaction to her presence, Jessica chose to believe that the hysterical outburst must all be part and parcel of Miss Draycott's state of distress and, setting out a chair in front of the dressing table, she begged Felicity to sit down and compose herself.

'Do let me bathe your eyes,' she said, reaching into a bowl for some of the cotton wool pads that had been so thoughtfully provided by their hostess. Then, tipping out the hairpins from a small dish nearby, she quickly filled it with water and, having dipped the pads into the cool water, she proceeded to apply them to Felicity's badly swollen eyelids. 'You will feel much better after this,' she soothed the now unresisting Miss Draycott, as she gently mopped away at the worst ravages of the girl's suffering.

As if in some sort of trance, Felicity made no comment as Jessica then concentrated her efforts on removing some of the damage that the constant scrubbing with a handkerchief had done to her nose and cheeks. But then, as soon as the puffiness around her eyes began to subside a little, she found herself watching the younger girl's patient ministrations with a deep sense of shame.

'So you are kind as well as beautiful,' she said, trying to smile. ''Tis little wonder that you are so well liked, Miss Beresford!'

A slight flush covered Jessica's cheeks but, as she looked up and caught Felicity's eye in the looking-glass, she merely shook her head and smiled and, after patting the other girl's face dry, she indicated the powder box.

'Possibly just the lightest dusting of rice-powder?' she suggested. 'Then you will be as good as new, I promise.' Then, after a slight pause, as she watched Felicity applying a powder puff to a face that had benefited greatly from her own dedicated attention, she added, 'Will you not tell me what has upset you so?'

Lowering her eyes, Felicity was at a loss as how to reply to Jessica's question. How could she tell this sweet young girl, who had come to her aid so ungrudgingly, that, scarcely half an hour previously, she herself had been involved in plotting her downfall! Her chest heaved and, before she could prevent them, tears began to fill her eyes once again.

Seeing that her unexplained misery still appeared to be causing Felicity considerable distress, Jessica could not think how best to assist the girl. There could hardly have been a death in the Draycott family, she reasoned, for, had that been the case, Felicity would not have attended the supper party. She frowned, as another thought occurred to her. Surely, no gentleman could have been responsible for such an extraordinary outburst of weeping? Suddenly, her heart stopped and, as the evident cause of Felicity's misery became horribly clear to her, she was forced to bite hard on her lip to prevent herself crying out in protest. Felicity Draycott was, quite clearly, pining over Wyvern's rejection! It had been impossible for Jessica to escape the rumours regarding the earl who, having been on the verge of offering for Felicity, had abruptly and without explanation, withdrawn his suit and retired from the running. How galling, then, for her to have to watch her lost love dancing with another! Small wonder that she had greeted Jessica's intervention with such dismay! And, as unwanted images of Wyvern's as yet still unfathomable behaviour towards herself came flooding into her mind, coupled with her own feelings of frustration and regret, a flash of anger ran through her. *Why,* she thought to herself, *I was right about him. It is clear that the man is nothing but an out-and-out philanderer!*

Then, without a thought for the welfare of her new evening gown, Jessica threw herself down at Felicity's feet and took the other girl's hand in hers. 'Please don't start crying again,' she begged. 'Else all our good work will have been for naught! He really isn't worth it, I promise you—you can do so much better!'

Felicity's brow wrinkled in a questioning frown at Jessica's final words, but instinct warned her that, whatever the other girl had imagined to be the cause of her misery, it might be more prudent to leave the matter as it was.

'You have been more than kind, Miss Beresford,' she said, rising to her feet and holding out her hand. 'I do hope that you will disregard my previous lack of courtesy towards you—a childish attack of the green-eyed monster, I fear! If you could bring yourself to forgive me, I would be more than happy to count you my friend!'

Although she had spent the previous few weeks ignoring Felicity's pointed rebuffs, Jessica, having recalled Imogen's remark that it might do her no harm at all to study the ways and manners of those such as this coolly elegant young woman and the other members of her select coterie, could not help but be flattered by her offer. Grasping the other girl's proffered hand in both of her own, she gave her a beaming smile, saying, 'I would consider it a great compliment to be numbered amongst your friends, Miss Draycott,' and finding, to her surprise, that she actually meant every word she had uttered. A friend with whom she might share her innermost secrets was just what Jessica was in need of, at this moment, and the knowledge that Wyvern appeared to have been playing fast and loose with Felicity's emotions, too, was in the way of being some sort of salve to her own mounting feelings of resentment towards the earl.

'Felicity, please!' returned her new friend, as she tidied her hair and briskly shook out her skirts. 'And now, perhaps we had better give some attention to your poor slipper—I could not help noticing that it seems to have suffered a good deal of damage—another careless gentleman, I dare say!'

And so it was that Jessica found herself taken up into

Felicity Draycott's top-drawer set, to begin a new, albeit slightly more sedate, phase of her stay in London.

If one or two of Felicity's more long-term acquaintances were a little surprised to find the previously disdained Miss Beresford admitted to their august ranks, they were far too polite and well bred to remark upon the strange occurrence. Even more gratifying was her half-brother's almost instant relaxation of his previously stringent control over her movements.

'Miss Draycott's escorts are known to be perfectly reliable,' he explained to Imogen, who had expressed considerable amazement at his having allowed Jessica to go off in a curricle in company with the Earl of Dawlish's younger son, the Honourable Walter Allardyce. 'They gain immense satisfaction from being seen about town with a series of attractive young women on their arms, but take great pains never to commit themselves! The plain truth of the matter being that, since the burden of procuring heirs for their family estates rests entirely on the heads of their older brothers, not one of these gentlemen feels compelled to alter his bachelor state and so, in consequence, they are all highly practised in avoiding compromising situations. Our little *enfant terrible* will come to no harm at their hands, I am certain of that!'

Chapter Thirteen

Tossing the butt of his cigar into the dying embers of his library fire, Viscount Digby Hazlett reached across his desk for the note that one of his paid minions had filched from the new Earl of Wyvern's jacket pocket.

Scowling, he perused the note's contents for the umpteenth time. Trust that scoundrel Theodore Ashcroft to have gone out of his way to make everything so deuced complicated, he thought savagely, pouring himself another bumper of brandy and tossing back half its contents in one careless gulp.

Having foolishly lost the title deed of what was now looking to be a highly productive gold mine to the late earl in deep play, Hazlett had spent the better part of the last five months endeavouring to retrieve the vital document. Several abortive attempts to track down the missing deed had left him beside himself with frustration and, since it had become obvious that not only did Wyvern not have the paper in his possession, it was also looking increasingly likely that the earl was oblivious as to its very existence.

It had been only by the merest coincidence that Hazlett had chanced upon the new earl and his two comrades in White's, but his gaze had been immediately drawn to the three men's unusual interest in the sheet of paper that lay between them on the table. At Wyvern's hurried removal of that same piece of paper, Hazlett's attention had grown even more pointed and he had taken great pains to note where Wyvern had secreted the document. Subsequently, this application to detail had proved to be of considerable use to the well-practised pickpockets whom the viscount had employed, affording the wily pair no trouble at all in their speedy distraction of the somewhat preoccupied earl, along with the nifty removal of his notecase. This, as Hazlett had suspected, had contained a document that had, in the first instance, appeared to be of great import.

Having had no difficulty in recognising the reference to the mine, Hazlett had then set his mind to trying to decipher the rest of Theodore's words but, to begin with, no matter how strenuously he had persevered, he had been unable to make any sense of it. It was of no consolation to him that both Wyvern and his friends, in their perusal of the note, looked to have been experiencing a similar difficulty.

Although the late earl had died owing Hazlett such an exorbitant amount, the viscount had decided not to press for payment, reasoning that the return of his deed of title, which Theodore had continually refused to relinquish, looked to be, potentially, of far greater value to him than a one-off payment of twenty-five thousand pounds. However, he was sufficiently shrewd to have reached the conclusion that the burden of such an enormous debt would remain a useful lever with which to intimidate Wyvern, should the earl happen to come across the title deed before he himself got his hands on it.

It had been an overwhelming dread of the latter occurring that had caused Hazlett to set his spies upon Wyvern, in addition to a frantic doubling of his efforts to try to decipher Theodore's garbled phraseology. Then, suddenly, almost like a bolt from the blue, it had hit him! The document was hidden in some place where the two Ashcroft brothers had, in their boyish pursuits, been wont to play! But where that favoured place might be, Hazlett had no way of discovering—not until his furtive conversation with Felicity Draycott, that is— and, no sooner had that lady's little gem of information worked its way into the equation, than the viscount had sent two of his back-street associates to scour every accessible inch of the ruined edifice that was once Wyvern Abbey.

That costly plan having failed to produce the elusive document, Hazlett found himself at a standstill. Eventually, having discovered that Wyvern was engaged in some sort of covert operation of his own in regard to mining stocks, he was reluctantly obliged to concede that, other than keeping a constant watch on the earl and his movements, there was little else he could do to further his own ends. And, after some weighty consideration of the matter, it occurred to him that leaving Wyvern to solve the problem in his own way might be by far the best solution to the problem. After all, he reasoned, once the earl had all the pertinent information at his fingertips, he would immediately understand

where to go to find the missing title deed and, as soon
as he had accomplished that task, Hazlett could move
in and demand reparation! To that end, he knew exactly
what to do to make Wyvern's job just that little bit
easier!

Having spent the past two weeks engaged in a fruitless pursuance of every single one of the possible leads
with which Charlie Fitzallan had, after a certain amount
of persuasion from his cousin Freddy, agreed to supply
him, Wyvern eventually found himself seated in a
small, dusty office tucked away in the back of Capel
Court's Stock Exchange.

Heartily weary of following endless trails that had
led to nothing, he had not held out a great deal of hope
that this latest excursion into the unknown backwaters
of London's business quarter would further his investigation in the slightest. Somewhat to his surprise,
however, it seemed that his tentative questions regarding the possibility of there being some sort of mine
somewhere to which the late Earl of Wyvern might
have claimed title were being taken perfectly seriously,
instead of being met with the unsympathetic and often
scornful incredulity that had generally been the case
thus far.

The elderly clerk had listened to Wyvern's somewhat
confused tale with great interest; at its conclusion, he
had reached into one of his desk drawers and brought
out a bulky sheaf of papers.

'Since we have, as yet, no fully comprehensive
register of mining companies,' he murmured, as he
rifled through the bundle and drew out several closely

written pages, 'it would, in the normal way of things, be quite impossible for me to assist you in this matter. However, given that, only just this morning, I received a very similar query from another gentleman in regard to a missing stock certificate, it has occurred to me that it is not beyond the bounds of possibility that the two matters may be linked in some way. The El Serena concession has, after all, been carving out some very worthwhile tonnage of late and production of a valid title deed looks likely to provide its owner with a considerable fortune.'

'El Serena?' repeated Wyvern, frowning. 'I am not familiar with the name—sounds foreign—South American, at a guess?'

Adjusting his spectacles, the man nodded. 'A small gold-mining settlement near Santiago, in Chile,' he explained. 'Your lordship is no doubt aware that, for the past few years, that country has been at war with the Spanish but, now that it is on the brink of achieving independence, those fortunate few who, before the onset of the hostilities, had the foresight to put their money into schemes to harvest its mineral resources are beginning to see vast profits from their investments.'

Peering down at the paper in his hand, he then went on, 'If my information is correct, the agent representing the El Serena management has been seeking information as to the whereabouts of one of its original shareholders—a Mr John Stavely, it would seem. However, my morning visitor has assured me that, not only has the title deed subsequently changed hands but, more to the point, it appears to have gone missing. Which, as I am sure you will agree, is something of a calamity, especially in view of the fact that considerable sums of money have already been deposited in an account with the Coutts brothers, on behalf of whosoever provides valid ownership of these shares!'

His eyebrows raised, he regarded Wyvern with interest. 'Do you have reason to believe that your brother might have been in possession of this title deed, your lordship?' he asked curiously.

'I wish I knew,' replied Wyvern, with a rueful smile. 'If he was, he seems to have gone to considerable trouble to prevent the blessed thing from being discovered!'

The man nodded sympathetically. 'A great pity,' he said. 'Nevertheless, should you happen to come across the missing paperwork, you may rest assured that it would be my pleasure and privilege to assist you with any difficulties that might arise in claiming the revenue.' He stole a quick glance down at his notes. 'Which, it may interest you to know, currently stands at something in excess of fifty thousand pounds!'

'Good God!' exclaimed Wyvern, as this somewhat staggering information filtered its way into his brain. 'If that's not the spur to a more diligent search, I'll be jiggered if I can think what might be!'

But then, as another thought came to him, he frowned. 'Did I hear you say that you have had other enquiries regarding this Chilean mine?'

'That is correct,' nodded the clerk. 'I was visited by another gentleman, only this morning.' But, immediately perceiving the question in Wyvern's eyes, he hastened to add, 'It would be quite out of the question for me to reveal my visitor's name, however. To do so would place me in breach of all the rules of my profession!'

With a rueful nod, Wyvern rose to his feet and thanked the clerk for his help, then, after assuring the man that he would keep him posted on any progress he might make, he walked out of the dusty office into the late afternoon sunshine. Although he was finding it hard to believe that his search might finally be over, the spring in his step was a good deal lighter than it had been when he had entered the building and he could not help feeling rather more positive about his chances of resolving his problems—particularly in regard to securing Jessica's hand.

Subsequent to the Berkeley Square teashop rendezvous, the earl's seemingly endless daytime excursions into the City had, for the most part, prevented his mind from wandering too far in Jessica's direction. The nights, however, had proved to be a very different matter for, whether sleeping or waking, he had found his thoughts being constantly bombarded with tormenting visions of Jessica in some other man's arms. To begin with, he had done his utmost to keep away from any social event that he knew that she and her family might attend and, with the support of his two stalwart companions, neither of whom had taken long to fathom the root source of their friend's discontent, he had, for the most part, been reasonably successful. But, last Friday evening, when the burning ache just to set his eyes upon her lovely face once more had overtaken his common sense, he had presented himself at Lady Henderson's supper-dance, hoping to claim a dance with Jessica, simply because this was the only way that he could think of where it would be deemed perfectly acceptable to be seen holding her in his arms. Having achieved that goal, however, it had left his emotions on such a knife edge that he had been obliged to quit the room, since the agony of having to watch some other fellow lay his hands on her might well have driven him to conduct himself in a not altogether acceptable manner!

And, if this predicament were not far more than enough with which to contend, he reminded himself gloomily, there was the added problem of his grandmother who, having taken umbrage with him over the Draycott affair, was now refusing to speak to him directly and had resorted to the somewhat farcical strategy of communicating with him by way of the servants!

Nevertheless, despite all of these mounting difficulties and, since his pride would not allow him to approach Jessica's guardian until he had something rather more tangible to offer her than the heartfelt promise of his own boundless and abiding love, Wyvern was ruefully aware that he had very little option but to continue with his present quest, which, until this afternoon's encouraging news, had looked to be turning into something of an odyssey!

Leaping up into his waiting curricle, he flicked the reins and headed back through the city towards Grosvenor Square, desperately trying to remember the final phrases in his brother's scribbled missive. Jessica had been perfectly correct in her assumption that, unless committed to paper, Theo's words would slip away from him, he thought grimly, knitting his brow in fierce concentration, as he wove his way through the interminable press of vehicles in London's West End.

What the devil had Theo written after the words *mine is yours now*? Just more apologies, as he recalled, along with some garbled nonsense about playing together as boys. Suddenly, he stilled and the reins fell slack in his hands, causing Berridge, his tiger, to shout a warning from his seat on the box behind. With an abrupt start, the earl jerked his mind back to the task in hand and, pulling hard on his left-hand rein, only just managed to avoid contact with an oncoming beer dray, the infuriated driver of which shook an angry fist at him, calling him a cork-brained young numbskull, an epithet that might well have been matched with one of a similar nature had not Wyvern's mind been more seriously engaged.

'Close one there, guv,' offered Berridge, a little shocked at his master's apparent lack of judgement. 'Nearly lost a wheel!'

'Yes, sorry about that, Berry,' returned the earl somewhat absently, as a wide grin creased his face. *Oh, Theo!* he exulted silently. *You clever old devil! You've hidden the damned title deed in one of our childhood haunts!*

But then, as the perplexing matter of just which childhood haunt his brother might have lit upon to secrete such an important document filtered its way into his brain, the grin slowly faded, to be replaced by yet another frown, as Wyvern's mind flashed from one favoured den to another. Until, finally, he was forced to conclude that he still had very little idea of where to look. This, of course, would mean another extended visit to Ashcroft

Grange—not to mention another week or so away from
Jessica, he thought gloomily, and, since her recent involvement with Felicity Draycott and her set, who knew
what might happen while he was out of town?

Felicity's taking-up of Jessica into her select clique
of upper *ton* females had come as a nasty shock to the
earl for, although he was aware that the group of gentlemen whom the Draycott set favoured as escorts were
generally regarded as confirmed bachelors, he found it
almost impossible to believe that any man could be in
Jessica's company for very long without eventually suc-
cumbing to her delectable charms. And the thought of
Jessica going riding in Hyde Park and being squired
about the capital by a series of well-to-do men about
town was a good deal more troublesome to Wyvern than
the sight of her dancing with one of the group of infatu-
ated young bloods who had previously gravitated to her
side.

As serious contenders for Jessica's hand, fellows
such as Harry Stevenage and his sort had been dismissed out of hand by the earl, although this had done
little to prevent the hot spurts of anger that had inflamed
him whenever he had found himself in a position to
witness one of them handling her in what he had considered to be a rather too familiar manner. And, even
though he was perfectly well aware that highly con-
nected men of Walter Allardyce's ilk were not the sort
to take that kind of liberty with single young females,
he was sufficiently astute to realise that, as possible
rivals, they were an altogether different kettle of fish
from the crass young sprigs with whom Jessica had
been wont to associate! With a scowl of vexation, he

found himself bound to consider the fact that, until he himself was able to woo her in the correct and proper manner, all of his carefully planned visions of future ecstasy might well be in peril of being prematurely nipped in the bud!

Drawing up his curricle outside the stable block at the rear of Ashcroft House, the earl threw the reins to the waiting Berridge, jumped down and hurried into the house, plagued by the unacceptable thought that one of those highly dashing and sophisticated men might win *his* beloved's heart and hand! Determining to seek out his two friends in order to petition them to join him at first light the following morning for a thorough search of the Grange's extensive grounds, he mounted the stairs to his bedchamber.

Chapter Fourteen

Despite her hasty re-evaluation of Wyvern's character, Jessica could not prevent her eyes from seeking out
his tall, broad-shouldered presence at every venue. Nor,
indeed, could she control the highly unsettling images
that pervaded her dreams, both day and night. Whilst
her new escorts were charming and attentive in every
degree, they none of them had Wyvern's red-blooded
vitality, nor did they smile at her in such a way as to instantly curl up her toes and set her pulse racing. It
seemed clear to her that Fate had doomed her to a
lifetime of falling for rakes and reprobates and other
such unsuitable characters.

This, she thought sourly, taking a quick peek at the
somewhat self-satisfied look on the face of her current
squire, the Honourable Gerald Pevensey, as he tooled
his carriage around the Hyde Park circuit, was presumably the penalty she was obliged to pay for having been
handed such beauty at birth, beauty that she had lately
come to realise had been apt to cause her a good deal

more trouble than it was worth. To think that she had once been perfectly content to bask in the admiration of the shallow young men who had constantly paid court to her—and even, to her utter chagrin, had actually considered it her due!

For the bald truth of the matter was that—apart from her half-brother, that is—Wyvern had been the only man in her life who had dared to challenge her actions; the only one who had sufficient confidence in himself to find fault with her behaviour and chastise her for it and, even though his occasional arrogance had infuriated her, it had not taken her long to realise that just one warm glance of approval from those deep grey eyes was worth more than a thousand pretty speeches from any other man.

As thoughts of this nature continued to occupy her mind, her shoulders drooped and her face grew wan, causing her escort to bring his carriage to a swift, albeit impeccable, halt.

'My dear Miss Beresford?' he exclaimed anxiously, as he peered down at her pale cheeks. 'Are you unwell? I trust that my manner of driving has not discomfited you?'

Jessica forced a smile. 'Hardly, Mr Pevensey—I declare that you are a most exceptional whip! It is merely that I have a slight headache. It was foolish of me to come out without a parasol, for the sun is very bright today, do you not agree?'

Already in the process of turning his equipage around, Pevensey gave a frowning nod, 'Still, dear lady, we cannot have you feeling poorly. It is clear that I must return you to your cousin without delay!'

Holding back the smile that threatened, Jessica could not help thinking that Pevensey's haste to return her to

Dover Street was rather more to do with his horror of being seen with a sickly companion than with any real concern for her well-being.

That was the trouble with Felicity's friends and acquaintances, she thought, as she watched the Honourable Gerald skilfully tooling his way back through the press of carriages on the Row. Although her association with them had been relatively brief, it had taken her no time at all to discover that they all cared far more for appearances than for character, which, she supposed wryly, was why they had been happy to take her up. The fact that that she had been voted 'Belle of the Season' amongst the more impressionable young men about town had been a point in her favour, especially insofar as Felicity's group of male escorts was concerned. To be seen with such a beauty on their arms seemed to do a great deal for these gentlemen's consequences, as a result of which, Jessica's days this past week had been filled to capacity, with early morning rides in the park, trips to the theatre, boating on the Serpentine, visits to art galleries and more carriage rides than she cared to remember. Added to which were the daily deliveries of so many extravagant bouquets of hothouse flowers that Mrs Simmons, their housekeeper, was having great difficulty in finding enough receptacles to accommodate them all.

Not that the recipient of all this consideration was in the least bit smug about any of it, having learned that it was all part and parcel of the Draycott set's need to create the right impression, which seemed to be far more important than simply enjoying oneself. Oh, so proper and, oh, so dull, she thought. It was difficult to imagine any one of her new female acquaintances ever having done anything so outrageous as to hop or skip, take the stairs two at a time or, heaven forbid, slide down the banisters, as she had been often wont to do back home in Thornfield!

With an inward grin, she allowed the Honourable Gerald to hand her down from his carriage and escort her to her front door. Politely declining her invitation to step inside for some refreshment, the gentleman raised his hat, executed a swift bow and, after extending his good wishes for her swift recovery, returned to his carriage with as much speed as dignity would allow.

'You weren't very long,' observed her brother, looking up from his broadsheet, as she entered the salon where he was sitting reading. 'Nothing wrong, I hope?'

'Just a slight headache, that's all,' returned Jessica, removing her bonnet and tossing it to one side. 'The sun is very bright today. Where is Imogen?'

'Upstairs resting—and I'd rather you didn't disturb her, if you don't mind.'

'No, of course I won't!'

Sitting down on the sofa opposite the armchair in which Matt was lounging, she patted her hair and made a play of inspecting her nails. Then, 'Have you happened to come across Lord Wyvern of late?' she enquired tentatively.

Matt raised one eyebrow and stared at her. 'Why the sudden interest in that fellow?' he asked.

'No especial reason, really,' she replied, trying to sound nonchalant. 'I thought you said that he might call, but he still hasn't done so.'

'But that was weeks ago!'

'True,' she nodded. 'But I never did get the chance to thank him properly for helping us that evening.'

Matt shrugged. 'Dare say the fellow's forgotten all about it—got more important things on his mind, I hear.'

Such as the loss of his brother's note, Jessica supposed, wondering if any mine had actually transpired after her conversation with him. 'He doesn't attend many functions,' she then observed.

Matt, who had returned to his perusal of the recent riots in Manchester, frowned and laid down his newspaper. 'As it happens, I played a hand of cribbage with him only last week at the Hendersons' soirée, while you were tripping the light fantastic with one of your many devoted swains. Appears there's a great deal of work to do on his recently inherited estate—although why that should be of any interest to you I can't possibly imagine!'

Having been perfectly well aware of Wyvern's presence on that particular occasion, Jessica thought better of the retort that she had been about to fling at her brother, since it was clear that Imogen had failed to mention the earl's having solicited her for a dance. 'I just wondered why it was that he never called,' she said hurriedly. 'If only for courtesy's sake!'

This time her brother raised both eyebrows and burst out laughing. 'Oh, at last I'm beginning to see the point of this conversation!' he guffawed. 'The one that got away! Poor old Jess! Finally come across someone who didn't immediately succumb to your rather obvious charms!'

'Don't be ridiculous, Matt,' protested Jessica, getting

swiftly to her feet and making for the door before her brother could detect the sudden rise of colour in her cheeks. 'It isn't like that at all—I was merely interested.'

Matt's eyes narrowed. 'Well, it beats me why you should be so interested in someone you've barely spoken to, unless…' Thrusting his newspaper to one side, he leapt to his feet and, crossing the room in two quick strides, he grabbed her by the arm. 'I trust that you haven't been up to your old tricks again, Jess!' he growled. 'Imogen will never forgive you if you get into another scrape like the last one!'

'No, Matt, I promise,' breathed Jessica fearfully. 'I would never do such a thing again, I swear to you!'

'No clandestine meetings of any sort?' he demanded. 'I swear to God that, if you upset Imo at this time, I'll—'

'No, Matt, no!' interrupted Jessica, now thoroughly frightened at the maddened expression in her brother's eyes. 'There has been nothing of that sort, I promise.'

'Well, just you make sure that there isn't,' he warned, as, only slightly mollified, he let go of her arm and, muttering a series of imprecations under his breath, stalked back to his seat.

Hurrying out of the room, Jessica uncrossed the fingers of the hand that she had been holding behind her back and, letting out her breath with a mixture of relief and guilt, tried to persuade herself that what she had told her brother was hardly an untruth in the real sense of the word. Meetings in the middle of Oxford Street and in full view of the public in Gunter's teashop could hardly be classed as clandestine, she reasoned but, nevertheless, felt the urgent need to offer up a swift supplication, praying that her brother would never have cause to discover her white lie.

When two whole days spent in a meticulous search of the Grange's numerous attics and stables, in addition to every single one of its many other outbuildings, failed to produce the desired result, Wyvern turned his mind to the consideration of all the outdoor venues in which he and his brother had spent their summer months.

The ruined abbey was an obvious choice, of course, but, as it happened, there had been only one especial spot that the boys had favoured for their games—the remains of a small cell in what had once been the monks' living quarters. And that, as he recalled, had been demolished during a violent thunderstorm, subsequent to which he and Theo had found themselves trapped beneath the fallen stonework of the cell's rear wall. Following their rescue, the two brothers had been banned from any future activity within the abbey's crumbling shell.

No, he decided, with a vehement shake of his head, as he ruefully rubbed his left elbow in painful recollection of the fracture that that calamitous escapade had earned him, Theo would never hide anything of import in that particular location! Which left only the woods— an enormous undertaking—and the river, the banks of which provided the estate's eastern boundary.

Late on the afternoon on the second day of Wyvern's excursion back to Ashcroft, after the three comrades had retired from their futile exertions of the day, the earl stood at his library window contemplating the extent of the morrow's search, his keen eyes noting that the sun was already well advanced in its downward descent towards the horizon.

'It's not too late to get back to London, if either of you have a mind,' he said, in a studiedly offhand manner, as he turned back towards his friends, who had installed themselves in a pair of comfortable armchairs, with a small drum table bearing a plentiful supply of liquor positioned handily between them. 'Take us less than half an hour, if we make good time.'

'Oh, Lord, no!' protested Fitzallan, easing his shoulders back into his seat. 'I'm just beginning to get settled—climbing up and down all those loft ladders in your outhouses has been more than enough exercise for one day. A five-mile canter back to town is the last thing I need at this moment!'

'Just happened to remember that it's the Duchess of Conyngham's ball tonight,' Wyvern persevered diffidently. 'Looks set to be the biggest function of the Season.'

After reaching out to pour himself another cognac, Sir Simon leaned back and surveyed his friend thoughtfully, having been aware of Wyvern's inward struggle for quite some time now. 'And one at which, unless I am much mistaken, you are hoping that the fair Miss Beresford will be in attendance,' he observed softly.

A faint tinge of embarrassment coloured the earl's cheeks but, in reply, he merely grunted and, throwing himself down on to a nearby sofa, picked up his own glass.

'You are going to have to face up to it at some point, old chap,' continued Holt, his eyes filled with sympathy.

'It's as clear as a pikestaff that you've fallen for the girl hook, line and sinker. What I don't understand is why you seem to be going to the devil's own lengths to stay away from her! You surely don't imagine that the chit is going to give you the cold shoulder?'

Wyvern bristled. 'You go too far, Simon,' he growled, glaring at his friend fiercely.

'Not far enough, perhaps,' retorted Holt, unperturbed. 'You've been mooning over the girl for weeks now, Ben, and Freddy and I can't be the only ones to have taken stock of your partiality. Both of us held our tongues after you pulled out of the Draycott arrangement, because we felt that you deserved our support. As your closest friends, we feel that we have earned the right to be concerned about you! The least you can do is to come clean with us!'

'Not a lot of point,' said Wyvern as, with a resigned sigh, he swallowed the remains of his drink. 'Whilst you are perfectly correct in your assumption that I have finally lost my heart—not to mention my head—' he then added, in a bitter afterthought '—you must see that there is not a damned thing I can do about it! Unless I can find these confounded documents, I'm ditched. I shall have to resign myself to marrying Draycott's daughter and there's an end to it! Whatever I may feel towards Miss Beresford is of little consequence in the greater scheme of things—besides which,' he then added, with a grim twist of his lips, 'I have no reason to believe that the young lady regards me as anything more than an overbearing jackass!'

'Not if I'm any sort of judge,' piped up Fitzallan, as he heaved himself out of his armchair. 'Got the distinct impression that she's just as smitten with you as you are with her. Don't seem able to keep those ravishing green eyes off you, in fact, you lucky devil!' Tossing back the contents of his glass, he placed it carefully down on the table then, raising an eyebrow, looked at his two companions and said, 'Well, are we going or ain't we?'

Chapter Fifteen

Earlier that same day, while the Beresfords were still in their sunny breakfast room enjoying their coffee, the butler entered to bring in the post, as well as announcing that several more floral tributes had arrived for Miss Beresford.

'Thank you, Clevedon,' said Jessica, with a warm smile, as she spread herself another slice of bread and honey. 'Ask Mrs Simmons to see if she can find somewhere to put them, will you please?'

'I will do that with pleasure, Miss Beresford,' intoned the manservant, in his usual stately manner. 'However, I did take the liberty of bringing this particular offering in to you as, being somewhat—unusual— in its make-up, I feared it might easily go astray if placed with the other, much larger bouquets.'

He handed Jessica a small and slightly damp package that appeared to have been wrapped in a simple square of muslin and secured with a length of dried grass.

'Smells like violets,' observed Matt, casting an interested eye at the package.

A sudden pounding started within Jessica's chest as she fumbled with the fastening and carefully separated the fragile offering from its muslin wrapping. There, on its own little bed of moss, lay a cluster of the most beautiful violets she had ever seen in her life, their leaves and petals still damp from the morning dew. Her pulse raced and a rosy flush warmed her cheeks, as she bent her head to inhale the intoxicating perfume.

'Fresh from the country!' exclaimed Imogen, in delight. 'What a sweet thought! Who could have sent them—is there a card?'

Shaking her head, Jessica stared down at the gift, her trembling fingertips gently caressing the delicate stems. She needed no card to help her identify the sender of these particular blooms. Her lips curved and a faraway look came into her eyes. *The man is a complete contradiction,* she thought, wonderingly. Surely, no mere philanderer would have gone to so much trouble to offer such a token of his regard? For some minutes, she gazed down in a contemplative silence at the fragile blossoms in front of her then, with a sudden straightening of her shoulders, she resolved that, on the very next opportunity that presented itself to her, she would confront the maddening Earl of Wyvern and demand an immediate explanation for his recent behaviour towards her. His continual absence from the social scene, only to turn up and torment her once again, was getting to be more than any sane person could stand and she vowed that, if he was not prepared to face up to her like the man she believed him to be, she would tell him exactly what she thought of his foolish games.

'Well, my dears,' announced Imogen, as she laid down her napkin and pushed back her chair. 'I have a great deal to do today. I am promised to Mrs Newton for morning coffee and I need to pay a quick visit to Madame Devy's to collect some new gloves for the Conynghams' ball this evening.'

So saying, she picked up her letters from the table, turned to leave the room and then, to the consternation of her watchers, gave a faint cry of dismay and promptly slumped to a heap on the carpet.

Leaping to his feet, his eyes wide with apprehension, Matt hurriedly cast aside the missive he had been perusing and sped to his wife's side.

'Imogen! Imogen, sweetheart!' he cried out as, kneeling beside her now motionless figure, he gathered her tenderly into his arms. 'Speak to me, my love, I beg of you!'

Opening her eyes very slowly, Imogen gave a great sigh and would have tried to sit up had her husband not prevented her from doing so. She blinked once or twice then, rapidly registering her husband's anguished expression, she reached out her fingers and placed them on his quivering lips. 'Please do not fret so, my darling,' she murmured. 'I fear I got up too quickly, that is all.'

'That's as it may be,' countered Matt, with a scowl, as he scooped her up and rose to his feet. 'But it's back to bed for you, young lady, with a visit from Dr Frinton as soon as I can get hold of him!'

'But, Matt,' protested Imogen weakly, 'what about

Mrs Newton and my visit to Madame Devy's? What about the Conynghams' ball?'

'To hell with the lot of them!' he returned savagely as, striding to the door, he kicked it open and proceeded to carry his still-protesting wife across the hallway and up the curved staircase into her bedchamber. 'You've had all the balls you're going to have this Season, my girl!'

Jessica, her eyes wide with concern and her fingers on her lips to still their trembling, was not sure whether to follow the pair or to remain where she was until her brother returned. *Oh, please don't let anything happen to Imo!* she prayed, as she bent down to retrieve the scattered letters and restore them to their place on the table. *I could not bear it if she…*

She stopped and turned swiftly towards the door as she heard Matt recrossing the marbled hall footsteps and making his way back into the room.

Flinging herself at him, she cried out, 'Please tell me that she is going to be all right, Matt!'

His face still pale with shock, he gave her a brief smile and patted her shoulder, before thrusting her away from him. 'She seems to have recovered somewhat,' he replied, with a slight tremor in his voice. 'Bertha is attending to her. However, I have sent for Dr Frinton and we will see what he has to say.' He paused, raking his fingers through his guinea-gold waves. 'But I've a mind to pack up and go straight back to Thornfield,' he then told her. 'I should have done so, as soon as she told me she was with child!'

'Pray don't upset yourself so,' pleaded Jessica, placing her hand on his arm. 'Imogen is awfully strong, you know—she throws off coughs and colds more quickly than any of us!'

Frowning, he stared down at her for some moments, then, 'Do you have any further engagements this week?' he asked her. 'Provided that the doctor considers Imogen fit enough to attempt the journey home, it is my intention to leave first thing on Saturday morning. That way we can take it in easy stages and be back home by Monday.'

'Well,' she reminded him, 'as Imo has just informed you, there is the Duchess of Conyngham's ball this evening. In addition, I am invited to accompany Miss Draycott and her friends to a supper party at the Vauxhall Gardens tomorrow evening—but I would not hesitate to send my excuses, if you would rather I did not attend,' she added hastily, having studied her brother's brooding expression.

Her breath held in fearful anticipation, she watched as her brother continued to frown and purse his lips. At the thought of having to leave the capital, with no likelihood of ever setting eyes upon Wyvern again, her heart was in turmoil, all previous notions of how she had intended to chastise him for his impudence instantly wiped from her mind. But to her unbounded relief Matt shook his head.

'No need,' he returned, with a satisfied smile. 'Your cousin is very keen that you attend the Conynghams' ball—it is said to be the biggest event of the Season and it would be a great pity for you not to have experienced at least one grand ball during your time in London. As for Vauxhall,' he continued, with another frown, 'I took the three of you there myself, before Nicky went back to college, so it is not as though you are missing anything of great moment.' He paused, considering, while Jessica, who, in this case, was quite indifferent as to whether or not she attended the supper party, patiently awaited his answer. 'Nevertheless, it would, perhaps, be rather impolite to cry off at this late stage.'

'You mean that I may go?'

Her brother gave a decisive nod. 'I cannot see why not. Miss Draycott's friends are all sensible and responsible adults. You have a suitable escort for this evening's entertainment, I take it?'

She nodded. 'Mr Lyndhurst and his sister are calling for me at half-past eight.'

'Rodney Lyndhurst? Oh, he's a most level-headed chap—you will come to no harm at his hands. That's settled, then—ah! I believe I hear the doctor at the door.'

And, turning on his heel, he left the room, anxious to return to his wife's bedside, leaving Jessica hugging herself in gleeful anticipation, as she pondered how best to utilise the totally unexpected opportunity with which she had just been presented. All that was needed now, she told herself, was for Wyvern to present himself at the duchess's ball and, regardless of what steps he might take to try to avoid her, she was determined that, this time, he would not escape her!

As she was soon to discover, however, the sheer size and opulence of the ballroom at Conyngham House was almost enough to daunt the resolve of even the most intrepid missionary.

From the moment of being handed out of the Lyndhursts' family coach by a powdered-haired and plum-suited flunkey, Jessica found herself quite overcome with awe at the unexpected richness and grandeur of the occasion. Never in her life had she seen such magnificent finery, such sparkling extravagance or such a heaving multitude of individuals gathered together in one room.

And such a room, she marvelled, as the little group that comprised the Honourable Rodney Lyndhurst, his sister Lady Sarah Lyndhurst and herself, having patiently waited its turn in the seemingly never-ending line of guests to reach the top of the great marble staircase, had gone through the usual offices of presentation and reception and was now descending the few shallow steps that led into the splendidly appointed ballroom.

On each side of the room, traversing its entire length, was a succession of white marble pillars in the Corinthian style, their capitals elaborately decorated with carvings of grapes and vine leaves and their tall columns artistically entwined with green ribbons bearing clusters of hothouse roses of every size and colour. Huge swathes of green-and-white silk were draped between the pillars, giving the room an almost Oriental tented effect. Four great crystal chandeliers hung suspended from the ceiling and dozens of ornate crystal sconces lined all four sides of the room, the light from their hundreds of candles shining on to the faces of the swarming assemblage beneath.

By craning her neck and standing on tiptoe, Jessica could just make out two pairs of doors at the far end of the room, their openings offering piquant glimpses of the balconied terrace outside and the huge formal gardens beyond, where a myriad of Chinese lanterns hung from the trees, lighting up the colourful scene with their radiant glow.

Feeling somewhat overwhelmed by such an abundance of sumptuous magnificence, Jessica began to doubt the chances of even catching a glimpse of Lord Wyvern, let alone speaking to him, given the teeming mass of humanity that surrounded her. But then, as the strains of the orchestra from the gallery above began to filter its way into the ears of the chattering masses below, the crowds began to disperse, many of them making their way out of the ballroom into the corridors and anterooms beyond, where a plentiful supply of refreshments and other amusements had been laid on to satisfy the needs of all but the most censorious of guests.

'Come along, ladies,' said Lyndhurst, offering an arm to each of his companions. 'I see Pevensey and Henderson have commandeered a set of chairs over in the far corner. Now, we shall all be able to sit together and view the proceedings in comfort.'

Upon arriving at the appointed place, they soon found themselves joined by other members of the Draycott set, including Felicity herself. Not having heard from Hazlett since her ill-fated conversation with him at the Hendersons', Miss Draycott had managed to convince herself that the hateful man must have been in his cups when he had sought her out and that his threatening behaviour had merely been his way to punish her for having refused his hand. Having done her best to curb her previous envy at Jessica's success with the members of the opposite sex and, contrary to what she had originally believed, it had soon become evident to Felicity that the younger girl made no effort to court such excessive attention. Reluctant as she was to have to face up to it, she knew that, no matter how long she waited, Wyvern would never look at her in quite the same way as she had seen him looking at Jessica. And, whilst she was aware that this somewhat forced association with Jessica could never really develop into a true friendship, the very sensible and highly correct Miss Draycott had been obliged to admit to herself that it had been unworthy of her to blame Jessica for Wyvern's obvious partiality for her. The net result of all this soul-searching was that Felicity had allowed herself to become quite attached to her new acquaintance and, this evening, had little difficulty in expressing her profound admiration for the cut of her young companion's ball dress, which was the most expensive gown that Jessica had ever owned.

Fashioned in the palest of figure-hugging green satins, with three deep flounces at its hem, its off-the-shoulder design sported a décolletage cut a good dealer lower than those of her other evening gowns. In fitting Jessica for the gown, however, Madame Devy had assured her cousin that, for a major occasion such as the Duchess of Conyngham's ball, a more daring style was positively *de rigueur*!

In the light of this highly auspicious occasion, Matt had been prevailed upon to splash out an enormous sum to have the famed modiste, whose creations were much in demand, fashion something slightly out of the ordinary for the two females in his life. Sadly, Imogen's lovely outfit was now in the depths of her wardrobe, still nestling in its muslin wrapper but when, earlier that evening, Jessica had tripped into her brother's study to show off her own finery, his summer-blue eyes had shone with pride and, putting his hands on her shoulders, he had held her away from him and, looking down at her, had said, somewhat huskily, 'There is little doubt who will be the belle of this ball, dear child! Off you go and enjoy yourself and…' He had then paused, hesitating, before adding, more severely, 'I am counting on you to remember your promise, Jess. Keep with Miss Draycott's set and try to behave yourself as Imogen would wish you to!'

But, despite her trepidation at the thought of stirring up the not-easily-forgotten might of her brother's wrath, Jessica, in the sure and certain knowledge that this evening looked set to affording her with her one and only opportunity to tackle Wyvern, was more determined than ever to proceed with her quest. To leave London without ever having discovered whether the earl's apparent regard for her had been anything other than transient, was more than she could contemplate. Nevertheless, she resolved, should it transpire that she had been totally wrong in her supposition that Lord Wyvern was secretly harbouring some sort of *tendre* for her then, although she knew that the ache in her heart would remain with her for ever, she would return home and endeavour to put the handsome but dastardly rogue out of her mind.

'You are singularly quiet, Miss Beresford,' remarked her current partner, Mr Pevensey, as he led her through the arches of clasped hands in the second set of country dances for which he had engaged her that evening. 'Not another headache, I trust?'

Summoning up some semblance of a smile, Jessica shook her head. 'Not at all,' she replied brightly. 'I was merely concentrating on the steps—it is so easy to lose count and mistake one's next movement.'

Since they had, by this time, reached their appointed positions in their respective lines, whereupon a relatively complicated manoeuvre whose steps consisted of much twirling and cross-handing with the pair standing next to them ensued, Pevensey could only smile and nod his agreement, leaving Jessica to her thoughts.

To her deepening disappointment, there had been no sign of Wyvern, even though the evening was already well advanced. Was she going to have to return to Thornfield without ever setting eyes on him again? she wondered dejectedly as, almost without thinking, she went through the tedious process of clapping the next couple around the outside of the set before reaching up to her partner's hands in order to form an arch for the couple to make its way back down the set.

Much to her relief, however, the music drew to a close at the end of that movement, whereupon, after tucking her hand into his elbow, Pevensey escorted her back to their group. Having performed the requisite two dances with him, Jessica was not in the least bit sorry that the Honourable Gerald had done his duty by her for, without a single sight of the earl, her initial excitement at being present at such a grand affair was beginning to wane. And, although, for Lady Sarah's sake, she drew the line at pretending another headache, which would have obliged her escort to take them both home, the thought that there were still almost two more hours to endure before the entertainments were brought to a close was more than enough to bring on a real one!

Hearing Felicity's sudden sibilant hiss in her ear, she

was jolted out of her reverie. 'Do wake up, Jessica,' whispered the other girl, from behind her fan. 'The Dowager Countess of Wyvern has been trying to attract your attention for the past several minutes! What can her ladyship want of you, I wonder?'

With an fascinated gleam in her eye, Jessica looked across the ballroom and there, on the dowager's podium, seated at the forefront of a group of the most senior and highly regarded members of the aristocracy, was the rather grand old lady whose soirée had brought about that rather memorable incident with Wyvern in the ladies' retiring room. The dowager was crooking her finger, imperiously beckoning Jessica to attend her. Her cheeks flushing in discomfiture, Jessica lowered her eyes and turned her head away.

'Well, she can beckon as much as she likes,' she replied mutinously. 'I barely know the lady and I certainly don't care for her high-handed attitude.'

Wide-eyed with astonishment, Felicity shot her a warning look. 'But, of course you must go to her, Jessica,' she cried. 'Lady Lavinia is the Dowager Countess of Wyvern—it would not do to ignore such a summons!'

With a deep sigh and doing her best to hide her exasperation at the discovery of yet another of London's upper set's, apparently, inflexible rules, Jessica rose to her feet and made her way across the floor to the podium. Dropping a polite curtsy, she raised her eyes up to the elderly dowager and asked, in the most dulcet of tones, how she might serve her ladyship.

'Come up here beside me,' replied Lady Lavinia, tapping the empty chair at her side with her fan. 'I wish to speak with you.'

With a slight sinking of the heart, Jessica acceded to her ladyship's request, which, as far as she was concerned, had been rather more in the nature of a full-blown command than a polite invitation. Having spoken to the dowager only very briefly on that earlier occasion, she could not begin to imagine what Lady Lavinia could want with her.

Hardly waiting for her guest to settle herself into her chair and arrange the skirts of her gown, the dowager leaned towards her and, raising her lorgnette, scrutinised Jessica carefully from head to toe.

'Well, you are certainly all they claim you to be,' she said as, with a haughty sniff, she snapped close her glasses and returned them to her reticule. 'I dare say you have your pick of all of the Season's available young bachelors—no doubt you have received any number of offers?'

At this rather surprising enquiry, a wary look crept into Jessica's eyes. 'I must assure your ladyship that I did not come to London to find myself a husband,' she replied cautiously. She had been long enough in London to have learned that, no matter how outraged she might feel at being questioned in such an impertinent manner, it would hardly do for her cross swords with a peeress of the realm, especially not in full view of a room packed with all the dignitaries and most notable members of the capital's high society!

Lady Lavinia let out a disdainful bark of laughter. 'Oh, really!' she retorted, scornfully. 'Then, perhaps, my girl, you might care to explain why you have been seen casting out your lures to my grandson!'

Jessica let out a gasp of disbelief and her cheeks

turned scarlet with a mixture of indignation and embarrassment but, before she could utter a word, the countess nodded her head in satisfaction.

'You may well blush and squirm, young lady, but, let me tell you, here and now, that your scheming little machinations will avail you naught—not if I have anything to do with it!'

Now thoroughly affronted, Jessica made as if to rise from her chair, determined to make as dignified an exit from the podium as she could reasonably manage, in such uncomfortable circumstances. The countess, however, leaned across and placed one hand on her knee, thereby effectively preventing her reluctant young companion from getting up. Her ladyship, it was clear, had not yet finished with her!

'Wyvern is not for you,' continued Lady Lavinia, her tone full of warning. 'He is all but betrothed to another. Whatever sweet nothings he may have whispered in your ear and whatever promises he might have made to you, you must undertake to put them all out of your mind. If you have any sense at all, my dear Miss Beresford—and I am advised that you have a great deal—you will undertake to set your cap in quite another direction! Do I make myself clear?'

Throughout this unjustified diatribe, Jessica had been doing her level best to keep control of her temper. Sweet nothings and promises, indeed! It would appear that the old witch was accusing her of having sordid assignations with her blessed grandson, when, in reality, she had scarcely spoken more than a couple of dozen or so words with the man! By taking several slow, deep breaths, she eventually managed to stop herself from

flying into one of her past rages but, no matter how hard
she tried, no amount of self-restraint could prevent her
from rudely thrusting away the dowager's hand from
her knee and rising to her feet in one swift movement.

'Perfectly clear, your ladyship!' she retorted, through
clenched teeth. 'And, now, if you will excuse me, I fear
that I must hie me away to find some other poor unsuspecting gentleman to lure into my web!' And, with the
most elaborate of curtseys, coupled with the falsest of
smiles, she stepped off the podium, inwardly marvelling at her own achievement—despite quite unbelievable provocation—of having succeeded in controlling
what had been, until not so long ago, a wild and unman-
ageable temper.

Ignoring the countess's gasp of righteous incredulity
and with her head held high, she started to make for the
nearest exit to the passageway, having no desire to
return to her own group and face the other females' inevitable questioning. Deciding that she would go and
find the retiring room and splash some cold water on
her cheeks to cool them down a little, she pulled open
the door and found herself face to face with the *bête
noir* of all her waking dreams, the Earl of Wyvern
himself!

Totally unprepared for the unanticipated phenome-
non of having the subject of *his* sleepless nights
suddenly cannoning into him at that moment, Wyvern
could do little more than reach out his arms to hold her
steady. Disregarding his own considerable unsteadi-
ness at the sight of her flushed cheeks and wide viridescent eyes, he gazed down at the appealing curves of
her naked shoulders, his eyes slowly travelling to feast

upon the irresistible temptation of the soft, creamy orbs rising, in almost unbearable perfection, high above the deep neckline of her satin gown.

As if they had a will of their own, his hands dropped from her elbows to slide over the satin encasing Jessica's rounded hips and, had not the warning sound of Holt's noisy throat-clearing restored him to his senses, it would have been quite impossible for him to prevent himself from pulling her towards him in a needful embrace. Hurriedly putting her away from him, he stepped back from the doorway and politely motioned her to proceed, achingly aware of the violent sensations that were ricocheting around his body.

'Miss Beresford,' he murmured, inclining his head. Knowing that all would be lost if he looked her in the eyes, he kept his gaze firmly fixed upon her lips. Another mistake, as he soon found to his considerable discomfort, when another pulsating bout caught him in the solar plexus, ripping his breath away.

Similarly affected by the unexpectedness of the reunion, not to mention the heady excitement of finding herself, once more, held in the arms of the man with whom, to her utter chagrin, she now realised she had fallen deeply in love, Jessica's initial instinct was to run away and hide herself somewhere where she could lick her wounds in private. But then, as she recalled the unpardonably high-handed remarks of the earl's grandmother, coupled with her own determination not to leave town without challenging him to explain his actions, her resolve stiffened. Had she been in a position to register Wyvern's totally unguarded expression of sheer rapture when he had caught hold of her, it was possible that she might have thought better of her next action.

Taking a deep breath, she conjured up her brightest smile and, flicking open her fan, she plied it coquettishly in front of her face, saying, 'My goodness, Lord Wyvern, I haven't seen you for *such* an age! What have you been doing with yourself all this time?' Then, fluttering her eyelashes at his two companions, she added, 'Won't you introduce me to your friends?'

Holding back his dismay at Jessica's extraordinary and quite unexpected behaviour, Wyvern, his jaw rigid with disapproval, presented Fitzallan and Holt to her, sourly noting how they were soon both fawning over her hand like a couple of mooncalves!

'Enchanted, gentlemen,' came Jessica's somewhat overblown response, along with another fluttering of her lashes. 'But, why have I not seen any of you dancing? I should have thought that ex-military gentlemen such as yourselves would have such expertise as to put a good many others in the room to shame!'

And then, before the bemused Wyvern had time to collect his wits, she turned to him and, with her head on one side, said impishly, 'Come, my lord, I see that a waltz is about to begin—shall we take to the floor?'

Finding himself under the highly amused and expectant surveillance of his two friends, it was quite beyond Wyvern to drum up a feasible reason to excuse himself from another bout of the exquisite torture that beckoned. So, after promising himself that he would on this occasion, at least as far as was reasonably possible, given the essential convergence that was part of the dance, keep her at arm's length, he held out his hand and led Jessica over to the ballroom floor, where several other couples were already in the process of assembling.

As the two of them passed the dowager's podium, Wyvern, looking across, was puzzled to note the expression of high dudgeon on his grandmother's face. Dammit! he thought resentfully. It is only a dance! And, taking Jessica's right hand in his, he placed his other hand lightly on her waist and swung her into the waltz.

Chapter Sixteen

In the normal way, being whirled and twirled around the room in the arms of the man she loved would have been more than enough to fill Jessica's heart with blissful contentment but, after one quick look up at Wyvern's rigid countenance, her heart descended to her dancing slippers. Superb dancer though her partner was, there was no pleasure to be gained from his skilful execution of the steps as, with almost mechanical perfection, he steered her expertly across the crowded floor and wove his way around less proficient pairs with consummate ease.

Finding herself being swept past the dowager's podium for the third time in succession, without a single word having crossed the earl's compressed lips, Jessica's dismay increased. And, in a growing alarm, she realised that, unless she thought of something soon, the longed-for opportunity would have come and gone and Wyvern would return her to her companions without giving her a single chance either to explain herself or, more importantly, to discover whether his regard for her was simply a figment of her imagination! Taking a deep breath, she threw back her head and, raising her eyes to the earl's expressionless face, she said abruptly, 'I apologise for that appalling scene, your lordship, but I could think of no other way to oblige you to dance with me!'

At her unexpected words, Wyvern's heart hammered almost to a stop, causing him to miss his step and necessitating the nearest couple to swing hurriedly out of harm's way. Stifling his exasperation, the earl corrected his error and guided Jessica to a less populated area of the floor, whilst racking his brains to conjure up some non-committal remark.

'I had not noticed that you were suffering from a dearth of dancing partners, Miss Beresford,' he managed eventually.

'I cannot imagine how you would know that!' she flung back at him. 'You only turn up when it suits you to do so!'

When he did not immediately respond, Jessica's indignation increased. 'Do you dislike me so much that you cannot even bring yourself to converse with me, sir?' she challenged him.

'I do not dislike you, Miss Beresford,' he replied heavily as, doing his utmost to ignore the tantalising feel of her soft, warm body beneath his fingers, he strove desperately to focus his attention on the manoeuvres of the dance.

'You went to enormous trouble to replace my broken fan!' she cried, glaring up at him accusingly. 'And then—' she took a deep breath, unable to still the trembling in her voice '—and then, after I had told you how much I missed them, you sent me those lovely violets!'

Wyvern's jaw tightened, recalling how, when he had spotted the delicate flowers growing in a clump beneath a tree beside one of the outhouses that he and his two friends had been in the process of searching that morning, Jessica's words had instantly sprung into his mind. Having had no fine beribboned box into which to lay his gift, he had carefully wrapped the fragile blossoms in a scrap of clean muslin that he had begged from his housekeeper, and had then instructed one of the stable lads to saddle up a fast horse and hotfoot it to Dover Street.

'You must be accustomed to receiving a great many far grander bouquets every day,' he replied, endeavouring to suppress the swell of satisfaction within his chest upon learning of the deep joy that his gift had given her. 'My simple offering was scarcely worthy of note.'

Her sudden stumble forced him to clasp her more tightly and, looking down, he saw, to his dismay, that two large tears had welled up in Jessica's lovely green eyes.

'You know perfectly well that that is not true,' she whispered. 'Your gift meant more to me than I can possibly say!'

As his heart thudded uncomfortably inside his chest, Wyvern was, once again, lost for words. Every nerve in his body was clamouring at him to be done with the whole hopeless charade, to come to the point and tell her how much he loved her.

'The flowers were meant to bring you pleasure, not cause you pain,' he said huskily. 'I would not have you sad, for all the world!' And, tightening his hold, he propelled her adroitly across the ballroom's polished surface and swung her briskly into a reverse turn.

Her breath almost shaken out of her body at the earl's sudden excess of vigour, Jessica could barely gasp out her next query. 'Why, then, have you gone out of your way to avoid me?'

A little frown sifted across his brow, as he came to the conclusion that, unless he meant to lose her trust for ever, it was no longer in his power to hold back. 'I fear that your observations have been perfectly correct, Miss Beresford,' he said, with a rueful grin. 'And, I do have to admit that I have been doing my level best to keep away from you!'

'But why?' she asked, staring up at him in frowning bewilderment. 'What possible reason could you have for behaving in such an extraordinary way?'

Barely able to concentrate on his steps, he let out a deep sigh. 'The fact of the matter is, you dear sweet girl,' he said softly, 'that I fear that I have found it well nigh impossible to resist you!'

Her brow puckering in incomprehension, Jessica asked, 'What are you saying—?' Then stopped, as she tried to weigh up the meaning of his words. Her cheeks grew pink and her heart seemed to be beating nineteen to the dozen. 'Can you be saying—?'

As the earl looked down at her expression of total mystification, his eyes grew warm; although he was conscious of the fact that he had, perhaps, already let slip a good deal more than was wise, given his still rather precarious circumstances, throwing caution to the wind, he drew her yet closer and, with expert precision, swung her into the flourishing twirl that brought the waltz to its close.

'I regret that I cannot say more at this moment, my sweet,' he murmured into her ear. 'But soon—very soon—I promise that I have every intention of so doing, you may depend upon it!'

Disregarding the curious stares of one or two of the other dancers nearby, the now highly agitated Jessica clutched at his arm. 'Very soon may prove to be far too late,' she cried, in desperation. 'My brother means us to return to Thornfield on Saturday!'

'Damnation!' muttered Wyvern, under his breath. This was an eventuality that he had certainly not taken into consideration in his carefully laid plan to seek out Beresford the minute he laid hands on the mine's missing papers of ownership. If he allowed Jessica to go back to Lincolnshire without having properly declared himself, it could be weeks before he found himself in a position to speak to her brother, during which time, he conjectured heatedly, one of those other smooth-talking bucks might easily worm his way into her affections! Incensed at such a possibility, he made up his mind. Such a risk was not worth taking!

'We have to talk,' he whispered, as he escorted her back to her corner. 'Is it possible that you could get away from your friends long enough to meet me out on the terrace?'

Although she was well aware that what the earl was suggesting was quite improper, Jessica could not prevent her heart from racing at the prospect of being alone with him. Giving a swift nod, she murmured, 'Give me ten minutes.'

Then, with a deep curtsy, she excused herself and returned to her seat next to the curious and highly envious Felicity.

'My dear, you must be beside yourself with satisfaction!' declared her recently acquired acquaintance, valiantly smothering her own rising feelings of envy and disappointment. 'Fancy Wyvern turning up again! I swear I was beginning to think he had turned his back on society!' Then, leaning more closely, she whispered, 'And what did her ladyship have to say to you? I dare say she had already instructed Wyvern to ask you and was telling you to accept his request?'

Recalling the countess's warning, Jessica's lips curved in a beatific smile. 'Not exactly,' she laughed. 'As a matter of fact, she did her best to warn me off her precious grandson so, of course, I made a beeline for him and asked him myself!'

'Jessica! You did not!' gasped Miss Draycott, visibly shocked to hear of her young companion's outrageous behaviour.

'I most certainly did,' replied the unrepentant Jessica. 'I don't care to have a complete stranger ordering me about!' Then, glancing about her, she remarked, in some surprise, 'I do not see any of our escorts on the dance floor—have they all deserted us for the card rooms?'

Shaking her head, the smiling Felicity explained that, owing to the expected rush for the refreshment room when the supper bell rang, many of the gentlemen had elected to forfeit the pleasure of the supper dance, which was now in progress, in order to be sure of securing an adequate number of tables to seat their group.

'Then, if you will excuse me for a few minutes, I shall take advantage of their absence to pay a quick visit to the powder room,' said Jessica, getting to her feet.

Having just that moment caught a fleeting glimpse of Wyvern exiting through the double doors that led out on to the terrace, she knew there was little time to lose for, in order not to arouse suspicion, she herself would have to make her way out into the gardens by quite a different route. 'I will see you in the supper room—I shan't be long.'

She whisked off across the ballroom and into the passageway, hoping to find another door out to the terrace, but the garden end of the passage revealed only a single narrow window. Trying to make herself as unobtrusive as possible, she sauntered down to the bottom of the passage and peeped into the last room, which turned out to be a library and, insofar as she was able to determine, since the room was in total darkness, appeared to be quite empty. However, the set of doors that she sought were, to her delight, clearly visible in the glow from the outside lamplight.

Tiptoeing carefully across the library floor, for fear that she might bang into or knock over some priceless work of art, she eventually reached the room's outer doors. In her deep concentration, she was blissfully unaware of the silent presence of Digby Hazlett who, seated in one of the library's high-backed chairs, glumly ruminating over his misfortunes, had been regarding her progress with deep interest. As Jessica let herself out of the room straight into the waiting arms of Lord Wyvern, a satisfied gleam came into Hazlett's eyes.

Getting to his feet, he strolled over to the doorway and spent some time studying the actions of the closely entwined pair. First-hand knowledge of such secret trysts could prove to be very useful ammunition, he grinned to himself, should Wyvern prove at all reticent to part with the papers! Having decided to leave the earl to discover the missing deeds, what had previously been proving to be a lengthy and fairly costly business for the viscount was now just a matter of him keeping his patience. In the light of all the activity that had gone on at Ashcroft Grange during the past day or so, Hazlett was supremely confident that it could not be much longer before Wyvern hit upon his brother's chosen hiding place. And, as soon as he did so, Hazlett believed that he now had the very lever with which to persuade the earl to deliver the deeds into his hands. With one last look at the shadowy pair, he gave a decisive nod, then exited the library and returned to his circle of friends in one of the card rooms.

Her heart pounding with expectation, Jessica stumbled into the welcoming circle of Wyvern's arms and, swiftly dismissing all of her previous doubts regarding his past negligence, she wrapped her arms around his neck and pressed herself against him more closely.

At this unanticipated embrace and the dizzying effect of Jessica's tantalising nearness, Wyvern let out a deep sigh of frustration, as he tried desperately to conjure up some hidden strength to pull himself away from her. 'God help me!' he groaned, his voice husky with emotion. Inner voices were clamouring that what he was doing was unforgivable and not at all the actions of an officer and a gentleman but, powerless to resist the sight of Jessica's luscious lips, parted so invitingly and so close to his own, he could do nothing other than to surrender himself to the overwhelming temptation.

A burning fire ran through Jessica's veins as soon as his lips touched hers and, as his hold tightened, she was inflamed by the urgency of his growing ardour. Somewhere in the back of her mind, she found herself marvelling on the divine intervention that had fashioned their bodies in such a way that they seemed to fit together in such sweet perfection. The more tightly Wyvern held her, the more closely she clung to him until, in a shudder of delight, she surrendered herself, heart and soul, to his embrace.

Almost overcome by the exquisite headiness of finding Jessica, at long last, in his arms, shivers of delight cascaded through the earl's trembling limbs and it was some little time before his innate sense of honour and fair play finally came to his rescue. But then, as he gradually became conscious of how close he was to losing all sense of reason, he forced himself to disentangle Jessica's arms from about his neck and thrust her firmly away from him.

'Oh, dear God, no!' he panted hoarsely, still struggling to quell his unfulfilled desire. 'I swear that I did not mean this to happen!'

The unexpected abruptness of his actions came as a dash of cold water to Jessica's spiralling ardour. And, as his frantic words of protest sank in, her eyes widened in shock. Had the embrace been a mistake and not what Wyvern had intended at all? And, as the sudden realisation of how the kiss had come about, she was overcome with embarrassment at her own wanton behaviour and more than ready to believe that, in her eagerness to join the earl out in the relative darkness of the terrace, it had been she who had initiated the embrace! She shrank away from him, unable to believe that she had encouraged the earl to treat her as though she were a little better than a light-skirt! By behaving in such a wanton manner, any respect that Wyvern might previously have felt for her must surely have been damaged beyond repair!

Her cheeks pale, her eyes large in her face and scarcely able to still the trembling that continued to assail her limbs, she staggered back towards the library door, intent upon removing herself from his presence with all speed.

Still fighting for breath, as he endeavoured to recover his own shattered equilibrium, Wyvern initially failed to register Jessica's agitated reaction. Hurrying after her into the still-darkened room, he closed the doors behind him and reached out his hands to her. Although his ardour had by no means evaporated, he had, eventually, regained his self-control and was determined this time to keep his head.

To his surprise, she shook her head and moved further away from him. With the soft glow from the Chinese lanterns in the trees outside the only source of light, it was difficult for him to fully register her expression.

'Jessica?' he whispered, unable to understand her sudden reticence. 'Don't be afraid, my love. We are quite safe in here—for the moment, at least!'

His hands still outstretched, he stepped forward, intending to calm her fears but, to his bewilderment, she continued her backward retreat towards the library's far side, clearly seeking for the door into the passage. Then, all of a sudden, she came to a halt, her progress impeded by the sharp edge of a small table. Reaching out, Wyvern was able to prevent her fall and hurriedly pulled her into the safety of his arms but, immediately conscious of her resistance, he frowned and stared down at her face. The sight of her trembling lips and wide-eyed apprehension, both now clearly visible in the lanterns' glow, caused his gut to tighten and sapped every vestige of breath from his body. *Dear God,* he thought, *what an insensitive oaf I am! The violence of my lovemaking has terrified the poor darling!*

Ignoring her obvious reluctance, he took both of her hands in his and pulled her towards him, being careful to keep the pair of clasped hands between them as some sort of a safety barrier. 'What just happened out there,' he began, somewhat hesitantly, 'was not at all what I intended, when I asked you to meet me outside. I really needed to explain to you why, for the moment, at any rate, it is quite impossible that we should be seen together!'

As Jessica's doubts about Wyvern's feelings for her continued to grow, her heart plummeted even further. His humiliating words were no more than she deserved. 'Yes, I see that,' she whispered, brokenly. 'I have given you a deep disgust of me.'

'Good God, no!' cried Wyvern, appalled. Then, as, with a sinking heart, he realised that her eyes were bright with unshed tears, he threw his carefully garnered caution to the wind and, letting go of her hands, he wrapped his arms around her and pulled her to his chest, burrowing his face in the fragrant softness of her silken tresses. 'How can you think such a thing when, surely, you must have realised by now that I worship and adore every single thing about you?'

Reluctantly releasing his hold, he held her away from him, a rueful smile on his lips, before continuing, 'Unfortunately, my sweet darling, until I am able to sort out my finances, I am in no position to offer for you. The way things are at present, your brother would have every right to laugh in my face and show me to the door.'

Her heart almost exploding with joy, Jessica lifted her questioning eyes to his face. 'Then you really do want to marry me?' she asked incredulously.

Raising his eyebrows in astonishment, Wyvern stared down at her. 'Haven't I just said as much, you delightful little widgeon? You may expect to find me on your doorstep as soon as I am in a position to approach your brother—which I can hardly do at the moment, since I have scarcely a penny with which to bless myself!'

'Then you have still not discovered whether your brother's mine exists,' she said despondently. 'And I had such high hopes for you!'

He smiled, squeezing her hands in appreciation of her concern. 'It most certainly does exist,' he assured her. 'It is a rather profitable gold mine in South America, as it happens. The trouble is that I am having difficulty laying my hands on the papers that will prove my ownership and, unless they turn up pretty soon, I look likely to face bankruptcy and the usual ignominy that goes with it.' Pausing, he raised his hands to her shoulders and held her away from him. 'The fact of the matter is, my darling Jessica, that I love you far too much to allow you to be subjected to such unpleasantness and disgrace.'

'Whether you are rich or poor makes not the slightest bit of difference, as far as I am concerned,' she replied, her earlier certitude now fully restored. 'I love you so much that I really do not give a fig for what the so-called polite world thinks or says about me!'

At her words, although Wyvern's heart swelled with a sweet mixture of pride and joy, he shook his head. 'But I do, my love,' he replied gently. 'How the world views the two of us is of vital importance to our future lives— giving me all the more reason to succeed in my present quest. Added to which, I have to admit that I would much prefer you to think highly of your husband's accomplishments!'

'I doubt that will be very difficult for me,' she said as, lifting his hand and cradling it to her cheek, she threw him a smile of such adoration that the earl was, momentarily, transfixed. But then, a small frown creased her brow and she let go of his hand, crying, 'But, what are we to do then? Matt is determined to go home on Saturday and, now that I know you truly love me, I cannot bear to be parted from you for weeks at a time!'

'It will be equally hard for me, my sweet,' groaned Wyvern, pulling her back into his arms once again. 'But, knowing that you return my love is all the spur I need to toughen my resolve.' Then, lowering his head, he kissed her tenderly upon her lips, drawing away before his baser instincts once more got the better of him. 'And now, dearest one, I fear that I have delayed you far too long. Your companions will wonder what has become of you.' He paused, considering, then, 'Are you, by any chance, engaged with Felicity's set tomorrow evening?' he asked.

'Lady Helen Grainger has arranged for a supper booth at the Vauxhall Gardens,' replied Jessica, with an indifferent shrug, but then, as the earl reached forwards to tuck back the one or two wayward curls which, during the fervency of his embraces, had strayed from their diamond clasps, she held her breath in awed fascination. To think that Wyvern really loved her after all! Her heart was almost bursting with happiness.

'Then I promise that I shall do my very best to meet up with you there,' he said, turning her to face the lights shining in from the garden, in order to inspect her appearance more thoroughly. 'Look out for me, my darling—it looks set to be our last opportunity to meet again before you leave town.'

Then, leading her across the library to the doorway opposite, Wyvern slid open the door, peered cautiously up the long passageway, and hustled her out of the room, closing the door behind her. Somewhat shaken at the rather sudden and abrupt ending to what had been the most momentous occasion, Jessica was finding it difficult to catch her breath and several moments elapsed before she was able to collect herself sufficiently to dwell upon how, in the space of barely a quarter of an hour, the entire tenor of her life had changed. Wyvern loved her and wanted to marry her! But then, as the shocking enormity of her impetuous actions, along with the totally unforeseen outcome of those actions, gradually began to sink in, she found herself beset by a mounting panic that Matt might find out about her fall from grace. And, since Wyvern had been adamant that he would not approach her brother until he had found the deeds to his mine, how in the world would she be able to justify her highly improper behaviour? Picking up her skirts, she sped towards the refreshment room, fearful that Mr Pevensey, concerned about her long absence away from the group, might have cause to mention it to her half-brother.

Luckily for her peace of mind, the press of people in the room was so great that, when she did eventually manage to rejoin her companions, very little was made of her non-appearance, save for Lady Sarah's less than sympathetic observation that fighting her way through such a crowd had brought an unfortunately high colour to Jessica's cheeks, in addition to causing considerable disarray to her, previously, much envied coiffure!

Chapter Seventeen

Having arrived back at Ashcroft Grange shortly after ten o'clock the following morning, Wyvern and his two friends were sitting at the kitchen table tucking into the hearty breakfast of steak and eggs that Mrs Hayward, the elderly housekeeper, had insisted in preparing for them.

The earl was finding himself obliged to endure a considerable amount of good-natured chaffing at the hands of his companions, as a result of the obligatory waltz of the previous evening, followed by his extended absence from the room—Jessica's subsequent disappearance having, also, been duly noted.

'I swear that you were gone a full fifteen minutes,' chuckled Fitzallan, as he reached over to help himself to his third slice of Mrs Hayward's succulent beefsteak. 'More than enough time to get any female out of your system, in my humble opinion.'

'Then allow me to assure you that, in this case, even fifteen years would not even begin to bring about that eventuality,' growled Wyvern, shooting his ex-comrade a glowering look. 'And I would be much obliged if you could bring yourself to desist from making offensive remarks about my future wife!'

'Your future wife?' chorused his friends, in wide-eyed astonishment.

'Are we to understand that you actually got as far as proposing to Miss Beresford?' asked Sir Simon, quite taken aback at his friend's unseemly haste to become leg-shackled. 'Whilst I realise that you are thoroughly smitten, dear boy, surely it is customary to involve oneself in a few weeks of dedicated courtship before one takes such an irreversible step?'

'Seeing that Beresford is set on returning his family to Lincolnshire in the morning,' returned the earl, with a wry smile, 'it would appear that time is a luxury I can ill afford. And, knowing that it might well be several weeks before I got another chance to speak to Jessica alone, I deemed it necessary to, er—stake my claim— if you will pardon the vulgarity!'

'All of which appears to have given us even more reason to get on with the business of searching for this blessed certificate!' observed Holt, quaffing back the remains of his porter and rising to his feet. 'Which reminds me…' He paused momentarily, considering his next words. 'I dare say that you were too distracted last evening to pay much attention to what was going on around you. I, however, did happen to notice Digby Hazlett emerging from the Conynghams' library shortly before you returned to the ballroom. It has subsequently occurred to me that he might well have been in a position to observe you dallying with

Miss Beresford, since you say that you were out on the terrace.'

'I hardly think so,' replied Wyvern, with a swift shake of his head. 'I, myself, spent quite some time in the library before returning to the ballroom and I can assure you that Hazlett was, most certainly, not present on that occasion!'

'Just a thought, old friend,' returned Sir Simon. 'It's as well to remember what a cunningly devious swine Hazlett is. It wouldn't do to give him anything to use against you. He would happily blacken not only your name, but Miss Beresford's too, just for the sheer hell of it!'

'Point taken, Simon,' nodded the earl. 'I promise to be extra-vigilant.'

Having debated the next best course of action, the three friends made their way to the stables and saddled up their horses, it having been decided that Fitzallan would investigate the hollows of certain trees that Wyvern had described to him, while Holt was directed to search between the crevices of the boulders in a small, rocky inlet that lay within a sharp bend in the Brent, the river that ran through the Ashcroft estate. The earl himself had elected to head for the Grange's dilapidated boathouse, which was situated on the banks of the Brent itself. After agreeing that a shot would be fired into the air should any of them happen to be successful in his search, the three men parted.

Wyvern made his way down to the riverside, directing his mount through the estate's badly overgrown copses. Such a lot of work to be done, he conjectured, dismally, shaking his head at the wilful neglect he could see all around him. If he could just get his hands on all that prime blunt that was lying so idly in Mr Coutts vault, he would not only be able to return his family home to its previous prosperity, but he might also invest in some of these new farming methods that he had been hearing about. If he was going to set himself up as a gentleman farmer, he decided, a wry grin creasing his face, then he might just as well do the thing properly. Other fellows were happy enough to spend their lives in some rural backwater—Matt Beresford, for one, it seemed, could hardly wait to get back to his farm and dirty his hands again. However, although he was more than keen to bring the Ashford estate back up to scratch, Wyvern was not entirely certain that he would care to be that closely involved in its day-to-day activities—that sort of thing had been much more in Theo's line.

As his thoughts flew once more to the tragedy of his brother's death, a puzzled frown crossed his brow. Why, he wondered, if Theo had been aware of the vast amount of money waiting to be claimed, had he not simply produced the deeds and collected it? Sadly, the answer to this question was not difficult to fathom. Having already gambled away his own fortune, in addition to a hefty portion of the estate's assets, Theo, in one of his saner moments, had been unable to trust himself not to flush away this final resource down the same sewer. Unable to contemplate a future without his beloved Sophie and having realised their potential value, he had managed to stay sober long enough to hide the documents, before taking his own life, in the certain expectation of his younger brother taking up the reins in his stead.

Whilst Wyvern could, by no means, condone his

brother's actions, now that he found himself suffering from a similar affliction—a condition somewhat akin to madness, he reminded himself ruefully—it was easier for him to begin to understand Theo's state of mind during that painful period. And, as the wholly unacceptable thought that he might never find the deeds, thereby losing his only chance to claim Jessica for his own, filtered its way into his brain, a comparable sense of hopelessness threatened to overcome him.

Steeling himself, he drew in a deep breath, knowing that, if he meant to win Jessica's hand, he had no option but to continue his search and, whipping up his horse, he set him into a fast canter along the riverbank towards the boathouse.

This building, when he reached it, turned out to be even more dilapidated than he had recalled, missing several of its roof timbers and open to the elements. There were, as he quickly realised, very few places within its damp and mouldy shell where a valuable document could be secreted. After searching every possible nook and cranny, including those within the rotting boat itself, he was almost ready to admit defeat.

Straightening up, in an attempt to ease the ache in his back, his eyes let upon the tiny ait situated in the middle of the river. Little more than a clump of willow trees set on a small grassy hump that rose above the placid waters of the Brent, it had provided the two brothers with many a happy hour of adventuring during their growing years.

With a doubtful frown, Wyvern gazed down at the vessel, somewhat uncertain as to its seaworthiness. And yet, he reasoned, as he looked over at the islet, calculating its distance from the shore, if Theo *had* chosen to secrete the missing deeds somewhere over there, the boat would have been his brother's only means of transport.

With a weary sigh, for he realised that he had no choice but to investigate the ait's possibilities, the earl stripped off his jacket and, rolling up his sleeves, climbed carefully into the leaky craft and untied the painter that secured it to its mooring post.

Mentally keeping his fingers crossed that the boat would prove to be far more reliable than it looked, Wyvern took hold of the oars and, his heart in his mouth—since he had no fancy for an unsolicited dip in the river—began to row the hundred yards or so that made up the distance to the islet. To his unbounded relief, in spite of the fact that there did seem to be a fair amount of water seeping through the aged timbers, the short voyage was eventually achieved without the expected disaster.

As he tied up the vessel to one of the many twisted roots that protruded from the trunks of the three or four willow trees that grew on the grassy hump, a swift smile of recollection creased his lips. Having reached the ait, memories quickly flooded back of the many wild adventures of beleaguered knights or marauding pirates that he and Theo, along with several of their school friends, had played on this tiny scrap of land, scarcely twenty feet across in either direction. However, in picking his way through the overhanging fronds of the willows, in an impatient search for some sign that his brother might have left for him, it soon became clear to him that there was nowhere on this little islet that anyone could possibly hide anything, let alone vital pieces of paper!

Deeply dispirited, he returned to the boat and, with a rusty tin that he had happened upon during his search of the islet, set about baling out the water that had collected in the boat's bottom, in readiness for his row back to the opposite riverbank. As he was doing so, his attention was caught by a gentle clinking noise, which seemed to be coming from somewhere further along the bank. With a puzzled frown, he climbed out of the boat and, by clinging on to the trees' overhanging branches in order to steady himself, the earl was able to make his way across the gnarled root system towards the source of the sound.

When, at last, he reached the spot, a wry smile twisted his lips for, tied to one of the ancient willow tree roots and bobbing about in the gentle movement of the water, was nothing more than an old wine bottle. Judging by its grimed and algae-encrusted exterior, it must have been there for years, he thought, recalling with perfect clarity how he and his friends had often provisioned their trips to the ait with pockets full of apples and sweetmeats, along with bottles of cook's homemade fizzy ginger drink that they would submerge in the river to keep cool. With a disappointed shake of his head, he bent down and undid the knot that secured the bottle to the root, lifted it out of the water and, pulling out the cork, gave it a quick shake, curious to see if its contents still gave off that satisfying froth of bubbles he remembered so well. To his surprise, the contents of the bottle merely rattled. His senses suddenly alert and scarcely able to contemplate the outcome, he tentatively tipped the contents of the bottle into his hand. A shower of pebbles cascaded forth, slowly followed by the tip of a twist of oiled paper. Hardly daring to breathe, Wyvern took hold of the end of the paper and withdrew a slim, tubular-shaped package. Although he was almost overcome with a mixture of relief and excitement at having finally found the lost documents, he wisely decided that there was no immediate need for him to unwrap the package, concluding that its contents were far too valuable to be lost to a sudden gust of wind or a destructive drenching in the river. Tucking the tube securely down into the waistband of his riding breeches, he felt for his pistol, which he had stowed into his pocket and, quickly priming the weapon, raised his arm and fired a single shot into the air.

Under the watchful and keenly interested gaze of Hazlett's paid minion, who had been hiding in the bushes beside the riverbank throughout his sojourn, the earl climbed back into the boat and, with the exultant grin on his face now clearly visible, proceeded to row back to the shore.

Chapter Eighteen

Lady Helen's supper party at the Vauxhall Gardens was in full swing—if such an epithet could be applied to the tightly controlled behaviour and restrained laughter of the somewhat supercilious group of individuals now assembled within her hired box! And, although Jessica's mind was, more or less, fully occupied with the tantalising question of when or whether Wyvern might choose to put in an appearance, she could not help wondering why Felicity Draycott and her friends ever bothered to attend such a cosmopolitan gathering, if all they intended to do was to mock or criticise the passers-by. They had refrained from joining in the choruses of the songs, as she had quickly discovered to her cost, her own short burst of enthusiasm having bought deprecating frowns from both of her female neighbours. Added to which, not one of them had made the slightest attempt to join the dancers around the Rotunda, openly averring that such over-boisterous performances were both unseemly and vulgar.

The earlier part of the day had gone so slowly that it had been difficult for Jessica to keep her simmering excitement under control. Luckily, her brother Matt had been far too involved with the tedious business of organising the packing up of the household belongings to bother much with his young sister. Short of asking her how she had enjoyed herself at the Conynghams' ball, he had paid her very little attention.

Imogen, however, had required a far more detailed recital of the previous evening's events and it had taken all of Jessica's descriptive powers to satisfy her cousin's eager questioning. Thankfully, there was no necessity for her to resort to untruths, since her vivid descriptions of the ballroom's exotic decorations, the spectacular lighting in the garden and the lavish choice of delicacies in the supper room were more than enough to bring a wistful smile to Imogen's face. And, if Jessica's eyes did seem a little overbright and her demeanour rather more agitated than of late, her cousin simply assumed it to be as a result of the excitement of the previous evening's entertainment.

Having already visited the highly popular pleasure gardens earlier in the Season, none of its attractions was of especial interest to Jessica, particularly since she, once again, found herself being squired by the Honourable Walter Allardyce who, in her opinion, had to be one of the greatest bores she had met during the whole of her time in London. If he mentioned the new gas lighting once more, she was quite certain that she would scream out loud! As for the music! To her dispassionate ears, the musicians in the Rotunda, striving to make themselves heard above the cacophony of shrill chatter that emanated from the diverse bevy of humanity passing by, seemed to be exhibiting far less proficiency than she recalled from her previous visit. The only advantage of being in a supper box, as far as she could see, was that it gave her a clearer view of the populace than if the group had chosen to join the confused jumble below.

Provided they could afford the price of the three-shilling entry ticket, the gardens were open to every single class of person imaginable, from the lowest costermonger to the highest duke in the land, not to mention a goodly smattering of the showy Birds of Paradise who plied their trade in the more dimly lit dark walks. Even the Prince Regent himself was said to be greatly enamoured of the place!

Politely declining yet another offering of the thinly sliced ham for which the Gardens were famed, Jessica's eyes travelled eagerly across the shifting countenances of the swarming masses below, desperately seeking out that one beloved face that had come to mean so much to her. But, alas, to no avail! Inexorably, the hands on the clock above the Rotunda crept onwards and still no sign of the earl. Finally, when the Master of Ceremonies announced that the firework spectacular that rounded off the evening's entertainment would commence in fifteen or so minutes, she was obliged to resign herself to the fact that, for whatever reason, Wyvern had found it impossible to join her, as he had promised he would endeavour to do. Now she would have to go back to Thornfield without any clear idea of when she might see him again. It was possible that he might write to her, she supposed glumly but, with Matt and Imogen overseeing the house's letters, she doubted whether, in view of his present lack of funds, that would be a very wise thing for him to attempt. Inwardly cursing the wretched Theo for having made his brother's task so difficult, she prayed that Wyvern would soon lay his hands on the hidden documents.

Deeply intent upon trying to think of some way to solve her difficulties, she was shaken back to reality by the angry voices of the four gentlemen who were tonight's escorts.

'Clear off, Hazlett!' Gerald Pevensey was saying. 'Leave Miss Draycott alone! You and your sort are not welcome here!'

Craning her neck, Jessica caught sight of a tall, scar-faced individual backing away from the box. His manner of dress seemed to indicate that he belonged to the upper classes but, when he turned to face her and gave her what could only be described as a knowing wink, she was immediately assured that he most certainly did not! Her cheeks flushed with embarrassment, she bent her head towards Felicity, who was seated next to her, intending to enquire as to the stranger's purpose in coming to their box. To her consternation, her friend's face had turned a deathly white and she looked as though she were about to faint.

Reaching out her hands, in order to prevent the swaying girl from falling out of her seat, Jessica called out, 'Some water, quickly, please, gentlemen!'

Unfortunately, since water was not a commodity that was readily available in the supper boxes, a choice of arrack punch or champagne was the best that any of their escorts were able to offer her.

Opting for the lesser intoxicating wine, Jessica

dipped her handkerchief in the proffered glass and dabbed it against Felicity's lips, noting, with considerable relief, that the other girl's cheeks were starting to regain their colour and that she seemed to be recovering from whatever had caused her distress.

'It was that swine Hazlett,' sniffed Sir Philip Henderson indignantly, as he leant forward and, somewhat feebly, patted Felicity on her shoulder. 'The sight of his evil face is enough to frighten even the strongest of stomachs!'

Summoning up every vestige of her former self-control, Felicity inclined her head. 'He did give me something of a shock,' she conceded then, getting to her feet, she added, 'What say we all take a little stroll about the gardens before the firework display begins? We have been sitting here so long that I am sure the exercise would do us a world of good, do you not agree?'

'Are you sure that you are up to it, Felicity?' questioned Jessica, rather taken aback at her friend's sudden bout of energy.

She was more than a little hurt when Felicity, instead of answering Jessica's well-intentioned query as to her well being, averted her eyes and, laying her hand on Mr Pevensey's proffered arm, stepped down from the supper box, leaving Jessica in a ferment of doubt and indignation. Surely, it cannot be out of bounds to enquire after someone's health, she thought, shaking her head in amazement. Had it not been for her painful disappointment at Wyvern's non-appearance, she was beginning to feel not at all sorry about returning to Thornfield on the morrow, for at least this would mean that she would be done with always having to defer to the complicated vagaries of Felicity Draycott and her wearisome set of friends!

Then, suddenly conscious that the Honourable Walter had been patiently waiting to assist her down from the supper box, she accepted his arm and allowed him to escort her across the crowded concourse in the wake of the other three couples, doing her best to close her mind to his inevitable remarks about the superiority of the new gas lighting, as compared with the garden's older and far less reliable system of oil lamps!

'Who was that gentleman who was pestering Miss Draycott?' she asked, as soon as she was able to get a word in edgewise. 'She seemed very put out by his appearance!'

'Nasty piece of work, name of Hazlett,' replied Allardyce, somewhat testily. 'Fellow had no business confronting Miss Draycott in such a brazen manner! Actually leaned right over the barrier and spoke to her! Nearly had a mind to call the scoundrel out!'

'Yes, but who is he?' persisted Jessica, who had been mulling over Felicity's rather odd behaviour towards her. Some inner instinct was telling her that the deathly pallor of the other girl's cheeks was not something that could be laid down to a simple affront at having been accosted by a passing roisterer. Nor indeed, could the terrified expression she had witnessed in the other girl's eyes. Clearly, there was some mystery here!

However, it seemed that Allardyce was not at all anxious to continue the conversation. 'Bad lot,' he said, abruptly. 'Not at all our sort of person—best not to worry your pretty little head about such things!' Then, with a puzzled frown, he added, 'Well, I'll be da—! Oh, pray excuse my language, Miss Beresford!'

'Is there something wrong, sir?' enquired Jessica, hiding the smile that threatened. As though she had not heard far worse language than his restrained expletive, she thought scornfully.

'Not at all, my dear,' came the Honourable Walter's swift reply. 'I was just a little surprised that we were taking this particular route, that is all.'

Not having been paying a great deal of attention to her surroundings, Jessica, too, was just a little taken aback at finding herself being led down what appeared to be one of the notorious dark walks of the gardens. Even Matt, as she recalled, had refused Imogen's teasing request that they might investigate the area and, laughingly pulling her away from the entrance down which she had been peering, had pretended to be deeply shocked at his wife's prurient interest in such matters. He had later explained that the more respectable elements of society tended to avoid such areas, since they were known to be the favourite trysting-places of some of the rather doubtful-looking characters who could be seen wandering about the gardens.

Only very slightly nervous, since she and Allardyce were still in close company with the other three couples in front of them, Jessica tightened her grip on her escort's arm.

'The gaslights are much further apart down here, aren't they?' she observed, her voice almost a whisper.

'Probably cost too much,' the Honourable Walter replied, patting her hand reassuringly. 'Can't think why Pevensey thought to venture down here—not at all the—*oof*!'

The remainder of Allardyce's words were cut off in midstream and, to Jessica's horror, he collapsed in a heap at her feet, blood streaming from a cut on his head. Before she could regain sufficient presence of mind to scream out for assistance, a vile-smelling blanket was thrown over her head, obscuring her vision and muffling her angry protests. Almost immediately, a pair of strong arms whisked her off her feet, dragged her backwards through the bushes that bordered the walk, tearing her skirts and ripping off one of her slippers in the process.

Oh, God, no! she thought, in dismay. Not another abduction! Matt will go berserk! Then, despite her far from laughable situation, she almost smiled at her own lunacy and, ceasing her frantic struggles to escape from her unknown captor, she let herself go limp in his arms. Knowing that it was in her nature to be a veritable spitfire when she was really roused, she had decided that it would be far more prudent to conserve her energy until a more suitable opportunity presented itself.

'The chit seems to have fainted,' she heard a coarse voice mutter. 'Best if we take off this 'ere blanket— whadyer say?'

'Nah!' came the reply from his associate, who sounded equally uncouth. 'Won't do 'er no 'arm— carriage'll be 'ere in 'alf a tick!'

Her heart pounding, Jessica realised that her captor had come to a halt then, moments later, as she heard the sound of horse's hooves and carriage wheels on a gravel surface, she recognised that they must have arrived at the roadway outside the gardens. The carriage door was opened and she felt herself being hoisted upwards and deposited, with no great civility, on to one of its seats. For several moments, she lay supine, as she waited to hear whether either of her abductors were intending to travel with her. To her surprise, and considerable relief, the door was shut and the unmistakable sound of someone vaulting up beside the driver was heard, indicating that at least one of her captors was travelling with them. Then the gentle rocking movements commensurate with those of her brother's finely sprung landau were soon to be felt. A gentleman's carriage, concluded Jessica, as she gingerly inched the foul covering from over her head, giving a gasp of dismay when she realised that, contrary to her expectations, she could see little more now than she had before! All the windows had been obscured and, when she finally managed to sidle across the seat to reach one of them, she discovered that the leather curtains had been securely taped to the framework. The door, as she had supposed, had been secured from the outside.

With a rapidly sinking heart, she realised that, until the carriage reached its intended destination, there was not a lot she could do to help herself and, although she did her best to keep track of its left and right-handed turnings, the only place that she could easily identify, thanks to the clear difference in sound, was when they crossed Vauxhall Bridge. At least they were now on the north side of the river, she thought with some relief and, judging from the carriage's regular forward progression at that point, they seemed to be making for the St James's Park area, but then, after several more twists and turns, she was obliged to admit that she no longer had any idea where they might be.

The carriage jolted to a halt, there was a scrambling from the roof and the door was pulled open. Despite her gasp of protest, the fetid covering was once more thrown over her head, but, instead of lifting her in his arms as he had done previously, her captor tossed her over his shoulder and carried her through a doorway, along a passageway and up a flight of stairs before dumping her, unceremoniously, down on to what she was soon to discover was a well-padded and expensively covered *chaise longue*.

Removing the blanket, a shabbily dressed, pock-faced individual leered down at her.

'Them windows is all locked,' he advised her, jerking his head to her rear. 'And there ain't any point in you 'ollerin' for 'elp, 'cos there ain't no one 'ere as'll 'ear you! Best you just sit there, nice and comfy-like, 'til 'is lordship gets 'ome!'

Then, tucking the blanket under his arm, he moved towards the doorway of what, to Jessica's astonishment, appeared to be a gentleman's library. A very large and grandly appointed library, it was true but, then, of course, the man *had* referred to his employer as 'his lordship'. She wasn't sure that she had actually made the acquaintance of many lordships—apart from Wyvern himself, of course, and she immediately discounted his involvement. She frowned, trying to remember which of her earlier corps of young devotees had laid claim to such a title, but could hardly believe that either of the, quite frankly, rather bird-witted Lords Covenham or Middleton had sufficient nous to dream up such a shocking caper! She then tried to comfort herself with the thought that the whole affair must have been some ghastly mix-up. Clearly, she must have been mistaken for somebody else and, as soon as the unfortunate error was discovered, she would be set free!

But, with a wry twist of her lips, she quickly realised that, even if it should transpire that her abductors had picked up the wrong female, her own release was far from assured, given the severe penalties for such crimes as kidnapping and—bearing in mind what had happened to Mr Allardyce—attempted murder! She did so hope that the poor man's injuries had not proved to be fatal.

Kicking off her remaining slipper, she walked over to the room's door, having made up her mind that it was up to her to try to extricate herself from this disastrous situation. To her surprise, she found that the door was unlocked but since, upon inching it gently open, she could clearly hear the voices of her two abductors, coming from a point somewhere over to her right, she supposed that, being so close at hand, her captors had judged it unnecessary to lock her in. Sidling out of the room and keeping herself pressed firmly against the wall, she caught sight of two men standing, luckily with their backs towards her, just inside the front door of the property. They appeared to be waiting for someone—presumably the master of the house and the unidentified 'lordship' of whom the pock-faced one had spoken.

Breathless with anxiety, Jessica inched her way slowly down towards the green baize door that she had spotted on the opposite side of the narrow hallway. It would, she was certain, lead down to the kitchens and the servants' hall. The majority of London's houses of this type, as she knew from the Dover Street property, as well as from her frequent morning visits with her cousin, had basement exits out into the main thoroughfare and, if luck were on her side, she had every reason to hope that such an exit might offer her a means of escape.

Her eyes intent upon the backs of her abductors, she tiptoed across the hallway and silently pulled open the baize door until the gap was large enough for her to slip through. The cheerful clatter of pots and pans from the kitchen below, along with some tuneless singing, greeted her ears and, as she had suspected, a flight of stone steps lay in front of her. Whether she would be able to make her way past the unseen vocalist without her presence being detected remained to be seen. Crossing her fingers, she crept down the stairway, her stockinged feet making no sound.

Breathless with anxiety, she was within two feet of the property's back door when an astonished voice hailed her from a small scullery on her right-hand side, the sudden shock causing her almost to jump out of her skin.

'Well, if it isn't my little lady from the tea-rooms! Whatever are you doing down here in my kitchen, my dear?'

'M-M-Mrs Barrowman!' gasped Jessica, still eyeing the rear exit and wondering if she dared to make a dash for it. 'H-how do you do, ma'am?'

'You will have to speak up, my dear,' returned Mrs Barrowman who, stepping forward, her elbows akimbo, was surveying her unexpected visitor with a puzzled expression on her face. 'I'm afraid I'm a little hard of hearing!' Then, 'Goodness me, my pet, you are in a mess! You look as if you've been dragged through a hedge backwards!'

Many a true word spoken in jest, reflected Jessica ruefully as, casting a nervous glance up at the door at the top of the stairs, she found herself obliged to raise her voice. 'A slight accident, I fear!' she enunciated carefully. 'I was hoping to find a door out into the street.'

But, when Mrs Barrowman gave a decisive shake of her head, Jessica's heart sank, only to rise again in unbelieving joy as she heard the rotund little woman declare, 'There's no way that I would allow you to venture out into the street looking like that, my dear! You'd best come along with me and I'll see what I can do to help you.'

And, so saying, she took hold of Jessica's arm and led her over to a nearby coat rack. 'Looks as though my gentleman has been up to his tricks again,' she muttered witheringly, as she rummaged through the assembled garments for something suitable for Jessica to wear. 'Seems to me that that nice husband of yours ought to take more care of a pretty little thing like you, but then…' she sniffed, unhooking a caped mantle and handing it to the open-mouthed Jessica '…there's no accounting for how some folk's minds work. I've seen things in this house as would shock the devil himself.'

'Then why do you stay here?' Jessica was curious to know.

'It's a roof over my head.' The woman shrugged. 'The work's not hard and the pay is fair. Plus, his lordship leaves me to my own devices. What more could an old woman like me ask at her time of life?'

There was no answer to that, so, after placing the serge mantle over her shoulders, Jessica merely nodded.

'Nevertheless,' Mrs Barrowman then went on, a kindly smile creasing her ruddy cheeks, 'I'm not one as tends to forget the generosity of other folk so, one good turn deserves another, as they say!' And, bending under the settle, she drew out a badly worn pair of ankle boots. 'Ahah!' she crowed jubilantly. 'Thought they was still 'ere! Belonged to the last housemaid they did and look to be about your size, too, unless I'm much mistaken, my dear!'

'But, won't she miss them?' exclaimed Jessica, accepting the footwear with a worried frown.

'Gone,' came the non-committal reply. 'Never stay long, any of them—can't say as I blame them, mind— luckily I'm too old in the tooth for him to bother with the likes of me!'

Thrusting her feet into the shabby boots, despite their proving to be at least two sizes too large for her, Jessica could not help feeling that the sooner she made her escape, the better. This master of Mrs Barrowman's, she reasoned, who was in all likelihood the very man who had ordered her abduction, did not sound to be at all the sort of gentleman with whom she would care to come face to face.

Wrapping her arms around the little housekeeper, she placed warm kisses on each of her cheeks and, reaching for the back-door latch, let herself out into the basement area.

'Take care, my dear,' came Mrs Barrowman's whispered admonition, as, crossing herself, she closed the door behind her.

Raising her hand in farewell, Jessica hurried up the metal staircase that led out on to the pavement. Pausing for a moment to get her bearings, it suddenly occurred to her that, in answer to Wyvern's questioning on that fateful day in Gunter's, Mrs Barrowman had given Half Moon Street as her place of work—barely five blocks away from Jessica's own address in Dover Street!

Hardly daring to believe her luck, she set off to walk the fifty yards or so down the street that she knew would lead her into Piccadilly but, after proceeding barely half the distance, it became necessary for her to toss back the hood of the thick woollen mantle with which Mrs Barrowman had provided her, for the late spring evening was still rather warm.

At the top of the street, and just as she was about to cross over into the main thoroughfare, she found herself having to step back quickly in order to allow a fast-moving carriage to swing into Half Moon Street. Glancing up as the carriage flashed past her, she was given a brief, but all too recognizable, glimpse of the scarred face of the same man who had accosted Felicity in Vauxhall Gardens! Her blood ran cold and, fighting down the sudden tremor of foreboding that threatened to paralyse her limbs, she dashed into the roadway. As she did so, she was aware of the screeching noise of the brake shoes hitting the metal rim of the wheels, the crash of the door against the carriage's bodywork as it was flung carelessly open and, most frightening of all, the sound of footsteps in rapid pursuit. Running for her life, as she was very much afraid that she was, Jessica had almost reached the opposite pavement when one of her too-large boots caught on the hem of her borrowed mantle, sending her flying to the ground, where she lay sprawled in an ungainly heap at the feet of her pursuer.

Hauled roughly to her feet and spun around to face her aggressor, she found herself staring up into the repugnant features of the man that Mr Pevensey had referred to as Hazlett.

'Well! Well! Well!' exclaimed the viscount, a malevolent grin on his disfigured face. 'Now, how did you manage to get out, I wonder? Certain persons are clearly not doing the job they were paid for and will answer to me for the consequences!'

Then, grasping Jessica's arm in a vicelike grip, he proceeded to drag her back down the entire length of the street, disregarding her panic-stricken insistence that his minions had mistaken her for some other female.

'You would do well to stop that caterwauling!' he advised her, in a cutting tone, as he dragged her up the steps to his front door and kicked at it.

It would be difficult to describe the looks of mingled apprehension and shock that swept across the countenances of Jessica's two abductors when, upon opening the door to their master, they found themselves face to face with such an indisputable confirmation of their total ineptitude.

'How the—!'

'Wha' the—?'

'You may well ask!' returned Hazlett savagely, as he hauled the still-protesting Jessica across the hall's marble-chequered floor back into the library from whence she had made her escape. 'I will deal with the pair of you later! In the meantime, if you value your lives, I advise you to stay by that door—I expect company very shortly. When he arrives, search him for weapons—and for anything else of interest that he may have about his person!'

Chapter Nineteen

Hurriedly dismounting from his horse, Wyvern tossed the reins to the waiting stable hand and, after instructing the man to have Berridge bring his curricle and pair round to the front of Ashcroft House in fifteen minutes, he strode quickly through the mews to enter the property by way of its rear entrance.

Taking the stairs two and three at a time, he was about to enter his chamber on the second floor, when he met up with his grandmother, who was just on the point of exiting her own set of rooms.

On a sudden whim of fancy, he darted to her side and, to the elderly lady's utter consternation, placed his hands upon her waist and proceeded to swing her off her feet in a wide circle.

'Put me down this instance, you foolish boy!' she gasped indignantly. 'Have you run quite mad?'

'Very probably,' grinned Wyvern, as he lowered her gently to the ground and swept her a deep bow. 'Allow me to inform you, dearest Grandmama, that our difficulties are at an end—our coffers will soon be overflowing!' At the dowager's frown of incomprehension, he paused momentarily then, looking her straight in the eyes and in a much more serious vein, added, 'Much more to the point, as far as I am concerned, I now find myself free to marry whomsoever I choose!'

Executing another bow, he would have turned to go had not Lady Lavinia reached out a hand to stay him. 'Explain yourself, Benedict, I beg of you!' she implored. 'I really have no idea what you are talking about!'

'A circumstance that you have brought entirely upon yourself!' he riposted gently, as he extricated himself from her grasp and held her away from him. 'Had you not been so eager to have me "sent to Coventry" during the last couple of weeks, you would have been in full possession of all the facts!'

'Nevertheless—!' began his grandmother, eager to point out that, in her opinion, her recent conduct towards him had been fully justified in the circumstances.

With a brisk shake of his head, Wyvern held up one hand to silence her. 'You must forgive me, Grandmama,' he interjected. 'I have no time to debate the matter at present—but I promise you that all will be revealed on my return!'

'But you have only just returned!' she retorted wrathfully, as she watched him turn back towards his own chambers. 'Where are you off to now?'

'Patience, dear lady!' he called over his shoulder, as he entered his room and closed the door. For some moments, he stood in silent contemplation for, if the truth be told, he was not altogether certain as to his next move.

His initial intention, after his afternoon peregrinations, had been to make straight for Vauxhall Gardens, for he could hardly wait to share his good news with Jessica but, having given the matter some thought on his journey back from Middlesex, it had occurred to him that, perhaps, a visit to Dover Street, to petition Matt Beresford for his sister's hand, might be the more sensible option.

Quickly making up his mind, he rang for Taverner and began divesting himself of his dusty travelling garments and, with that erstwhile gentleman's assistance, he readied himself for what, as far as he was concerned, looked set to be one of the most important interviews of his life.

Seated at his dressing table stool, clad in his best jacket of dark blue superfine, grey waistcoat and buff-coloured, thigh-hugging pantaloons, he thrust out each leg in turn to allow his valet to ease on the highly polished Hessians that the man had just that minute brought up from the boot-room, then, getting to his feet to survey himself in the looking-glass, he pronounced himself reasonably well satisfied with his appearance.

After a minute adjustment to the already perfect arrangement of his master's snowy-white neckcloth, Taverner stood back with a contented smile, saying, 'There you are, sir, and, if you will pardon my saying so, not even the most pernickety female on the planet could find any fault with you this evening, if I am any judge!'

'Then you will no doubt be relieved to hear, Taverner,' replied the earl, with a cheerful nod, 'that the

young lady in question is not in the slightest bit pernickety! Unfortunately, however, the whole point of all
this extra attention to detail is to impress her guardian,
who may well be so inclined!'

Picking up his hat and gloves, he turned to leave but
then, as his eyes fell on the twisted tube of oiled paper
that still lay on his dressing-table, a slight frown creased
his forehead. Having already studied the contents of the
package with his two comrades, along with subsequent
enquiries on his return to the capital, he had learned that
the shares had, in the first instance, been owned by the
missing Jack Stavely who had, some five years earlier,
transferred his rights to the mine to Digby Hazlett.
Scarcely two months before Theo's death, the viscount
had, in his turn, transferred the rights to the then Earl
of Wyvern. All of the transfers, including the final one
from Theo to himself, had been duly signed and witnessed and seemed, insofar as the three friends were
able to judge, to be perfectly valid.

Knowing that it would be impossible to visit the
bank until first thing on Monday morning, Wyvern
picked up the package, his anxious gaze flying around
his bedroom in search of the best place to hide such a
valuable object but then, as he recalled all the trouble
that Hazlett had gone to in order to try to retrieve the
documents, he decided that it might be rather more
sensible for him to keep them about his person. But,
having already had his pocket picked on one memorable occasion, and realising that this, perhaps, was not
the best place to carry them, he opted to tuck the slim
tubular package down the outside leg of one of his
boots.

Hopping up into the waiting curricle, some time later than he had anticipated, the earl made his way through London's busy Mayfair and drew up outside Number Twenty-Four Dover Street, feeling rather less confident than his dress and demeanour would seem to indicate.

After being shown into the somewhat surprised Matt's study and hurriedly explaining the purpose of his visit, he assured Jessica's brother that, now that his financial difficulties were resolved, he need have no qualms about the suitability of the match.

'Good Lord!' gasped Beresford, who was thoroughly taken aback by this unexpected turn of events. 'Apart from that unfortunate incident last month, I had no idea that you were even acquainted with my half-sister!'

'I have—er—found it rather difficult to get her out of my mind,' returned Wyvern uncomfortably. After Jessica's plea that he should refrain from mentioning the Oxford Street incident, he judged that it might also be as well to desist from drawing attention to their other meetings—especially last evening's episode out on the Conyngham's terrace! 'May I take it that you have no objections to my paying court to her?'

'Well, no, I suppose not,' replied Matt, distractedly drumming his fingers on his desk. 'It's just that we are due to travel back to our estate in Lincolnshire tomorrow and I cannot, for the life of me, see how you expect to conduct such a courtship. I shall, of course, put your proposal to Jessica as soon as she returns. She is, at this moment, along with several of her friends, enjoying the entertainments at Vauxhall.'

Glancing over at the marble clock on the mantelshelf, which indicated that the time was almost ten o'clock, he shook his head. 'I don't expect her home much before midnight—far too late an hour for any serious discussion, wouldn't you say?'

'Then, with your permission, sir,' said Wyvern, getting to his feet, 'it clearly behoves me to be on my way to the Gardens with all speed—I would prefer to present my case in person, as I am sure you will understand?'

'Point taken,' grinned Matt, as he held out his hand. 'I suppose I ought to wish you luck, old chap!' *And, in taking on that little bundle of mischief,* he then thought to himself, as he showed Wyvern to the door, *you are certainly going to need it!*

Back on the driving seat, Wyvern whipped up his horses and set them into a smooth canter, estimating that it would take him the better part of twenty minutes to make his way across the river into Vauxhall and, having recalled the vast number of supper boxes that bordered the walks around the Rotunda, who knew how long to track down the Draycott party?

Nevertheless, the thought that he would soon, with perfect legitimacy, be once more holding his beloved in his arms, added extra zeal to his determination and, after concentrating his efforts on winding his way through the never-ending streams of traffic, he eventually arrived at Vauxhall Bridge. Checking only very slightly at the toll-bar, in order to toss the required payment at the waiting keeper, he whipped up again and pressed on towards the gardens, now scarcely five minutes away.

Flinging the reins to Berridge, he leapt out of the

still-moving carriage, leaving his startled groom in charge of the equipage, and made his way through the entrance to the pleasure gardens. Having decided that the Rotunda would be the best place to commence his search, he pushed his way towards the centre of the gardens, cursing the many groups of revellers who were standing about enjoying the closing firework spectacular for which the gardens were famous.

Upon reaching the Rotunda, he was surprised to see a large group of people, each of them nodding and exclaiming to their neighbours in a most animated manner, gathered outside one of the boxes. Craning his head to see what all the excitement was about, his eyes were drawn to a scene that had the effect of stopping his heart in mid-beat.

Stretched out on the top of the buffet table in the booth lay the supine figure of the Honourable Walter Allardyce, blood trickling from a nasty-looking wound at his temple. Grouped around the dead or unconscious man—at this angle it was difficult for Wyvern to ascertain which—he was able to distinguish the faces of Gerald Pevensey, the Lyndhurst siblings, Sir Philip Henderson supporting a weeping Lady Helen Grainger and Felicity Draycott herself. But, of Jessica, there was no sign!

A sudden sense of dread swept over Wyvern and, as icy fingers seemed to clutch hold of his heart, he fought his way through the tightly knit throng of morbidly curious bystanders and leapt up into the supper-box.

'Where is she?' he demanded hoarsely. 'Where is Jessica?'

At the sight of the earl, Felicity, her face ashen with

shock, flung herself towards him, her unexpected action almost knocking him off his feet.

Steadying himself, and gripping her by the shoulders, he thrust her away from him, his grey eyes dark with anger.

'Answer me, Felicity!' he commanded the trembling girl. 'Where is Jessica?'

'Oh, Ben!' she wailed, reverting, in her panic, to the name she had used when the two of them were children. 'He has taken her and it is all my fault—I am so very sorry!'

Wyvern's throat tightened. 'Who has taken her?' he asked urgently, although it was not as though he did not already know the answer.

'It has to be Hazlett!' she replied, with a low moan, as she registered the expression on his face. 'He insisted that we all take a stroll down one of the dark walks— Sir Philip heard Mr Allardyce cry out, but, when we got to them, Jessica was gone!' Breaking into a fresh torrent of tears, she indicated the solitary blue satin slipper on a nearby chair. 'I found it on the ground next to Mr Allardyce! Oh, Ben! What can have happened to her?'

Although he was still confused as to why Felicity should have felt it necessary to follow orders from Hazlett and, more to the point, why any of the gentlemen present had considered it advisable to take a party of gently bred females down one of Vauxhall Gardens' notorious dark walks, Wyvern knew that, if he meant to save Jessica, he could not afford to waste precious time in questioning the deeply distressed girl as to her involvement in the affair.

Jerking his head towards the motionless figure on the

table, he asked, 'Is he dead?' knowing that an answer in the affirmative would provide him with all the information that he needed as to exactly what lengths Hazlett might be prepared to go in his underhand machinations to regain the ownership of the Chilean gold mine.

With her hand on her mouth, Felicity gave a little shake of her head. 'We are waiting for a doctor to attend him,' she sobbed. 'His pulse is very weak and he has lost a great deal of blood—Mr Lyndhurst does not believe that he will survive!'

His lips pursed in anger, the earl nodded. 'I shall need to speak to you later, Felicity,' he said, turning on his heel. 'Now, however, is not the moment—I have to find Jessica before that devil does her any harm!' Then, offering up a fervent prayer that this all too likely possibility had not already taken place, and cursing his own folly at having gone to visit Beresford instead of seeking out Jessica, as had been his original intention, he strode rapidly back to the gardens' main exit.

Fortunately, Berridge had managed to secure a parking spot quite close to the gates and, within a very few minutes, they were on their way back across the river. *If only I had had the sense to ride straight to Vauxhall instead of wasting all that time tricking myself out to try to impress her brother!* groaned Wyvern to himself as, almost in despair, he found his curricle boxed in by two slow-moving vehicles.

Cursing at their drivers' incompetence and ignoring their outraged shouts, he steered his cattle straight up on to the street's narrow footpath and, ignoring his shocked groom's yell of protest as the curricle's wheels bounced with a jarring crunch as they hit the kerbstones, he brought his equipage back on to the road's gravelled surface, some distance in front of the now-infuriated dawdlers.

Slamming his vehicle to a screeching halt outside the front door of Hazlett's mansion in Half Moon Street, the earl leapt out of the driving seat and, dashing up the steps, was all too ready to kick down the door had it not, all of a sudden, occurred to him that, dressed as he was, in all his finery, he did not even have a weapon at his disposal!

Hurrying back down to his waiting groom, he instructed him to go directly to Sir Simon Holt's chambers at Albany, inform the baronet that Miss Beresford had been abducted and that both his and Mr Fitzallan's immediate assistance was urgently required at this address.

In the meantime, Wyvern decided to make his way round to the mews at the back of the property, hoping to find an unopened window or some other means of access into the house but, to his utter frustration, all such entrances appeared to be securely barred and bolted.

Returning to the front street, he peered down into the basement area, wondering whether the viscount's servants—as had often been the case in his own household, until the recent attempts at a break-in—might not always take the precaution of locking the kitchen door behind them. He sidled down the stone steps and was just about to test the door's latch when, to his astonishment, the door was flung open and the unmistakable figure of the elderly lady of the teashop incident appeared before him. Clad in her outdoor garments and carrying a large and cumbersome wicker hamper, it was clear that something had occurred to put her in a considerable fret.

'Why, Mrs—er—!' exclaimed the earl, who could not, for the life of him, recall the woman's name. 'What in God's name are you doing here?'

'Oh, sir!' she gabbled breathlessly, having recognised him on the instant. 'You have come at last, thank the Lord! I promise you that I did my best for your poor little lady, but the master must have caught hold of her again on his way back home—he has locked her in the library and is hollerin' at those two bully boys of his something dreadful. I thought it best to pack up and leave before he finds out that it was me what helped her get away before!'

Relieved to hear that Jessica was still, for the moment at least, relatively unharmed, Wyvern reached into his pocket, withdrew a sovereign and, handing it to the bemused housekeeper, instructed her to find a hack and make her way to Ashcroft House where, if she explained that Lord Wyvern had sent her, she would be made comfortable until his return.

'You may leave your heavy valise,' he advised her, crossing his fingers as he did so. 'I shall have it sent over as soon as my business with Lord Hazlett is completed.'

No sooner was he inside the kitchen than he did a quick search for some sort of weapon with which he might arm himself but, short of the usual array of saucepans and rolling pins and the like, the only item that seemed likely to be of any use to him in any sort of confrontation—apart from the poker, which he dismissed as ineffectual—looked to be one of a collection of evil-looking knives. Not his favourite weapon of choice, he thought distastefully, as visions of his frequent night-time sorties into the enemy's camp during his years in the Peninsula sprang into his mind. Nonetheless, and praying that he would have no need to resort to such bloodcurdling tactics, he picked up what appeared to be the sharpest of the set and, wrapping the tip carefully in his handkerchief, slid the weapon up inside his coat sleeve.

Chapter Twenty

Back in the library once more, the much-subdued Jessica soon realised that, now that Lord Hazlett had returned, any further attempts at escape would serve no useful purpose. From the man's patent disregard of her protestations that his servants had committed a grievous error, she had, reluctantly and rather fearfully, been obliged to admit to herself that it would seem that they had not. Clearly, she *was* Hazlett's intended victim and she was no longer so green and so foolish as to fail to recognise what his intentions were likely to be! An icy dread washed over her as her mind replayed the terrifying gamut of events that encompassed the whole sorry escapade of the previous year. Surely she was not destined to relive the nightmare! With a shiver of apprehension, she realised that on this occasion, there was no possible chance of her half-brother racing to her rescue and, since Wyvern had not turned up at the Gardens, he would not even know that she had gone missing.

She drew a deep breath and, whilst recognising that any action she took was likely to prove to be a mere delaying tactic, she vowed that she would, just as on that previous occasion, make every effort to fight her abductor tooth and nail and, should she lose her life in the process, then it would, at the very least, be a merciful release from a far worse fate!

Endeavouring to consolidate her thoughts to that end, she looked around the room to find some object with which to arm herself. Books aplenty, of course, but those that might do any damage to a person were far too heavy for her to lift, let alone throw at her attacker. Her eyes flew to a large oak desk in an alcove between the library's two rear windows but, on investigation, she discovered that its drawers were locked and that the only objects on its green leather surface were a blotting pad, a small wooden tray holding several freshly trimmed quill pens and a glass inkstand, with two of its three pear-shaped inkpots filled with ink. And, whilst she was heavily conscious of the fact that any plan to make use of these items, along with the various other ornaments that she had noticed dotted around the room, would merely put off the inevitable, taking note of their positions for future use might give her a much-needed breathing space.

Turning her attention to the wide, oak-mantelled fireplace, she picked up each of the displayed artefacts in turn, carefully weighing up their possibilities as potential missiles. She was just stooping down to test the relative weights of the fire irons in the companion set on the hearth, when she heard the library door being unlocked. Picking up the poker, she stood up to face her aggressor.

A sour-faced Hazlett entered the room and, after surveying Jessica's defiant stance for several moments, he gave a short laugh. 'You may put down your weapon, Miss Beresford,' he advised her. 'Let me assure you that, as things stand, I have no designs on your person—you are far too valuable a commodity to me.'

Then, walking over to a small drum table, he reached for one of the decanters and poured himself a drink, saying, 'Would you care for a little something, my dear? To steady your nerves, perhaps?'

When she did not reply, he simply shrugged his shoulders and, walking over to the fireplace, threw himself down into one of the leather armchairs that straddled it. Jessica, meanwhile, still clutching the fire iron, had retreated to the alcove at the far side of the room.

Hazlett sighed. 'You really have nothing to fear from me, dear lady,' he said. 'Do please dispose of that ridiculous poker, otherwise I shall be obliged to come over and remove it from you, which would be a great pity, since it really would not be in my best interests to damage you in any way!'

Growing more puzzled by the minute, Jessica laid the poker down on the desktop, still within her reach, should she have need of it, and lowered herself on to the very edge of a nearby chair, poised for flight.

'If it is not your intention to hurt me,' she said carefully, 'may I ask why you employed those two brutes of yours to manhandle me so roughly?'

A brittle laugh issued from Hazlett's lips. 'Certain circumstances require rather more forceful solutions,' he replied. 'I cannot imagine that you would have acceded to their polite request to accompany them!'

She frowned. 'But why have you brought me here?'

'All will be revealed very shortly, my dear. Suffice to say that we are about to receive a visitor—someone very close to your heart, if I am not much mistaken. If matters go according to my plan, as I have every reason to suppose that they will, I dare say that both you and he will be free to leave without a single hair of your pretty little heads being damaged in the slightest!'

Stiffening, Jessica realised in an instant to whom Hazlett referred and was quick to work out for herself the meaning behind his words. That he was using her as some sort of bait to draw Wyvern into his web was patently clear, but she still could not understand what it was that he wanted of the earl, unless…?

Then, out of the blue, it hit her. Of course! The wretched fiend was after the earl's missing deeds of ownership! But, surely, she thought, much mystified, the whereabouts of Wyvern's promised solution to their future happiness together had still to be discovered.

Getting to her feet, she glared angrily at her abductor. 'You mean to use Lord Wyvern's affection for me to blackmail him into handing over that to which you have no right! What kind of a man are you?'

He laughed again, a chilling sound and, tossing back the remains of his drink, he ground out bitterly, 'A rather desperate one, as it happens, my dear. And you are mistaken about my rights. Until very recently, the title deeds and share certificates were in my possession but then, unfortunately, I fear that I lost them to Wyvern's brother in a game of chance and, even though the black-guard went on to owe me a considerable sum of money, he refused to hand back the deeds.'

'But, only last evening,' she responded, in a tone of protest, 'Wyvern himself informed me that the whereabouts of these documents has not yet been discovered!'

'Ah, yes!' he nodded thoughtfully. 'Last evening, it is fair to say that your sweetheart spoke nothing but the truth. Today, however—'

The rest of Hazlett's words were drowned by the sounds of a violent altercation, accompanied by the smashing of china and the splintering of woodwork outside the library door. Leaping to his feet, the viscount was at Jessica's side before she had time to consider what he was about. Quickly withdrawing a length of cord from his jacket pocket, he motioned her back in her seat and proceeded to bind the cord about her waist, securing her firmly to the chair's uprights.

'Just to keep you in your place, my dear,' he grinned, before strolling nonchalantly to the far side of the room and, after putting his ear to the door, rapped upon it three times in quick succession. On receiving the agreed signal from without, he pulled out his pistol, cocked it carefully and, unlocking the door, beckoned to two of his stalwarts to bring their prisoner inside.

As Jessica's shocked eyes registered Wyvern's bruised and bloodied countenance, her eyes filled with tears and she could not prevent her cry of dismay. As soon as he caught sight of her and even though his arms were both being held firmly and none too gently behind his back by Hazlett's two pugilists, the enraged Wyvern renewed his attempts to free himself.

Raising his eyebrows questioningly at the pock-faced one of the pair, Hazlett received a brisk shake of the head from him. 'Just tha' there chiv,' growled the man, kicking the earl's recently purloined weapon across the hallway. ''Ad it up 'is sleeve, so 'e did!'

Frowning slightly, Hazlett motioned the men to release their captive and, prodding the point of his pistol into Wyvern's side, he directed the earl farther into the room, kicking the door shut in the faces of his henchmen.

'Now that is a bit of a setback,' he drawled as, still keeping his pistol pointed carefully at the earl's chest, he stepped away from him and moved backwards to the centre of the room. 'I felt sure that, once you found the damned things, you wouldn't let them out of your sight!'

'Possibly not as clever as you think you are, then,' returned Wyvern, through clenched teeth. His eyes flew across the room to where Jessica was sitting and he shot a questioning look at her. At her tremulous nod, a shudder of relief ran through him. 'So, what now, Hazlett?' he then asked, briskly wiping away the trickle of blood that had seeped down into his eye from the vicious-looking cut on his forehead. 'More action from your bully boys, until I divulge the deeds' whereabouts, I assume?'

'Not at all, my dear chap,' rebutted the viscount with a sneering laugh. 'It is clear that you have totally failed to get my measure. I have no intention of subjecting *your* well-honed muscles to another pounding—I have in mind a far more tender target!'

His face suffused with anger, Wyvern took one pace forward, causing Hazlett to jerk his pistol threateningly. 'Touch one hair of her head,' the earl ground out, 'and I swear that you won't live to see another daybreak!'

'A somewhat idle threat from where I'm standing, I would say!' sneered the viscount. 'I'll give you just two minutes to decide, Wyvern. Either you tell me where you have hidden those blasted papers or I will call my men in to take their pleasure with the luscious Miss Beresford! And, naturally,' he added, with a prurient grin, as he registered the riveted expression of shocked horror that had appeared on the earl's face, '*you* will be allowed to stay and feast your eyes on the whole delightful procedure!'

With a wry twist of his lips, for to him, there was no other choice, Wyvern leant down and, sliding the slim package from his boot, held it out invitingly towards Hazlett, desperately hoping that the other man's impatience to lay his hands on the eagerly sought paperwork would tempt him to drop his guard. For one split second, as he held his breath, poising himself in readiness to spring, it did indeed seem as if the viscount might be on the verge of dashing forward to rip the packet from his outstretched fingers. Sadly, it was not to be, for Hazlett suddenly checked, clearly having decided that to do so would be unwise.

'None of your damned tricks, Wyvern,' he panted, his eyes still on the wrapped tube in Wyvern's hand. 'Toss it down here, in front of me.'

Still struggling in her chair, Jessica, her stomach churning with terror as the dreadful implication of Hazlett's threat sank in, had made every effort to release herself from her bonds, but the viscount had cleverly tied the knot well out of her reach. Frantically casting her eyes around for something that might help her in her quest, her glance suddenly fell on the glass inkstand and its almost globular inkpots.

As the wildest of ideas flew into her brain, she slid her hand carefully across the desktop and lifted the empty pot out of its housing. Desperately trying to remember her half-brother's instructions, as he had patiently endeavoured to teach her to throw in a straight line, she kept her eyes intently focussed on the weapon in Hazlett's outstretched hand and, at the very same instant that Wyvern tossed the package at the viscount's feet, she lifted her arm and hurled the missile directly at the pistol.

Her actual intention had been to try to knock the pistol out of Hazlett's hand, in order to give Wyvern a fighting chance to defend her honour, as she was certain he would have no hesitation in so doing. But her aim, whilst straight enough, was high off the mark and, when the gun went off and the viscount's howl of anguish echoed across the room, she saw, with a curious mixture of relief and chagrin, that the inkpot had hit him squarely on his left temple, the resultant pain of which had caused him to stagger forward, lowering his right arm in the process. Hazlett, it soon became obvious, had shot himself in the foot!

Ignoring the viscount, who was now writhing on the floor in agony, clutching at his bloodied boot, Wyvern dashed to the door, locked it and dropped the key into his pocket, thereby preventing any possible entry by Hazlett's two partners-in-crime. Then, scooping up both package and pistol, he sped to Jessica's side and, unfastening her bonds, pulled her up into his arms.

'My dearest love!' he cried, his voice choked with emotion, as he buried his face in her hair. 'Are you all right? Please tell me that the swine did you no harm!'

'Just a few bumps and bruises,' she assured him, as she revelled in the comfort of his embrace. 'But you, my love? Those dreadful men must have hurt you so very badly!'

'Nothing like the pain of finding out that that villain had you in his clutches,' he replied savagely, as, manfully disregarding the painful bruising around his ribs, he tightened his grasp. 'How can you ever forgive me? If I had come to the gardens as I promised you, none of this could have happened!'

Raising her hand, Jessica placed her fingers over his lips and shook her head, saying, 'No recriminations, Ben, my love. I'm just so thankful that you found me.' Then she paused, a look of wonderment in her eyes. 'You were really prepared to give up your mine just for me?'

'Of course I was, you silly little goose!' groaned Wyvern into her ear. 'Haven't I already told you that you are everything to me—without you my life would be meaningless—as the past few weeks have most clearly demonstrated!'

Her wide green eyes moist with emotion, Jessica slid both of her hands to the back of his neck and, pulling his head down, she pressed her lips against his. Wyvern's response was sweet and instant. For several minutes, oblivious to the banging on the door coupled with the moans of the injured man, the pair clung together, lost in the rapturous world of their newly discovered love for one another.

As the kiss deepened, their embraces became more passionate and urgent, sending shudders of excitement and delight cascading throughout their entwined bodies. Very gradually, however, and despite his rapidly mounting ardour, the earl managed to regain sufficient self-control to realise that, unless he found the strength to force himself away from the wondrously compelling magic of Jessica's lips, he would be in serious danger of losing himself entirely!

'Neither the time, nor the place, my sweet,' he grimaced, as he reluctantly disentangled himself from Jessica's entwining arms. 'I believe there is the rather vital matter of a marriage ceremony to deal with before we take this any further!'

'But that could be months away!' pouted Jessica as, with a temptingly mischievous gleam in her eyes, she looked up at him.

'Not if I have any say in the matter,' he groaned, sweeping her into his arms once more and planting a fervent kiss upon her forehead. Then, stepping away from her, he jerked his head in the direction of the still-moaning viscount.

'Better attend to the invalid, I suppose?'

Although Jessica wasn't entirely sure that, after the way he had behaved, Hazlett deserved any sympathy, she was sensible enough to realise that something ought to be done to help him, if only to send for a physician. The banging on the door had ceased, so she could only assume that the viscount's two henchmen had taken to their heels.

Wyvern had gone over to the viscount and was bending down to examine the cut on his temple, the blood from which, to his relief, was already beginning to congeal.

'Great shot, by the way!' he grinned up at her. 'Couldn't have timed it better myself!'

Biting back a smile, for she did not have the heart to confess that she had actually missed her intended target by a considerable margin, Jessica asked him what he meant to do with Hazlett.

'Well, I suppose I had better try to get the villain's boot off and see the extent of the damage—I advise you to look away if you have no stomach for it!'

'Nonsense!' replied Jessica, defiantly. 'Somebody has to hold his leg while you pull!' And, kneeling at the viscount's side, she gripped hard at his lower thigh while Wyvern eased off the damaged boot, hastily swallowing back the bile that rose at her first sight of the bloodied stocking.

'Shot clean through to the woodwork!' exclaimed Wyvern, in surprise, indicating the hole in the splintered floor beside him. 'Bit of luck, really—less likelihood of blood-poisoning!'

'Get me to a doctor, you bloody young fool!' vociferated the enraged Hazlett.

'Not until we have sorted out our differences, old chap,' responded Wyvern cheerfully as, having unwrapped his neckcloth, he proceeded to bind it tightly around the viscount's still-seeping wound. 'Luckily for you, the pressure of your boot seems to have helped reduce the bleeding.'

Then, with, Jessica's assistance, he lifted the still querulous Hazlett to his feet and, after settling him in a nearby armchair, along with a large glass of brandy to help dull his pain, he led Jessica to the *chaise longue* and bade her sit down. Positioning himself at the fireplace, one foot resting on the wrought-iron fender, he folded his arms and scrutinised his adversary.

'According to my sources,' he began, 'the Earl of Aylsham purchased the original shares for his son, young Jack Stavely, who lost them to you in a game of poker—and his disappearance was not, as is commonly believed, due to any duel to which he may or may not have challenged you on some lady's behalf, but to his own fear that his father would come to learn of his heavy gambling losses.

'My brother Theodore,' he went on, 'having won the deeds from you in a similar fashion, then proceeded to lose large sums of money to you and several others of your cronies. And so, when you learned of the mine's sudden success, you went to a great deal of trouble and expense to buy up all of Theo's outstanding vowels— am I, thus far, correct in my premise?'

For answer, Hazlett merely shrugged and glared at him.

Wyvern took a deep breath and, after tossing a swift smile of reassurance at the wide-eyed Jessica, who had been avidly drinking in his words, he continued, 'Having amassed a debt of over twenty-five thousand pounds against him, you then appeared to assume that you had every right to demand the return of the deeds?' Here the earl raised his eyebrows questioningly.

'I offered to cancel out the debt!' the viscount burst out wrathfully. 'Instead of which the damned fool chose to blow his brains out!'

Wyvern's lips tightened. 'Cancelling out the debt *and* taking the deeds would have left my brother with nothing,' he said heavily. 'My guess is that Theo, having also discovered that the mine was making a profit, but having little heart to carry on himself, opted to take his own life in the firm belief that I would take up the cudgels on his behalf which, I must assure you, I have every intention of doing!'

Narrowing his eyes, he stared down at the scowling viscount. 'I will have every one of Theo's vowels from you, Hazlett,' he ground out. 'And, although on Monday morning you will find yourself some twenty-five thousand pounds or so better off, you may also discover that it will not do you a whole lot of good, where you are going!'

'What are you implying?' asked the other man warily.

'Well, for one thing, there is the possible charge of conspiring to commit murder!'

'Murder? Whose murder?'

'Walter Allardyce,' returned Wyvern, somewhat unwillingly, as he shot an anxious glance at the horrified expression on Jessica's face. 'Seems that one of your hired minions took a cosh to him before dragging my betrothed off into the bushes—which brings me to your second offence—kidnapping!'

'You'll have a job proving that I had anything to do with any of that,' sneered the viscount.

'Wouldn't be too sure of that, if I were you, Hazlett,' drawled a voice from the doorway and, as three pairs of eyes swung in his direction, Sir Simon Holt entered the room, accompanied by the Honourable Freddie Fitzallan. Squirming on the floor of the hallway behind them, amidst the wreckage of Wyvern's earlier failed attempt to rescue his betrothed, could be seen the heavily bound and gagged figures of the viscount's two bully boys.

'Well, you certainly took your time!' grinned Wyvern, strolling forward to grasp his friends by the hands. 'Very welcome, nonetheless—how did you get in?'

'Caught these two just as they were coming out of the basement—carrying a couple of bags of rather valuable-looking silver, they were,' returned Holt, his eyes glinting with amusement. 'Thought it looked rather odd, so we collared the pair of them and, after a bit of—er—friendly persuasion, shall we say, they were happy to direct us up here. Freddie found another set of keys in the housekeeper's room, and there you have it! Hope we didn't make too much noise?'

'Nary a sound,' chuckled Wyvern. 'You've neither of you lost your touch, it would seem—help yourself to some of Hazlett's fine cognac, gentlemen!'

It was well into the early hours of Saturday morning before Jessica, at last, found herself on the driving seat of Wyvern's curricle, ready to begin the short journey back to Dover Street. The physician had come and gone, the night watchmen had been called and a black, windowless carriage had arrived to ferry the three much-deflated miscreants to the Newgate Street prison.

Snuggling happily into his side, the highly contented Jessica asked the earl when he had first known that he loved her.

'What a question!' He laughed, as he leant over and planted a kiss on the top of her head. 'I can hardly remember a time when I didn't!'

'Even though I was so very beastly to you?' she persisted. 'I find it hard to believe that you found such obnoxious behaviour particularly attractive!'

'Well,' he said, considering, 'I was much struck by your beauty, of course.'

Her shoulders sagged. 'Was that the only reason?' she asked plaintively.

'Almost certainly—at least to begin with,' returned the earl, smiling down at her. 'But I *remained* in love with you because I very soon learned that you are also the sweetest, bravest, most compassionate and generous-hearted young lady that I have ever come across. The fact that you are, in addition, rather easy on the eye, is now merely a rather satisfying bonus!'

At such fulsome praise from the man she adored with every bone in her body, Jessica's heart swelled with joy and, her lips curving in a tender smile, she murmured contentedly, 'I doubt that anyone but you would ever dream of describing me in such glowing terms!'

Raising one eyebrow quizzically, he commented, 'Now, that, I do find hard to believe.'

She shook her head. 'You would not have loved me a year ago,' she said, in a small voice. 'I was considered to be the most conceited, pig-headed and selfish brat on the planet! Up until my other abduction I...'

Her voice trailed away in confusion as Wyvern suddenly yanked at his reins and, grabbing hard at the brake lever, brought his equipage to a grinding halt, tipping the unwary Berridge out of his seat at the rear in the process, as well as oversetting his horses.

'Please explain yourself, Jessica,' he said, very deliberately, as his groom righted himself and flew to steady the restless thoroughbreds. 'Did I really hear you say "other abduction"?'

Nervously registering the steely note in his voice, Jessica began to wonder whether she had been entirely wise to refer to that earlier attempt but, squaring her shoulders, she reasoned that, if she and Wyvern were going to spend the rest of their lives together, as she desperately hoped they would, then surely he was entitled to know of this rather dark episode from her past?

She raised her head and her anxious eyes met his—so grey, so clear, so full of loving concern. Swallowing her apprehension, now confident that, no matter how disgraceful and humiliating her tale might prove to be, Wyvern's love for her would not falter, she began to relate the horrifying events of the previous autumn, with particular reference to Jake's having spotted Wentworth carrying her off. 'Had it not been for him recognising Papa's scarlet curricle,' she concluded, stifling back a little sob, 'Matt would never have known how to find me!'

Reaching across to take hold of her hands, Wyvern made no attempt to interrupt as he continued to hear out the rest of Jessica's halting description of the failed abduction, although it was impossible for him to prevent the surge of hot anger that coursed through his veins at the unwelcome thought of anyone laying their filthy hands upon his sweet innocent darling! Suddenly, he tensed, and an expression of sheer self-disgust crossed his face. Dear God in heaven, he reflected bitterly, he himself had just been responsible for his beloved having almost suffered a similar fate for the second time in her short life! Releasing her hands, he leaned back against the squab, striving to regain his composure. 'I trust the blackguard got his just deserts,' he ground out, unaware that the sudden removal of his comforting touch had left Jessica feeling somewhat bereft.

'He was transported, I believe,' she replied shortly and, somewhat discomposed by the fierce expression on Wyvern's face, coupled with his continued silence, she began to fear that her impulsive confession must have given him cause to regret his earlier words of love.

'Good!' he said impassively. 'I hope that the devil rots in hell!'

Then, to her unbounded joy, he gathered her tightly in his arms, saying, 'I intend to spend the rest of my days making sure that no one ever hurts you again, my dearest love—you are more precious to me than life itself. I cannot wait to make you my wife—tell me that you will soon be mine for ever!'

Assuring him that this, too, was her dearest wish, Jessica surrendered herself to Wyvern's lips and, oblivious to everyone and everything about them, the pair were soon transported back to Love's glorious wonderland where only passion and excitement rule, until the earl was, once again, obliged to call upon every one of his resources to draw away.

'Enough of this, my love!' he cried reluctantly. 'You really must allow me to focus my attention on delivering you back to your brother!' And, with his lips curving upwards into the roguish grin that Jessica found so appealing, he added, 'I fear that we have some serious explanations to attend to!'

Chapter Twenty-One

Despite his many grumbles and protestations, it was not until mid-December of that year that the Earl of Wyvern was, at long last, able to claim Miss Jessica Beresford as his wife. Whilst Matt would have been more than happy to deliver his headstrong half-sister into another man's tender keeping, he had remained obdurate in his refusal to contemplate any marriage celebrations until Imogen was safely delivered of their first child, which happy event had occurred on the fifteenth of November.

As a result of Matt's intransigence, the impatient earl had been constrained to journey up and down the Great North Road in order to snatch the occasional few hours of sweet salvation in the company of his betrothed. Luckily for his peace of mind, the refurbishment of Ashcroft Grange took up much of his free time. Having paid off all of his brother's creditors, including Viscount Hazlett, who was now languishing in a cell in Newgate, the gradually increasing profits from the mine were now being poured into the more serious business of, not simply returning the estate to its former glory, but also in introducing the many new farming methods that would bring it more up to date. Much to his surprise, Wyvern had found that he quite enjoyed the overseeing of these procedures and this recently discovered occupation, along with the estate's mounting prosperity, was proving to be a great source of satisfaction to him.

In answer to a placatory entreaty from Lady Lavinia herself who—now that her own coffers were, once more, overflowing—had quickly revised her former opinion of her grandson's intended wife and was now doing her level best to heal the unfortunate breach between Jessica and herself, Matt had given his consent for his sister to pay two short visits to the Grange.

Although neither he nor his wife were able to accompany her on either of these occasions, ostensibly arranged in order that Jessica might select the colours and any new furnishings that she might require in what was to be her marital home, her brother had been quite satisfied that the dowager's chaperonage would be perfectly adequate in the given circumstances.

The sheer size of Ashford Grange and its surrounding grandeur had, initially, filled its soon-to-be-mistress with feelings of awe and dismay but, after Wyvern had proudly conducted her through the Grange's sprawling splendour and driven her several times about the estate in his carriage, relating to her the many happy incidents from his childhood, she had come to appreciate the deep love and enthusiasm he felt for his childhood home.

Having made her peace with the new countess-in-waiting, and despite Matt's supposition that they would remain always within her sight, Lady Lavinia had been content to leave the young couple to their own devices, merely demanding that they should arrive, suitably dressed, at the dinner table at the predetermined hour. Whether or not the pair had chosen to take advantage of the dowager's somewhat lax chaperonage to anticipate their nuptials during either of these two visits, it would be impossible to say, but there was certainly no diminishment of ardour in Wyvern's eyes when he turned to watch his heart-achingly beautiful bride, as she proceeded up the aisle towards him on her smiling brother's arm, when the day of their wedding finally arrived.

The little church in Kirton Priors had seldom been so well attended as it was on that bright, crisp day. Having dismissed all suggestions of a high-society wedding at St George's Church in Hanover Square, Jessica had elected to be married by Mr Boscombe, the local vicar, whom she had known since her childhood.

The pale winter sun shone through the stained-glass windows, casting a myriad of colourful patterns on the stone floor beneath, enhanced by the soft light from the tall wax candles in the brass candlesticks standing on the altar and in the brackets that hung from the walls. Fragrant sprays of winter greenery, entwined with white Christmas roses, bedecked the windowsills and oak rafters of the building and every pew end was hung with either a lavender or rosemary-filled muslin bag, their combined delicate perfumes pervading throughout the pretty little church's interior.

Seated in one of the church's front pews, clad elegantly in a tasteful ensemble of lavender-coloured velvet and silver fox fur, with the Honourable Freddie Fitzallan as her escort, was her ladyship the Dowager Countess of Wyvern. The whole of the second row was taken up with an assortment of Wyvern's more distant relatives, whose arrival from Ireland, late the previous evening, had caused the village innkeeper a considerable headache in trying to accommodate them all. Behind this party stretched rows of pews filled with high-stepping luminaries and other ex-comrades from Wyvern's military days, including the great Duke of Wellington himself who, upon hearing that his one time aide-de-camp was finally about to take the plunge, had expressed his deep delight, declaring that it was high time the fellow settled down and started up his nursery.

Miss Felicity Draycott, along with several of the ladies of her set, accompanied by their dedicated escorts, including the now fully recovered Mr Allardyce, had elected to sit on the bride's side of the church. Having had a private chat with Wyvern, full of tears and self-recrimination, Felicity had been more than grateful to learn that he could see no reason to divulge any of what had passed between Hazlett and herself either to his betrothed or any other party. And, having found that Jessica still counted her amongst her friends she had, subsequently, declared herself to be amongst Jessica's staunchest supporters, when the news had broken of the now very wealthy earl's intention to marry a girl whom some of the older diehards amongst the *ton* had regarded as a flighty little nobody.

Even the elderly Jane Widdecombe, one-time governess to the family, had travelled all the way from the school in Kendal, where she now taught, to hear her formerly rather headstrong pupil undertake her marriage vows. The moment that her dearest Widdy had stepped down from her chaise, Imogen had confessed her secret hope that the little governess could be persuaded to remain at Thornfield, in order that she might administer her admirable methods of education to the Beresford nursery's newest occupant, when that young gentleman should reach a suitable age to warrant it.

Having finally relinquished his sister's hand for the ceremony to commence, Matt slid into his seat on the front pew and captured his wife's. 'I can't believe that this is really happening,' he whispered, leaning forward to beam a smile of encouragement at the tearful Lady Beresford who, as well as being Jessica's mama, was also his stepmother. She, along with Jessica's brother, Nicholas, was sitting on Imogen's left-hand side. 'Never thought I would live to see the day when I would actually be sorry to see the back of the young scamp!'

Squeezing his hand, Imogen gave him a tremulous smile. 'It is hard to believe that a year could have made such a difference to her,' she replied softly.

'Made quite a bit of difference to us, too,' pointed out her husband, his bright blue eyes glinting with mischief. 'As a certain Master John Matthew Beresford would, no doubt, be quite prepared to confirm, were he able to do anything other than gurgle!'

'Perhaps this time, next year, our dear Jessica will have a baby of her own to cherish,' remarked Imogen. 'She has been so keen to pet and cosset our little John that I swear I have had hardly a moment alone with him since he was born!'

'By the look on Wyvern's face when he set eyes on her,' grinned Matt, looking towards the altar in front of which the bridal couple stood, 'I would be highly surprised if as much as a year passed before that happy event occurred!'

'Oh, shush!' his blushing wife admonished him. 'You should not say such things in church!'

'Nonsense!' he retorted, with a soft laugh. 'Mr Boscombe himself has only just informed the entire congregation that the whole purpose of marriage is to procreate—an admirable objective and one which I most heartily endorse and which—if last night was anything to go by—so also do you, my darling Imo!'

'Oh, do hush, Matt!' protested the now scarlet-cheeked Imogen, struggling to restrain the gurgle of laughter that threatened. 'Someone will hear you!'

Luckily, at that point, the congregation were invited to stand and join in a hymn of praise to God's bountifulness and the rest of the service passed without undue comment from either Matt or his wife.

As he escorted his new bride back down the aisle past the smiling faces of their many friends and well-wishers, Wyvern's wide grin of pride and happiness could hardly have been missed by any one of them. Not that any of the onlookers could have doubted that the match was, indeed, a love match—a little unusual amongst the higher echelons, as they were quick to point out to one another. But, having seen the way the handsome young earl looked at his wife, almost as though he were about to ravish her on the spot, a goodly number of the females in the congregation could not help but feel rather envious of the new countess.

'Have I told you how much I love you, my dearest darling wife?' he whispered, as he handed Jessica up into the open landau.

'Not since we parted last evening, sir,' she replied, impishly fluttering her lashes at him, causing an immediate reaction in the pit of his abdomen.

Unable to stifle his desire, Wyvern leapt up into the carriage beside her and, to the combined gasps and laughter of the assembled congregation, he pulled her towards him and, pressing his lips against hers, kissed her long and thoroughly.

'Then, perhaps that will convince you, madam wife!' he grinned, as he finally tore his lips away. 'And, you may rest assured, my own sweet love, that there will be a good deal more of that to come in the not too distant future!'

Overwhelmed with love for her new husband, Jessica raised her glorious green eyes to meet his and said softly, 'For which I can hardly wait, my lord!'

* * * * *

On sale 6th June 2008

THE MAN FROM STONE CREEK
by Linda Lael Miller

There was trouble in Haven, Arizona, and Ranger Sam
O'Ballivan was the man to sort it out. Badge and gun
hidden, he arrived posing as the new schoolteacher – and
that led to a call on Maddie Chancelor, older sister of
a boy in firm need of discipline.

Maddie was a graceful woman whose prim and proper stance
battled with the fire in her eyes. Sam's job had always kept him
isolated and his heart firmly in check. But there was something
about Maddie that had him unwittingly tempted to start
down a path he'd sworn he'd never travel.

'Miller paints a brilliant portrait of the power of love
to bring light into the darkest of souls. This is western
romance at its finest.'
—*Romantic Times BOOKreviews*

MILLS & BOON

Historical

On sale 6th June 2008

THE DUKE'S DESIRE
by Margaret Moore

The Duke of Deighton returns to England, expecting
to marry. Seeing Verity again stirs his passion, yet she seems
reluctant to be close to him. But what the Duke desires,
he usually gets…

VIKING WARRIOR, UNWILLING WIFE
by Michelle Styles

The dragon ships of warriors had come for battle and glory.
It wasn't the threat of conquest that shook her – Vikar,
the leader of the invading force, was once Sela's husband!

PRAIRIE WIFE
by Cheryl St John

Amy Shelby had the perfect marriage until tragedy
struck. Amy knows she cannot give up on her husband,
and with the promise of a new family she finds the
strength to fight for his love!

A delicious addition to the
Moreland family novels!

Gloucestershire, 1878

Ever since Anna Holcombe refused his proposal, Reed
Moreland has been unable to set foot in the home that
was the backdrop to their romance – Winterset.

But when Reed has dreams about Anna being in danger,
he heads back to Winterset, determined to protect the
woman he still loves. Once again passion flares between
them, but the murder of a servant girl draws them deep
into deadly legends of Winterset…and a destiny neither
Anna nor Reed can escape.

Available 18th April 2008

Immerse yourself in the glitter of
Regency times and follow the lives
and romantic escapades of
Stephanie Laurens' Lester family

15th February 2008

21st March 2008

16th May 2008

20th June 2008

www.mirabooks.co.uk

Celebrate 100 years of pure reading pleasure with Mills & Boon®

To mark our centenary, each month we're publishing a special 100th Birthday Edition. These celebratory editions are packed with extra features and include a FREE bonus story.

Plus, starting in February you'll have the chance to enter a fabulous monthly prize draw. See 100th Birthday Edition books for details.

Now that's worth celebrating!

15th February 2008

Raintree: Inferno by Linda Howard
Includes FREE bonus story Loving Evangeline
A double dose of Linda Howard's heady mix of passion and adventure

4th April 2008

The Guardian's Forbidden Mistress by Miranda Lee
Includes FREE bonus story The Magnate's Mistress
Two glamorous and sensual reads from favourite author Miranda Lee!

2nd May 2008

The Last Rake in London by Nicola Cornick
Includes FREE bonus story The Notorious Lord
Lose yourself in two tales of high society and rakish seduction!

Look for Mills & Boon 100th Birthday Editions at your favourite bookseller or visit
www.millsandboon.co.uk

FREE

2 BOOKS AND A SURPRISE GIFT!

We would like to take this opportunity to thank you for reading this Mills & Boon® book by offering you the chance to take TWO more specially selected titles from the Historical series absolutely FREE! We're also making this offer to introduce you to the benefits of the Mills & Boon® Reader Service™—

- ★ **FREE home delivery**
- ★ **FREE gifts and competitions**
- ★ **FREE monthly Newsletter**
- ★ **Books available before they're in the shops**
- ★ **Exclusive Reader Service offers**

Accepting these FREE books and gift places you under no obligation to buy; you may cancel at any time, even after receiving your free shipment. Simply complete your details below and return the entire page to the address below. You don't even need a stamp!

YES! Please send me 2 free Historical books and a surprise gift. I understand that unless you hear from me, I will receive 4 superb new titles every month for just £3.69 each, postage and packing free. I am under no obligation to purchase any books and may cancel my subscription at any time. The free books and gift will be mine to keep in any case.

H8ZEE

Ms/Mrs/Miss/Mr...Initials ....
BLOCK CAPITALS PLEASE

Surname ....

Address ....

....

....Postcode ....

Send this whole page to:

The Reader Service, FREEPOST CN81, Croydon, CR9 3WZ